Ken and Reg Prosser strolled a little unsteadily through a narrow alleyway behind Fleet Street – one of those alleyways that's dark even on the brightest day. They'd been doing some serious lunchtime drinking in The Inkwell. Surely, Ken thought, if two words were ever made for each other, they were 'lunchtime' and 'drinking' . . . the unique pleasure of going out, during the day, on the pop. He now regretted all those years he'd wasted on milk and sandwiches, just because he hadn't wanted to fall asleep at his desk. Down Reg's end of the Street, lunchtime drinking almost constituted an Olympic event! The after-effects even had their own names: there was the 'Tower of Pisa', where you tilted to one side; the 'Hibernating Mole', where you buried your head in your arms . . . and the 'Scouse Kiss', which was a head-butt straight onto the desk. Anyway, Ken decided, he was in just the mood for a little nap. And Reg agreed.

STAN HEY and ANDREW NICKOLDS

HOLD
THE BACK PAGE!

Based on original screenplays by
Stan Hey and Andrew Nickolds
with Joanna Willett

Futura

A Futura Book

First published in Great Britain in 1985 by
Futura Publications,
a Division of Macdonald & Co (Publishers) Ltd
London & Sydney

ISBN 0 7088 2992 9

Typeset in Times by Fleet Graphics, Enfield, Middlesex

Reproduced, printed and bound in Great Britain by
Hazell Watson & Viney Limited,
Member of the BPCC Group,
Aylesbury, Bucks

Futura Publications
A Division of
Macdonald & Co (Publishers) Ltd
Maxwell House
74 Worship Street
London EC2A 2EN

A BPCC plc Company

AWAY FROM HOME

Somehow Ken had hoped for more of a send off. He'd not really enjoyed the drinks party his colleagues – or rather his ex-colleagues – had thrown together for him. The hearty back-slapping and raucous jokes wear a bit thin when you're rather the worse for wear. As he emerged bleary-eyed and a little unsteady on his feet from the upholstered comfort of El Vinos wine bar, a procession of faces wished him well, shook his hand, and abandoned him to the relentless Fleet Street traffic; it began to rain. There was nothing for it, he would have to hail a cab.

London cabs are difficult to get at the best of times, but in the rain in Fleet Street on a Friday afternoon, flagging one down is about as easy as hitching a ride from Concorde.

His clouded brain took a few moments to register the shock therefore, when only seconds after he had raised his hand there was a squeal of brakes and he fell into the open door of a black cab.

'Where to, guv?'

He was not too far gone to name his destination. This was a taxi ride to a new chapter in his life.

The taxi described a U-turn and pulled up on the other side of the road. There was a long pause while Ken waited for something else to happen. Had he just imagined it? In his present state it was difficult to tell. The driver wasn't behaving as if anything was odd. Ken got out of the cab, and fumbled in his pocket for some change. A large brown-paper parcel, his leaving present, slipped from his hands and clattered to the floor.

'That'll be eighty pence, guv,' announced the taxi-driver, as Ken pulled an ashtray out of his pocket. He looked at it mystified, wondering how it had got there. As he handed a torn note from a ball of currency through the driver's window he focused slowly on the sign of the building opposite. 'El Vinos' it announced proudly. Ken paused while the truth sank home.

'Oi – why didn't you tell me I was already here?'

'I was taking advantage of you 'cos you're drunk,' the driver explained, unabashed. It was simple, really. In spite of himself, Ken couldn't help but be impressed. Honesty seemed such a rare commodity in the 1980s, particularly among London taxi drivers. 'Here, have a drink,' he told him, handing him another crumpled banknote. 'And a smoke,' he added, pushing the ashtray into his outstretched hand.

'Thanks very much, guv,' replied the bemused taxi-driver who was obviously polite as well as honest. 'You leaving the paper, then?' he asked, nodding at the brown-paper parcel and its accompanying card. Ken handed him a folded newspaper from his pocket and pressed it into his hand as well.

'Yeah.'

'No, I didn't mean that one. I meant leaving *here*,' said the driver, jerking a thumb at Ken's destination with obvious distaste. 'It must be a great relief to get away from that toilet-roll . . . '

There was an awkward pause. 'If you must know,' said Ken, mustering what little remained of his dignity, 'that toilet-roll happens to be my new place of employment.'

'Gawd. No wonder you're drunk. What are you going to be doing there, then? Calling the bingo or running a wet T-shirt contest?'

Ken paused again, this time for effect. 'Actually,' he replied. 'I'm a writer.'

'Oh yeah?' retorted the taxi-driver acidly. 'Branching out, are they?' Ken forced his brain to think, seeking a defence for what must have looked like pretentiousness on his part. 'Look, between you and me – I know it's got the reputation of being a bit of a rag . . . '

'A bit of a rag . . . !' scoffed the driver. 'It's a rag alright. A rag soaked in chloroform. You know what, guv? Newspapers like yours have taken over from religion as the opium of the masses.'

'That,' explained Ken, adopting a lofty tone, 'is why I am going to work there – so I can inject a bit of intelligence and get the public thinking about what they read.' A point to Ken.

The taxi-driver thought for a moment. 'Which department?'

'Sport.'

The cab rocked as the driver exploded with laughter. 'SPORT!!!'

Now Ken was really offended. 'What's so bloody funny about that?' He didn't feel so drunk any more either. Here was somebody decrying the profession he'd spent the last twenty years mastering.

'Because, my old china,' replied the driver, 'in the words of Thomas de Quincey – "Sir, 'tis an idle mind that wouldst spend itself in dalliance with sporting pastimes. For if thou wouldst truly flex the brain . . . ".'

'Don't tell me,' interrupted Ken. 'Thou wouldst get a job as a taxi-driver, right? You know what? Ever since you bloody lot won "Mastermind" you've become more ignorant than ever.'

The taxi-driver was touched to the quick. 'No, no,' he replied. 'We do The Knowledge, mate . . . The Ignorance is *your* speciality. And' he added, determined to kick a man when he was down, and looking at the meter which was still running, that'll be another twenty pence.'

Ken tossed a twenty pence piece at him. 'Here – get a copy of Monday's rag . . . see if you notice any improvement. Wordsworth's the name. Ken Wordsworth.'

He turned and strode into the building behind him.

Nobody was in the Sports Editor's office so he made himself at home. A frosted glass partition divided it from the rest of the Sports Department with the name 'REG PROSSER SPORTS EDITOR' in capitals on the door and a yellowed cut-out headline that read 'You Must be Bonkers' underneath it. The walls of the dingy little office were plastered with workcharts, a holiday planner with nothing on it, racing pages from the *Sporting Chronicle* (deceased 1983) and framed autographed photos of sport-and-showbiz personalities. Buried among the dusty heaps of old newspapers and sporting handbooks were a drinks cabinet and Reg Prosser's desk, piled high with unread press releases, chewed biros, shoes, illegible handwritten notes and completely legible losing betting slips.

Ken unwrapped his farewell gift ruefully. It was a dictionary with a drawing on the flyleaf of a skull and cross-bones and the words 'Ken Wordsworth R.I.P.' inscribed beneath.

'You won't be needing that here,' announced a voice behind him. Ken turned and took in his new boss with a measured stare. He'd met him before, of course, most recently when they'd talked about Ken's taking the job, and naturally at various sporting events over the previous years. But this was different; this was a working relationship. Reg Prosser was small and wiry, of, as they say, an indeterminate age somewhere between forty and sixty, with sharp features and an indefinable accent.

'Good send off from the *old* office, I take it,' asked Reg at his most tactful. It was a significant meeting for him too. This was the fruit of his efforts to inject a bit of class into his Sporting Pages. Ken Wordsworth was known as one of the best sportswriters in the business. He'd been underused in his old job on the Sunday and Reg had seen his chance and taken it. Apparently Ken had some problem with his marriage – a divorced wife and child to support – and was looking for more money.

Ken explained that the 'do' had been a bit low-key, in keeping with the style of a Sunday newspaper and his ex-colleagues' bewilderment at Ken's move: hence the caustic note in the dictionary.

'Well, you'll find a big difference here, Ken,' boasted Reg. 'We may look like a dump from the outside . . . *and* the inside . . . but we've got our priorities right! Your old place might have all the fancy furniture . . . cork tiles, chrome karzis, etc – but we spend money where it's most needed – on our writers. Which is why we attract the cream.'

Ken blushed suitably as Reg rooted among the debris on his desk for a piece of artwork, which he held up for Ken to see. At last, at the edge of forty-one, Ken Wordsworth was to have his own masthead! It turned out to be a caricature of him, his huge face superimposed on a tiny body wearing one of everything conceivable to do with sport – one football boot, one cricket pad, one rugby shirt, one tennis-player's headband. His right hand clutched a quill pen and the lettering above the picture read 'Ken Wordsworth – Poet Laureate of Sport'. This was to appear above every feature that Ken wrote for Reg. Ken's heart sank in dismay but Reg continued enthusiastically, oblivious of his horror at the appalling cartoon.

'Come Monday morning this face'll be grinning out at four million people!, he announced and proceeded to brief Ken on his first assignment. It would be a good idea if Reg's new signing introduced himself to his new readers, because not too many of them would have been familiar with his previous work in the higher reaches of journalism, unless they'd happened to find it wrapped round their chips. Ken was to complement the FA Cup match report with a few reminiscences about some of the great semi-finals he had seen – celebrations in the dressing room from the brown ale fifties to the champagne eighties. Ken suggested that it might be more interesting to write about the sides that *didn't* make it to Wembley, but this was shot down immediately. 'A piece about losers on a Monday morning, Ken? We don't want to depress everybody.'

'We wouldn't be depressing em, though,' argued Ken, keen to assert his position early in the game. 'We'd be tapping a rich vein of nostalgia. I mean, some of the most famous players have never made it to an FA Cup Final – this is as far as they got . . . George Best, Trevor Francis, Kenny Dalglish.'

Reg paused for a moment. He hadn't realised that. There might perhaps be a competition in it. Few old photos – 'Spot the Loser and Win Two Tickets to the Cup Final!'

In the meantime, here was Ken Wordsworth's travel warrant for Liverpool. First class of course. Ken brightened. This was more like it – a cut above the Big City Savers he'd been used to travelling on.

'Fancy a quick pint?' said Reg. 'Let's go down The Inkwell and meet a few of the boys.'

It was half past three – Happy Hour.

Ken followed Reg through dark, Dickensian passages off Fleet Street. He noticed Reg's jacket displayed a colourful logo: 'Val d'Isere 1985' surrounded by sponsors' flashes, and assumed Reg had been covering the Men's Downhill. The Sports Editor snorted derisively at the suggestion.

'Our readers don't want to know about winter sports . . . load of rich playboys posing around in the snow . . . I wasn't going to turn down the trip though. I mean, twelve hours ago there I was, brilliant sunshine, fresh mountain air, draught Martini, beautiful women . . . I felt really homesick.'

Peering into the gloom of The Inkwell, Ken saw Reg's point – Val d'Isere and this stygian tavern were worlds apart. The Inkwell, one of many drinking clubs off Fleet Street, was exclusively for journalists. It was constantly threatened with closure by the police, because of its long opening hours, but managed to save itself by making the police members. Ken descended through the smoke into the dank, converted cellar. Boxing posters were peeling off the walls. Some tables in the low-ceilinged alcoves boasted candles. Stubbed-out cigarettes smouldered in ashtrays. Sodden beermats promoted brews of all nations. The room was full of journalists, standing drinking together in groups, slumped in old sofas and armchairs, or watching the afternoon's racing on a television set mounted above the bar. Some were eating food from a dingy counter at one end of the bar. On a sign reading 'today's special' were chalked the words 'Pie and Beans'.

Leaning against the bar was a red-faced, late-middle-aged man who was clearly drunk, his hands clasped firmly round the plastic pint of lager on top of the Carlsberg tap. This was Frank McNab, Reg Prosser's deputy editor.

'Hey, Ruby, called Frank in a thick Scottish accent which got thicker as the day wore on. 'When are you going to clean this bar? It's getting very sticky. I can't even lift my pint.'

Ruby, a wafer-thin young barmaid standing on the other side of the bar watched his ritual performance sardonically.

She couldn't help thinking Frank must get tired of trying the same joke every day – she was certainly getting tired of hearing it. Now he was coming out with his other joke – 'Wasn't "Today's Special" "Yesterday's Special" as well?'

'Yeah. Mum didn't have time to bake this morning,' explained Ruby. 'She's gone to visit Dad in Chelmsford nick.'

Meanwhile Reg was showing off The Inkwell to Ken. 'Favoured haunt of sportsmen and artists throughout the ages . . . step up from El Vino's eh, Ken?' Half-expecting to find the Thames lapping round his feet, Ken couldn't help thinking it was several steps down. Hanging on the bannisters was a book with a biro attached to it by a piece of string. Reg signed it with a flourish. 'Reg + 1'.

'I want you to meet someone who's going to play a vital part in your life from now on,' he announced, steering Ken towards Frank.

'Frank McNab, my deputy – meet your new colleague, Ken Wordsworth.' Reg had been hoping to show off in front of Ruby, but she'd darted off to change a barrel.

'Oh aye – the six million dollar man,' muttered Frank, beadily. Ken went to shake hands, but Frank's were full. 'I won't be earning quite as much as that, Frank,' Ken replied, mildly. Frank glowered at him. 'Well, whatever it is, you're going to have to justify your transfer fee. Because it'll be a bit of a change from the fancy Sunday routine you've been used to – no more two-day weeks, sitting around on your arse contemplating your navel.'

'You're right,' said Ken. 'I can see it's going to be a hard life of afternoon drinking and free skiing holidays.'

Reg stepped in diplomatically and tried to lighten the atmosphere. 'I got a nice fifty words out of that trip, as it happens – the British competitor didn't finish the downhill, but went over a cliff and came fourth in the ski jump! What was it you came up with, Frank?' "Piste Off"? See? Frank's the best headline writer in the business.' Ken winced, unimpressed.

'Believe it,' said Frank with a certain forceful finality.

Reg could sense more trouble. 'And now he's going to work alongside the best writer in the business,' he smiled, putting an arm around each of them. 'That's what I call a crack team.'

But the so-called Poet Laureate of Sport rose to the bait. 'A "crack" team? I thought "crack" teams only came from Europe . . . The crack East Germans . . . the crack Hungarians . . . the crack cossacks from Krakow. Isn't that so, Frank?'

Frank had to admit defeat grudgingly. 'He's right, gaffer.'

Reg beamed with satisfaction. 'There we are – a creative partnership forged already. Get 'em in, will you Frank?'

Frank was surprised when 'Sunday Jim' didn't order a Pina Colada with a cherry and a furled umbrella . . . it seemed he was just a bit suspicious that Ken might be slumming it, for the money.

In fact this was only partly the truth – the move from the Sunday paper had been largely a career decision. Ken had had enough of playing second fiddle to certain of his colleagues who achieved greater fame by constant blowing of their own trumpets. The twenty-seven-and-a-half thousand plus expenses was an inducement, of course, but as Ken pointed out to Reg, there wouldn't really be much left for himself once the ex-wife had taken her chunk. Talk about adding injury to insult.

When Ken and Alison first came down to London from Yorkshire he'd told her what to expect. She knew he'd be working odd hours, travelling up and down the country, drinking with the lads, bumping into the odd woman now and then. Ken saw them as occupational hazards but Alison had seen them rather differently. She was determined that she was going to live life as well. And so they had got divorced and Ken had found himself, in his own words, 'forking out for her bloody acupuncture lessons and Open University course . . . Open Wallet University, more like.' Ken had moved out from their house in up-market Wandsworth to a flat of his own in downtown Bayswater, leaving Alison with their son Charlie. 'Your *tug-of-love* son, Charlie' said Reg, gently reminding Ken of the sort of newspaper he'd be working for from now on.

Ken's first job coincided with his weekend to have Charlie, and the family had arranged to meet on Euston station. Ken was late: after the trouble he'd had with the taxi-driver he'd taken the tube. 'Trust your father,' said Alison. 'Still, what do you expect from somebody who can't even remember his son's birthday.' Charlie took his dad's side, as was usual in these situations, and thought Ken was late because he'd stopped on the way to buy him a present.

Ken finally arrived and gave Alison a peck on the cheek. She noted that his breath smelled – 'Have you been working?' Irritated, Ken questioned the need for Alison to accompany Charlie across London. After all, he was fourteen. 'He was fifteen – yesterday.' A point to Alison. Ken had to think fast. He rummaged in his bag.

'Ooh, look,' said Alison, sarcastically, 'A hip-flask.'

'Just drop it, eh, Alison. As if I'd try and pass off one of my possessions as a present,' said Ken, producing his leaving present dictionary. 'I want words to be as important to you as they are to me, Charlie. And don't read the inscription yet. I'd only get embarrassed.'

Alison handed Ken a lunchbox containing some sandwiches for Charlie. Last time Ken had him for the weekend he'd lost three pounds. She'd even taken the precaution of weighing him on a machine this time. And now he was Ken's responsibility.

Once safely aboard the train, Ken promised Charlie he'd buy him a proper present as soon as they got to Liverpool. Anyway, the dictionary would come in useful with the weird John Fowles books Alison kept buying Charlie in an effort to educate him. Charlie was intrigued by the inscription 'R.I.P.' 'Rest in Peace'?

'Perhaps they thought I was committing professional suicide or something,' said Ken, keen to change the subject. Did Charlie want a drink? Ken was just persuading Charlie to have something other than a slimline tonic on the day after his fifteenth birthday when he was interrupted.

'Kenneth, my son! I hear you're one of us now! You

going to the bar? Get us a vodka and Perrier.' The owner of the voice disappeared towards an attractive woman further up the carriage. 'Away goals count double.'

Steve Stevens. '*The Times* Chess Correspondent' explained Ken. But Charlie wasn't fooled. Now he saw what they meant by R.I.P.

Steve Stevens was the sort of journalist who gave the gutter press a bad name. The sort of journalist who was proud to have the occupation 'Hack' in his passport. The more he tried to chat up the attractive woman however, the more he realized that she'd treat any revelations of who he was or who he worked for with the contempt both deserved. So he merely introduced himself as 'a sportswriter for a well-known national newspaper'. But that didn't cut any ice either, so Steve tried again.

'Now isn't that a coincidence – both of us going to Liverpool!'

'On the Liverpool train, yes,' came the sharp reply.

When Ken returned with the drinks and made as if to join them, Steve Stevens seemed rather put out. They were having a conversation, he said.

'About Liverpool,' said the woman, smiling at Ken. 'Roz Knight.'

Ken introduced himself and Charlie, his, er . . .

'Nephew,' Charlie came in promptly. 'Uncle Ken's taking me up to see the match.' Gratefully, Ken opened his wallet to give Charlie a tenner to buy a packet of crisps.

Determined not to lose ground, Steve made a suggestion. Why didn't Roz, Ken, Charlie and himself make up a foursome and go to the game together. He could get them into the press box. Roz, however, announced that she already had a seat in the directors' box. It turned out she organized the Manager of the Week Award on behalf of Bison Aftershave. Bison were having a presentation in the morning and Roz had been invited to stay on afterwards for the match.

Steve, trying to recover poise, asked who'd won it but Roz wouldn't say. Ken though, explained it must be Ron Bishop. After all, it would have to be one of the semi-final managers and it couldn't be Lennie Neves, as he had a beard. Steve couldn't understand what difference *that* would make but Ken didn't choose to enlighten him.

'Are you sure you aren't one of those investigative journalists, Mr Wordsworth?' breathed Roz.

'Ken, please,' said Ken. But just at that moment their tête-à-tête was abruptly ended. The barman hadn't believed that Charlie was eighteen. Ken and Roz decided to move onto wine instead and Steve, knowing when he was beaten, went to buy it. Charlie opened his sandwich box. He was obviously going to have to keep himself amused.

When they got to Liverpool and arrived at the hotel there was a swarm of footballers emerging from a coach parked in the forecourt. A few kids were hanging round collecting autographs. Always on the look-out for an exclusive, Steve sidled up to one of the players to ask if his hamstring was going to stand up to the game the next day, and was told that it would cost him fifty quid to find out.

Ken and Roz passed on into the hotel foyer, ignored by the autograph hunters, but Charlie got caught up in the melee surrounding an imposing figure opulently dressed in a camel coat and smoking a cigar. Scattering autographs around like maundy money, the man pulled Charlie's dictionary from his hand, signed it with a gold pen, handed it back and swanned into the hotel, leaving Charlie open-mouthed behind him.

'Something tells me your Manager of the Week has just blown into town,' Ken said to Roz, inhaling the aftershave-heavy air. She smiled, and left him with Charlie.

'Who's Ron Bishop?' asked Charlie, studying the autograph in his dictionary.

'He's the City Manager,' explained Ken. 'One of football's Mr Bigs.'

'Mr Big Head,' I reckon,' said Charlie.

'Erm – about dinner.'

'Don't panic – I know when I'm not wanted.'

'Good lad. I'll do the same for you one day. I tell you what – we'll call room service, get you a nice fat hamburger . . . '

'No thanks,' said Charlie, pulling a face. 'Not after your beer and Mum's sandwiches.'

Back in Fleet Street that same afternoon Reg and Frank were looking for a lead story. It was a toss up between a semi-final preview or a Grand National injury scare. It was the jockey not the horse who was injured, but on the other hand it was a woman jockey, which might make a good story. Reg sifted through the Press Releases. 'Listen to this, Frank. "City Manager Ron Bishop is again winner of the Bison Manager of the Week Award. Commenting on the Award, City Chairman Mr Feisal Akbar said 'This award represents yet another testimonial to the superb managership of Ron Bishop. The club would like to take this opportunity of putting on record its full support for the manager and expressing every confidence in our joint future.' "'

Reg looked at Frank meaningfully. Frank didn't get it. 'They're giving him a vote of confidence . . .'

Frank still didn't get it. 'Why not? He'd got them to the semis, they're in the top three of the first division . . . last four in the UEFA Cup . . .'

'Exactly! He doesn't *need* a vote of confidence. . . . A football chairman saying this is like a Fleet Street proprietor saying "I guarantee there will be no redundancies". I think I'll let Ken Wordsworth cut his teeth on this.'

'Him?' said Frank, with disdain. 'He couldn't find a pub in Glasgow.'

But that evening Ken wasn't looking for pubs, and certainly not in Glasgow. He sat in the hotel restaurant waiting for his dinner guest to arrive. Steve Stevens dropped by wanting him to go down the Continental for a bit of a leer but when Roz arrived Steve quickly realized his mistake and left the two of them alone. Ken had taken the liberty of ordering a bottle of champagne.

The atmosphere was so conducive to confidences that he even admitted to Roz that Charlie was in fact his son, not his nephew. Roz, however, had already deduced this for herself.

'How many uncles do *you* know who carry their nephews' photos around in their wallets?'

Just as things were going really well a waiter arrived with a portable phone. A call for Ken. It was Reg. No, Ken had heard nothing at all. It seemed a bit unlikely didn't it? All right, Ken would ask around . . . without talking to anybody. He apologized to Roz. 'Sorry about that. Just my new editor flying a kite.'

The waiter was told not to disturb them again and Ken launched into reminiscences about the old days on the *Northern Echo*.

'Friday nights before the match were spent on a pub-crawl of Darlington with the local centre-forward . . . twelve pints, a meat-and-potato pie, then back to his digs for a blast of Gene Vincent till three in the morning . . . No wonder they were in the Fourth Division . . . I'll just make a note of that if you don't mind – nostalgia's a theme of my first piece.'

'It's funny,' mused Roz. 'The more I become involved with sports people, the more I realize how obsessed they are with the past.'

'That's simple,' explained Ken. 'Most people see their lives as moving towards something . . . in sport, the best years are nearly always behind you.'

'Present company excepted, of course.'

Ken was just scanning the menu for meat-and-potato pie à l'orange when a white face appeared at the door. It was Charlie in his dressing gown.

'Why didn't you answer the phone, Dad? I've been sick. Three times.' He announced loudly. 'I told you I was too young to drink.'

Ken got up, exchanging a resigned look with Roz.

'Didn't expect to see you around this morning.' Steve whispered in Ken's ear in the hotel reception the next day, as he gave him a friendly nudge.

'No,' agreed Ken. 'I could have done with a few more hours in bed.'

'I bet. Up all night were you?'

'Most of it. Running backwards and forwards to the wash-basin.'

Steve's eyes nearly popped out of his head. 'Cor, she sounds a right raver. You jammy Arab! What about this Bison do of hers – you gonna go?'

Ken said he thought he might look in. It was being held in a youth club for under-privileged children and it might do Charlie good to see how the other half lived.

'Under-privileged? Does that mean there won't be any booze?' asked Steve. 'I don't think I fancy listening to Ron Bishop bunnying without a drink in my hand. Anyway, he isn't going to make the big announcement till just before kick off.'

Ken had a moment of panic. 'What big announcement's that?'

'About Wayne Jarvis' hamstring of course. I think I'll go and get a few hairs of the dog inside me before *Football Focus* . . . otherwise it'll be *Football Out of Focus*, eh?'

Charlie, meanwhile, was going to accompany his father, even if he hadn't felt well enough for any breakfast. Ken was anxious Charlie put some weight back on before they met up with Alison again. They decided to share a taxi to the Youth Club with Roz. The three of them were just about to leave when the hotel manageress pressed an ornate charm bracelet into Roz's hand. She'd apparently left it in her bathroom. Ken wished she'd left it in his.

The presentation went smoothly. Ron Bishop held forth at length to the boys of the Swanside Road Boys' Club about how providing sports facilities for city kids was very close to his heart, and went on to match the Manager of the Week money – 'the rhino from Bison' – with a cheque of his own. Ken enjoyed this, even though there didn't seem to be any sort of story here that Reg would be interested in. But then Russell de Vries walked through the door. Russell

18

was one of the reasons Ken had changed jobs. His life was a blurb-writer's dream: journalist, columnist, occasional novelist . . . there was nothing Russell couldn't turn his hand to – except perhaps a stint on the subs' desk on a Saturday, when lesser mortals like Ken had to wrestle with Russell's ornate and multi-lingual copy. Ken hated him, and Russell knew it, but that didn't stop him sidling over.

'Ken mate,' he whispered to his ex-colleague. 'So sorry to have missed your leaving bash yesterday, but I had a prior engagement.'

'That's alright Russell,' Ken whispered back. 'You weren't invited anyway. I'm amazed you're here, let alone interested. It's a bit unpromising, even for someone who once compared a Joe Bugner fight to Grand Opera.'

'Oh yes "The Ring Cycle" – I'm flattered you remember it.'

'I also remember the two hours it took me to rewrite it in English,' said Ken darkly.

'Well, that's all behind you now, Ken – you've emerged from the shadows after labouring so long in my vineyards. Buona fortuna, mate . . .'

'Thank you, Russell . . . I'd like you to know that, whatever happens, there's nobody whose grapes I'd rather tread than yours.'

Ken decided to show Russell how a real journalist operated. While Ron Bishop was autographing a football for the Boys' Club so they 'could get as big a kick out of him as he did out of them', Ken managed to get a quick word with him.

'Ron, there's a bit of a rumour going around, probably nothing in it of course, that the City board might be, well, reconsidering your position . . . as manager that is. Have you any comment?'

Ron exploded. 'Yeah! You're like bloody vultures you lot. Fancy asking me that at a time like this – two hours before the biggest match in my life! Here's something you can write – see you at Wembley, okay! Talk about gutter press . . .'

'Settling in nicely I see,' Russell observed, as Ron stormed out.

* * *

At the ground, the only way Ken could get Charlie into the press box was by making him pretend he only had one arm, and pinning the empty sleeve to Charlie's shoulder. This gained the instant sympathy of the one-armed commissionaire, who showed them to two seats together in the front row, gesturing to Russell de Vries with his remaining arm to make way for them, much to Russell's annoyance. Not that Russell was watching the match – he was trying to concentrate on the new Iris Murdoch, having already written his report. Charlie didn't like the atmosphere in the press-box: there was no sense of excitement or enthusiasm, not even when City scored the goal that took them to Wembley. Charlie forgot where he was and started to wave and cheer . . . until Ken reminded him of his empty sleeve.

In the Press Room afterwards Russell was phoning through his copy. 'There were two football matches here today . . . point. By far the more rewarding experience . . . was provided by . . . the Swanside Road Boys' Club . . . point. It is this song of innocence . . . I propose to describe to you, comma, . . . rather than the dirge of the grown-up game . . . you will find bruited elsewhere . . . *Bruited* . . . That's "B" . . . "R" . . . '

'Same old Russell,' Ken confided in Charlie. 'Catering for the Bloomsbury Boot Boys as only he can. Well, at least ten years of listening to that made going home to your mother seem like light relief.'

Charlie was mildly offended. It wasn't much fun being a one-armed boy from a single-parent family.

Steve Stevens was wolfing the sandwiches, complaining that all the sausage rolls had gone and that the game itself had been poxy – one goal and the worst player on the park scoring it. Charlie couldn't help adding that he thought Wayne Jarvis had played rather well, which unnerved Steve slightly. He'd thought Jarvis had just headed the ball down for Williams. Still, he'd get it off *Match of the Day* that night.

Ron Bishop finally arrived, carrying a crate of champagne and Steve set to work interviewing him. No, Ron didn't think the fact that City were going to Wembley would sink in until a few of the glasses of champagne had. Yes, he'd been into the dressing room to see Lennie Neves and Neves was gutted, feeling as bad as Ron felt good. Yes, he'd spoken to Mr Akbar and yes, Mr Akbar was over the crescent moon. So happy, in fact, that he'd offered Ron a new five-year contract. Ken listened attentively. And finally, Yes, Ron Bishop would be wearing his lucky charm on his right arm as always for the match at Wembley. Ron raised his right arm . . . which sported the very bracelet that Roz Knight had left behind in her bathroom. 'It's what your right arm's for,' boasted Ron.

Ken couldn't believe his eyes. He looked across to the door of the Press Box. There was Roz Knight. She exchanged a glance with Ron and disappeared outside. Ken filled two glasses with Ron Bishop's champagne and headed after her.

He found Roz sitting alone in the Press Box watching the lights go out.

'Do you come with the award, then?'

'Ken, I think you're chasing the wrong story.'

'Am I? Seems fairly straight-forward to me . . . your dinner date gets called away to look after a sick child, so Ron Bishop gets called off the substitute's bench, and what do you know? Suddenly he's lucky charmed his way into your . . . bathroom!'

Roz looked at him. 'Ken, why do you think Ron's won so many of our Awards? I've been having an affair with him for eighteen months.'

Ken paused. 'Oh, terrific! I beg your pardon, I got it wrong again – *I* was the substitute. Or was I just warming you up on the touchline?'

'You were holding my hand while Ron was deciding his future, and whether I was going to be part of it. City are very proud of their reputation as a family club . . . so it wouldn't be much good for their image if the manager suddenly deserted his wife and two kids. They finally found out about us this week. Ron was hauled in and the chairman gave him a choice – either I went or his job did. He's made his decision now . . . or rather it's been made for him out there this afternoon. I mean, which would you rather choose – "The love of a good woman" or leading your team out at Wembley?'

'I'm sorry,' Ken said. 'If it's any consolation I put sport before a relationship once . . . and look what a shambles I am.'

'I wouldn't mind,' Roz smiled bitterly, 'But it was such a crummy goal! So now all I can do, the same as any other jilted girl, is to run home to mum in Huddersfield.'

While Roz took the train to Huddersfield, Ken, Charlie, Steve and Russell de Vries headed back to London. Steve was unable to get a drink from the bar which was closed because of the football fans on board. Steve called them all the insulting names he could think of – conveniently ignoring the fact that most of them were his readers – before settling down for a nap. Russell looked at him with contempt. 'I drink, therefore I am'.

Without realizing it, Ken had started to think of Steve as a colleague – more than Russell had ever been, anyway, and defended him. After all, Steve had got to write seventy-five words about the game by the next day and he'd already summed it up in two.

Russell saw the way for a quick burst of reminiscences. 'Ah yes, the Sunday afternoon treadmill. I remember writing essays at Oxford then – the hush of the library, the dappled shadows slowly lengthening across the desk, the chapel bell languorously announcing vespers . . . Have you thought what you're going to write about? Do tell.'

'You'll only sneer.' But Russell seemed genuinely interested, so Ken went on. 'You know that cliché about "nobody remembers the teams that lose semi-finals"? Well I do. I identify much more with Lennie Neves and his lads going home on the motorway desperately trying to organize a sing-song, than with the Ron Bishops, all champagne, phoney awards and five-years contracts. And don't get the idea that I'm just miffed after my little contretemps with Bishop . . . Ron Bishop only got his new contract because he agreed to ditch his girlfriend. He kept winning the Bison Award because it was the only way his girlfriend could keep seeing him. Do you see what I mean? Losing seems so much purer somehow . . . '

Russell had to agree. 'And there's certainly a piece to be written – "Losing as an Ethic. Discuss".'

'Hands off, Russell,' warned Ken. 'I've already bagged a seat in the library . . . '

But any seats had already been bagged by Steve Stevens. As luck would have it, he hadn't been able to drift off to sleep. And he wouldn't be writing about the ethics of losing, or worrying about the ethics of exposing Ron Bishop's affair.

Ken was wrestling with his piece on Lennie Neves when Alison dropped by to pick Charlie up. It was the first time she'd been to his new flat and she found it difficult to hide her distaste at the chaos of half-unpacked suitcases, tea chests full of books, and piles of bedclothes on the sofa. At least it was compact. As she wasn't going to get much of a response from Ken, she asked Charlie, what he'd done all weekend.

'Well,' replied Charlie carefully, 'I had a lot of beer on the train up. I was sick in the hotel room while Dad was downstairs trying to pull some woman, I've had nothing to eat all weekend and I could only get into the match by pretending I had one arm . . . ' Ken stopped typing for a moment but luckily Alison didn't recognize the truth when she heard it. He couldn't help wondering why she had come round. They had arranged that Ken would drop Charlie off later. However, when she started asking him about his new job and about how many columns he'd be writing each week, the truth dawned on him. She wanted money. As he handed her fifty pounds, it passed through his mind that he ought to get his typewriter fitted with a till. The money was for cello lessons for Charlie, so that, as Charlie put it, if he didn't get into Oxford he'd have another string to his bow.

'Don't you be railroaded, son,' advised Ken. 'Do exactly what you want to do. If you want to be a sportswriter, don't let anyone try and stop you – I'll back you all the way.'

But a sportswriter was one thing Charlie never wanted to be. What was the point of being read at everyone's breakfast tables if it meant you were never at your own?

Ken couldn't stand the suspense of waiting to see his words in print under his own masthead, and came in early to pick up the first edition. He caught up with Reg in The Inkwell. Reg shook him by what Reg described as his talented right hand. It was so good, Reg said, that he had read it twice and from now on anyone who told Reg Prosser that his sports pages lacked quality was going to be chinned. He was just ordering a bottle of champagne when Frank turned up, clutching early editions of Steve Stevens handiwork. Reg read it in horror. 'Wembley Boss in Love Tangle' announced the headline. 'Glamorous Roz Knight, 32, the girl in the life of top soccer boss Ron Bishop, last night spoke exclusively to me about their torrid affair as she sat and wept in the Huddersfield home of her mother, 59 . . . ' It was the headline that distressed Frank most. He could hardly bear to think what he could have done with that story – 'Bishop Falls From Grace' . . . 'Bishop Takes Knight'. Reg, however, was more virulent. 'He's aced you, sunshine!' he yelled at Ken. 'He gets the girl to nobble Bishop on the front page then the club to nobble Bishop on the back! Classic pincer movement!'

Neither Reg nor Frank appreciated Ken's defence. It may have been just a sad story about the private lives of two people who just happened to be involved in football, as Ken claimed. True, if Ron had been a *bank* manager if wouldn't have gone on the financial pages. But that sort of story sells papers. Who was going to notice Ken's piece with a splash like that around?

* * *

As luck would have it, who should Ken come across as he emerged from The Inkwell after this heated discussion but the Brain of Britain taxi-driver.

'You haven't got a spare brain to lend me have you?' asked Ken, climbing into the taxi.

'Where you going, guv?' chuckled the driver.

'Downhill I'd say.'

The driver had taken his advice and invested a few hard-earned pence in his rag.

'That's right,' moaned Ken. 'Kick me when I'm down . . . '

'Great stuff!'

'What?'

'The column – I loved it. I mean, I still hate sport, but I like the way you write.'

'It's nice to know someone still appreciates me . . . come on, head for Smithfield and I'll buy you breakfast.'

'Thanks very much, guv – I'm a vegetarian, mind. No, I was most impressed – I reckon you've got a great future . . . have you ever thought of working for one of the quality Sunday papers?'

Ken shut the dividing window. He wanted to be alone with his thoughts.

GRASS ROOTS

'That's right, Frank, make yourself at home,' Reg told his Deputy Sports Editor one Sunday lunchtime as he swaggered into his office. But Frank already had. He was sitting in Reg's Sports Editor's Chair, munching a take-away hamburger and reading one of the Sunday papers which served as a tablecloth underneath. Frank's excuse was that he'd been keeping Reg's seat warm for him while his boss was out playing pro-celebrity golf with Tarby and Parky. Not that Reg was either a pro or a celebrity. He was the hyphen in the middle – he brought the two worlds together. The trouble was, he'd got back from a quiet round to find some bastard had swiped his new Gucci loafers. Souvenir hunters no doubt. The price of fame. The worst part was driving back to Fleet Street – he must have been doing 90 down Ludgate Hill with a spiked golf shoe stuck on the accelerator. He'd have to have words with Jimmy Tarbuck about the company he kept.

Which is why his hamburger and chips were cold. Reg and Frank were not there, however, just to eat take-aways. This was an editorial meeting to discuss the week ahead the prospect of which looked bleak. The Second Test was starting that Thursday and one of the Aussies had a drink problem, but, as Reg said, find one that hasn't, there's the story. It was Royal Ascot as well. The thought of having that blue-haired cow from Fashion in to discuss silly hats filled them with dismay. And then there was Wimbledon. Reg was relying on Frank to come up with some fresh angles. They couldn't do 'Spot the Moustache' in the Ladies Doubles *again*. Trouble was, Steve Stevens had already beaten them to it in offering five grand to any of the British players who got past the first round, the unpatriotic dog. Reg's only solution was to put The Poet Laureate on to it. He could write an Ode to the Death of British Tennis. Poetry, thought Frank, was all Ken Wordsworth was fit for.

Still, Ken was probably a lot more strawberries-and-cream than hamburger-and-chips.

At the time Ken would probably have rather been eating strawberries or even hamburgers than quarrelling over a tennis match. He and Alison had decided to play a friendly game, Alison with Charlie against Ken and Ben Smith, a schoolfriend of Charlie's. Ben happened to be tall and strong for his age, besides being black – a whizz-kid of a tennis player – but Ken's game was so poor that he had to indulge in a little cheating to prevent Alison and Charlie from doing too well. Unfortunately he over-played his hand. When Alison served what was pronounced by Ken as her seventh double fault she lost her temper. It was all very well Ken explaining it away by saying that Alison was terrified of his forehand return, his *dream* of a forehand return as they said in the trade; his trade was a professional liar.

Alison agreed to continue, reluctantly. Three set points to Ken and Ben. While her opponents were still discussing the score Alison turned and smashed a lethal serve at Ben. Ben, however, turned casually and smashed it back with equal force, neatly bisecting Alison and Charlie for a perfect winner. This was too much for Alison. She stalked to the bench at the side of the court and started putting her track-suit on. Ken left Charlie and Ben to carry on themselves for a bit while he sorted the little tantrum out.

'Bit on edge, aren't we, old girl?' he asked, sitting down beside her. 'I'll get the butler to fetch you a lemon tea from the house, shall I? Why are you so overstrung? You didn't invite me over for a nostalgic look at my legs – so what does that leave? Let me see – money?'

He was right. Alison had plans to send Charlie to a private school. He was turning into a right Cor Blimey where he was. There were no facilities, it was run down, the teachers didn't care. Ken, needless to say, didn't agree. He remembered Cuthbert Street Juniors – fifty in a class, ten to a desk, sharing books and toilets. Just the incentive you needed to make something of yourself. And here was

Alison trying to persuade him he should stop seeing Charlie for six months at a time because she wanted his only son to be stuck in some three-in-a-bed public school somewhere in the middle of nowhere – and at his expense. Alison, though, had already thought of that. Firstly, Charlie would be a day boy. The school she had in mind was in the middle of Wandsworth. As for the expense, couldn't his paper help him out with the fees? Ken could see he wasn't getting through.

'Alison, I don't believe in public schools – they're mainly for parents who aren't responsible enough to look after their own children.'

Alison looked at her ex-husband, his wild hair held out of place by a sweatband, dressed in a muddy track suit and dilapidated sneakers. 'Responsible. Listen, Ken – bloody sportswriting broke up our marriage so it can bloody well pay for Charlie's education.'

Ken and Alison weren't the only ones quarrelling. Reg and Frank had been enjoying a nice quiet game of darts in The Inkwell, joking about how Reg should be playing with Ken, rather than Frank, who kept missing the board altogether, because Ken's limp wrist would be aero-dynamically suited to darts, when who should lumber in but Steve Stevens and his cronies. Reg signed them in on chalk on the blackboard: '3 PRATTS'.

Steve was looking for champagne and The Inkwell was the only place that served it at five o'clock on a Sunday afternoon. Reg couldn't help voicing his surprise Steve could afford it with the prospect of having to fork out so much prize money at Wimbledom.

'What, us? Fork out?' jeered Steve. 'Haven't you ever heard of laying off, Reg? To give away five grand, all you do is stick a few bob on at the bookies, and if the geezers get through, we're covered! If they don't, it's still been worth the money in terms of flying the flag – *our* flag, that is.'

'There's a word for that sort of thing, Stevens, immoral.'

'That's two words, innit?'

It was then that things got heated. Steve was shown the

door by Ruby but not before he'd accused Reg of being cheesed 'cos he hadn't thought of the idea first and Reg had found himself boasting that Steve would wish he were back on the Beano once he saw what Reg and his crew had up their sleeves for the coming week. Reg just hoped The Poet Laureate could come up with a good idea.

Ken was dropping Ben home. it seemed like the perfect opportunity to find out the truth behind Alison's stories about Charlie's school. Ben wasn't very complimentary.

'It's a dump, with a capital "D" – although we do have a lot of laughs. I mean, there's one hard court, but it's got so many weeds growing through it it looks like a grass court. The history teacher takes games and he must be over forty.'

'That's old, huh,' said Ken, tactfully.

''Course, he's even worse at history. As for other subjects, if I get an O-level next year, it'll be for tennis – just drop me at the next corner, thanks.'

'It's okay, I'll take you to your door.'

'We didn't have one last time I looked. I'm serious. If you value your hub-caps, just drop me here.'

Ben got out and Ken watched from his car as he turned into the seedy South London street, his sports bag over his shoulder. So much for leaving the jungle. To make it worse, the kid obviously had great talent as a tennis player.

When Reg asked Ken to come up with something that would put Steve Stevens' story in the shade, Ken did have an answer. He'd write about the need to solve the problems of British tennis by putting the money in the right places instead of into promotional stunts like Steve's. Of course, he wouldn't mention Steve's paper by name . . . 'You may have read elsewhere this week' . . . then he'd go on to write about the need for new facilities – tennis courts on Hackney Marshes as well as football pitches, encouraging city kids to start playing and producing champions from among them, putting an end to the custom of having the game run by a load of amateurs as a private club. The one problem – as Reg saw it – was how to make the story interesting. The only solution a stunned Ken could come up with was to type it topless.

It was while thinking over what Ben had told him that inspiration grabbed him. Which is why, two days later Ken and Ben drew up in Ken's car at a smart, private London tennis club and took out their rackets. Ken shut the car door and, followed by Ben, walked along the gravel path, by the hedges and trim verges, towards the grass courts in front of the elegant clubhouse: a complete contrast to the municipal court they'd played on with Alison and Charlie. As they passed one or two members in crisp white tennis gear they were given rather odd looks, but nothing was said. Ben was starting to get uneasy.

'Don't worry,' Ken assured him, 'we're not doing anything illegal. Just conducting a little experiment in social mobility.' That may have been why Ben felt like running away.

Ken walked confidently onto the nearest grass court and positioned himself at the far end. Ben waited reluctantly as Ken ostentatiously bounced the ball up and down ready for a knock up. Again they attracted curious glances from players on an adjacent court. Ken served to Ben, who returned the serve easily. Ken just managed to get it back. By now a middle-aged woman had appeared in the doorway of a portakabin office next to the clubhouse and was staring in their direction. Seeing her, Ben let Ken's shot pass him. In the distance, the woman walked quickly into the clubhouse. Ken could see this out of the corner of his eye. He, for one, was enjoying the situation. He served again and Ben started to get into the swing of things, effortlessly winning every point even though Ken was trying by now.

'Ace playing surface,' Ben remarked as a serve whizzed past Ken. 'What do they call it?'

'Grass, I think . . . makes all the difference, doesn't it?'

'Yeah – even makes *you* look average.'

By this time they were so engrossed in their game that

they hadn't noticed the approach of a man in his early forties, dressed in a sports jacket and flannels.

'Um – I think we may have a problem,' the man announced.

' 'Course – I beg your pardon,' and Ken fetched some cash out of his track suit pocket. 'How much is it? Two pounds an hour or so?'

'Slightly more than that, I'm afraid – this is a Members Only club you see.'

'All right, we'll join then. Ben – gent here wants us to join. Where do we go?'

'It isn't as simple as that either, sir.'

'Ken. And you are . . . ?'

'Boyes. Warren Boyes – I'm a member of the committee.'

'Oh, we can sign up with you, then!'

'No, to join the club you have to be proposed and seconded by two members . . . '

'Well, they'll do, won't they?' Ken started signalling at the players on the next court.

' . . . Who know you and can vouch for you,' Boyes added quickly, his voice rising nervously. 'Also, I fear the fees might be outside your range. You see, it's £200 per annum, excluding the entrance fee and for under-18s it would be £75.'

After a moment's thought Ken made as if to set off for the car. 'I suppose it's worth it,' he told Boyes. 'I'll just get my cheque book.'

'No, don't do that.' Boyes looked even more agitated. 'You see, even if you are accepted for membership, there's also a waiting list. Three years.'

'But he'll be over the hill by then! Not to say over 18.'

'If he wants to make it to Wimbledon, he's going to have to try elsewhere. I think that's much the best idea, don't you?'

Ken's eyes gleamed in the afternoon sunlight.

Reg's gleamed too when he saw the piece Ken wrote on the afternoon's exploits. If you ain't got the money and the right connections, you ain't got a prayer. Ken had said it all.

31

It was then that Ken's scheme for adopting Ben Smith, paying for his coaching and all his equipment and giving him all the financial back-up he needed to become a top British player really caught Reg's imagination. They could, as he put it, 'groom the kid for stardom'. Once Ken's piece about the Private Club appeared, they'd get hundreds of letters of protest, even if Frank did have to write most of them, and then they could step forward to give tennis new balls. Ken could do a 'Who is Ben Smith?' personality piece and then write regular reports on his progress. A second *Pygmalion*: Ben Smith *shall* go to the ball. Ken's half-hearted attempt to get Reg to agree to the paper's subsidizing Charlie's school fees as well didn't meet with quite the same approval. 'What do you think we are, made of money?'

Alison, meanwhile, had been doing her own research and fund-raising. On Tuesday afternoon she had an appointment to look at Emanuel School, Wandsworth. She was shown round the lavishly-equipped, modern classrooms by a young teacher in a gown, who talked of seminars and audio-visual aids. Alison's quip that for Charlie audio-visual aids meant Bugs Bunny cartoons to keep him quiet, was rather lost on the teacher, who didn't have a vast knowledge of cartoon rabbits. Alison was more reluctant to look at the sporting facilities – the indoor swimming-pool, tennis and squash courts – Charlie, she informed the teacher, was more academically inclined. One sports maniac in the family was enough. Not that he *was* in the family exactly. The teacher was quick to reassure her that it wouldn't count against Charlie at all that his parents were divorced. In his opinion the public school system couldn't survive without the illegitimate offspring of peers of the realm. He was curious though, as to what Ms Rathbone's ex-husband actually did. Reluctantly Alison admitted that Ken was a sportswriter, though she was careful not to mention the paper. The teacher was impressed. One of their better-known old boys was a Fleet Street sportswriter – a certain Russell de Vries . . .

Which is why Alison served tea and cake to Russell de Vries in her living-room the next day. Russell was only too flattered to have his brains picked about Emanuel, though he had to admit that it was more years than he cared to remember since he had been head of Lyons. Alison didn't dare let on that she wasn't quite sure what Lyons were, though they sounded quite a responsibility. Russell would be delighted to get Charlie into his old House, just as he was happy to renew his acquaintance with Ken's ex-wife. The last time they met had been a couple of years before at the office outing to Goodwood. Russell had gone on to Glyndebourne in the evening and Ken and Alison had come back early to watch a pre-season friendly at Millwall.

Russell did his best to be polite about Ken's new job.

'How is Ken settling into, er, his new career? Painting on a broader canvas?'

Alison was equally careful. 'He seems to find it quite challenging.'

'I can imagine it must be. I couldn't do it. I'm more of a miniaturist I suppose.'

Before the conversation could get any stickier, Charlie arrived. He wasn't at his most polite to Russell. Yes, he remembered him. Ken used to rewrite his stuff. Charlie had hoped to get stuck into Bugs Bunny but Alison insisted he sit and chat for a bit first. She seemed pleased when he told her Ken had come round that day after school but then she asked all sorts of stupid questions about whether he'd talked to the headmaster or spoken to Charlie's form teacher or just walked around looking at the state of everything. She seemed a bit put-out when he explained that Ken had traipsed half-way across London just to take Ben to play tennis.

To ease the awkwardness, Russell started telling Alison and the boy about the marvellous tennis facilities at Emanuel. This went down like a concrete custard. Alison hadn't wanted Charlie to know anything about her plans until *they* were concrete. By now he *must* be suspicious.

* * *

It was decided that it should be Ken's job to persuade Ben Smith's father that his son would be perfectly safe as a newspaper protégé. Rupert Smith lived in a grotty council flat. He showed Charlie's father Ben's room proudly. It was covered with posters of tennis players, and even the wallpaper had a raquet motif. Ken noticed that there weren't any posters of Buster Mottram, though naturally enough Arthur Ashe featured heavily.

As a way of easing the atmosphere with Rupert, Ken started reminiscing about the Ashe versus Connors match. He'd been at a wedding reception in Durham and everybody had stopped drinking to watch it. Arthur Ashe got more tears than the bride. Ben remembered it, too, Rupert explained, because although he was very young at the time, he'd been asleep on his father's lap. When Arthur won, Rupert had jumped up and Ben had fallen off. He'd been nuts about tennis ever since.

Rupert seemed worried that the sponsorship might mean that Ben and he would be separated, but Ken was keen to point out that there was no danger of that. At this stage all it meant was a few hours' coaching and some extra competition, and perhaps the odd photographer turning up . . . at the school sports day, for example. Nor would the pictures go over the top. Ben wouldn't be dressed up as Man Friday, like Viv Richards had been. Ken had his principles. He didn't believe in ruining the next generation. He would give Rupert his word that Ben would be presented exactly as he was, not turned into something he wasn't. So would Rupert accept a gentleman's agreement? He still wasn't sure. Could Ken have a word with Mrs Smith? Ben's father smiled. He'd have to go to Trinidad for that. He was a single-parent family. Ken seized on the coincidence.

Funnily enough, so was he, he assured Rupert. They made a single parent's agreement.

It was when Ken let slip that Ben Smith, the Great White Hope of British Tennis, was actually black that things started to go wrong. Reg went mad. What difference did it make? About a quarter of a million readers, that was all. The fact was that they had to pander to those readers' tastes – tastes which Reg called patriotic and Ken called downright racist. Nor would Reg be swayed by a mention of Daley Thompson. He was different. He sold newspapers. What was more, half the birds in the country wanted to boff him, Ruby included. It was only when Frank came in on Ken's side, relating it to his own experience as a Scot in facing racial prejudice, that Reg changed his tune. Nevertheless, the boy's name would have to be changed. Ben Smith was too boring. What they needed was a combination of Caribbean charisma and the British bulldog. Something more ethnic, with a tennis flavour. When Ken suggested 'Robinson Barley-Water' Reg and Frank didn't realize he was joking.

Frank set to work. Zola Budd, he explained, was a perfect name. Reg had heard she'd originally been called Joyce Duckworth but they'd had to change it. By now Frank had closed his eyes and was in a sort of semi-hypnotic trance. 'You want to watch this,' Reg confided in Ken. 'He's a human word processor.'

'First name . . . Winston.'

'I'll buy that . . . Keep going, Frank . . .'

'Bingo!'

'Yeah . . . so what's the name?'

'Bingo! Winston Bingo! The man who's gonna win a million pounds!'

Reg thought about it. 'Right . . . *and* it sounds like it comes from the jungle. You know, N'Bingo!'

They turned proudly to Ken. 'In the words of another tennis star – "you cannot be serious". And if that kid's called anything other than Ben Smith, I'm resigning.'

Frank looked quite hopeful at this. Two birds with one stone. But Reg felt he owed a certain loyalty to Ken. Ken in turn was relieved at having protected at least this part of Ben's journey from SW9 to SW19. He was beginning to realize that Reg was a bit more sensitive than he first appeared. He went off to order three pints of *Sam* Smiths in celebration, while Reg tried to appease his deputy. 'Never mind, Frank. He'll always be Winston Bingo to us. Tell you what – get onto that photographer pal of yours . . . see if he's got a junior version of that Man Friday costume.'

Ken ran into Russell de Vries in the Press Marquee at Wimbledon the next day. He very rarely watched tennis when he was at Wimbledon. They tucked into strawberries and cream, ignoring the live tennis match on a small television screen in one corner.

'I hope you'll be steering your protégé clear of such temptations,' ventured Russell as he balanced seven strawberries on his desertspoon.

Ken chose to ignore the reference to Ben. 'Ironic, isn't it, Russell, this stuff being associated with tennis. Not to mention lager and fags . . . if the average player lived on them and clotted cream, he'd drop dead on court!'

'Because,' continued Russell, doggedly, 'It would be tragic if such a promising youngster fell into the clutches of Mammon. While he's in your tender care, that is.'

Ken could just imagine what Ben's story would have looked like on Russell's Sunday pages – a mass coach-in for the disadvantaged in Hyde Park . . . and a professor of sociology explaining why blacks look good wearing white. But Russell didn't rise to this, praising instead Ken's skill at discovering a new 'Wilson of the *Wizard*' out in the wilds of South London. It struck Ken that he might be being a bit hard on old de Vries. 'I'm just off to see Ben now, actually,' he confided, 'Knocking spots off my son Charlie in the 400 metres . . . just like the "Tough of the Track".' Then he left, not realizing how Ben's journey from Wandsworth to Wimbledon had suddenly been made all the more difficult and dangerous by that one chance remark.

Russell was won over by Ken's responsible attitude to the young lad, so when Steve Stevens came in to watch a bit of telly, Russell couldn't resist telling him that far from going off to buy Ben his first diamond earstud Ken was supporting him at the most down-to-earth of events: a school sports day. 'Which school would this be?' asked Steve, innocently. It seemed such a waste to Stevens, Captain Sensible getting hold of a kid like that. Steve could have done so much more with him . . . he'd have been a superstar by now. Books, TV, smart girlfriends . . . and Ben himself would have done all right out of it too! Captain Sensible was about to meet Captain Invincible.

The Sports Day started stickily for Ken when Alison buttonholed him about asking Reg about Charlie's school fees and he had to admit that Reg had seen his heart wasn't really in it. Ken just didn't want any son of his not having the disadvantages he'd had as a lad – and judging by the state of Charlie's school, he wouldn't be. Alison couldn't help taking out her bitterness in Rupert Smith's presence: 'You must be very pleased with Ben's success. Good old Ken. It's amazing what he can do when he puts his heart into something.' Ben, meanwhile, was having his photograph taken for Ken's story, and enduring lots of ribbing from the other kids.

'We must be the only newspaper in Fleet Street covering a school sports day,' said Ken . . . and promptly saw Fleet Street appear in the shape of none other than Steve Stevens striding rapidly across the field, stopping on the other side of the track, looking hard at Ben, then looking at his watch. At that moment an ominously large, black BMW came into vision, driving across the field towards them.

The four hundred metres' race began. As Ben and the others started along the track the BMW drew up alongside Steve, he jumped in, and it set off round the inside of the track in pursuit of the runners. The truth dawned on Ken. This was an attack of cheque-book journalism in its purest form!

By now Ben had a long lead. The car pulled up alongside him and Steve hung out of the back window with an unfolded document in one hand and a pen in the other.

'Oi, kid,' cajoled Steve, 'Do yourself a favour and sign for a real newspaper! We're gonna make you seriously rich . . . I've got five grand in readies in here – just get in the car . . . do you like the car? You can have it if you want it! Just get in . . . '

37

But Ben Smith had been told never to accept lifts from strangers, particularly strangers who then set about trying to carve him up. Steve and his cronies jumped out of the car, grabbed Ben and started bundling him into it when Charlie arrived, kicked Steve unceremoniously in the groin, and fought the cronies off Ben. Steve's men half-carried their groaning friend back to the car, pushed him in and roared off, but not before some of the spectators from the school had 'tarred and feathered' the car with whitewash and anything else that came to hand.

Luckily Ben was only a bit shaken. Charlie, meanwhile was over-the-moon at his own heroism. 'Look, dad, action replay. He's Steve, right and here's me. Right in the tabloids.' Ken was anxious to prevent this sort of thing happening again. Ben must stay with Alison and Charlie at the house in Wandsworth. He mustn't answer the phone or sign anything if it came through the letter-box, and he must keep well away from the front-door.

It had to be said that he was very grateful for Alison's help at a moment like this. Ben could stay as long as he liked with them, she said. After all, he'd be good company for Charlie. Then there were more hushed interchanges between Ken and Alison on the pros and cons of public school, which Charlie was supposed not to overhear. They must think he was deaf as well as stupid. He didn't know what his feelings were towards changing schools, but he did know that he would have liked to be consulted first. Adults always had to be so sensitive. Look at Ben. His ambitions were simple. He wanted to be the Michael Jackson of tennis and any chance that came along, he'd grab it.

Even Reg was rattled at Steve's tactics – the unprincipled bastard! was his mildest reaction. It was later the same day and the Sports Pages were in abeyance while they waited on Virginia Wade's tie-break at Wimbledon. Frank was exasperated at the selfishness of these British players, not losing in straight sets. Still, if the impossible happened and she won, he'd just have to change the headline from 'Wade Out' to 'Wade In', 'crashes' to 'crushes' and the picture on the masthead from the frowning Willmot to the smiling Willmot. Reg turned his attention to the important matter of getting Ben Smith nailed down. It was all very well Ken talking about his gentleman's agreement but strokes like that were no good when you were dealing with the gentlemen of the press.

Frank had his own ideas on how they should handle Ben from now on. He'd get on to a mate of his who'd been the minder for the Scotland football team in 1974. If they picked Ben up in Wandsworth they could get him down to Brixton and then they'd never be spotted. This didn't go down too well with Reg. Kidnapping, he said, wasn't in their line. And besides, they owed it to Ken to do this the right way. Thanks to Reg Prosser's pro-celebrity handbook, do it the right way they would.

Which is why the journey from SW9 to SW19 included a stop-over at the very club Ken and Ben had been turfed out of, for Ben to get some expert coaching from Mark Cox, watched over by Reg, who sat smoking a cigar, ensconced in the umpire's chair. Ken was just savouring the sight of Ben Smith playing in such elevated circumstances, when he was bear-hugged from behind by Ben's new bodyguard. Reg had to tell the heavy to drop Ken, whose suit looked as if it had been pressed for a second time that day. Reg was adamant that they couldn't be too careful. At least he could scan the horizon from his umpire's chair. Ben was playing a series of perfect forehand drives while Mark Cox returned them . . . but he was being made to play.

'Who *is* that Ben's giving a game to?' Ken asked Reg, but Reg didn't get the irony.

'Mark Cox,' he whispered, proudly. 'It's a sort of final MOT before we get this show on the road.' Reg didn't get his metaphors from the world of tennis.

Ben and Mark finished their knock-up and went over to the other two. Mark Cox seemed rather impressed to be meeting the man who had discovered such a promising new player, even if Reg did take the credit. While Ben was huddled off to the dressing room, in case he caught anything expensive, (closely followed by the faithful heavy) Ken listened to Mark Cox himself telling him that Charlie's schoolmate was a genuine prospect as an international tennis player, provided he had the right handling. At this Reg beamed. 'We'll make sure he gets a barrow-load of that, right Ken?' But Ken wasn't sure of this at all. He and Mark exchanged apprehensive glances.

Ken's suspicions were proved right when he and Ben were asked to attend a meeting in Reg's office with Warren Boyes – the very man who'd first thrown them out of the club. Warren Boyes featured in Reg's pro-celebrity handbook as a golfing partner. In fact, Reg's golf-swing had hit Warren Boyes so hard on the head the last time they played that Warren still felt touches of dizziness now and then. Warren's reunion with Ken was a trifle frosty.

'That piece you wrote caused quite a problem for us,' he told The Poet Laureate, who he noticed was rather more smartly dressed on this occasion. 'We were flooded with applications all seeking the very exclusiveness you found so offensive.'

Reg tried to ease the atmosphere. 'And we were swamped with letters of support,' he breezed, 'So we all did well out of that. The perfect relationship. Shall we all sit down?'

Ken and Ben felt like a couple of schoolboys, rather than a journalist and a tennis star. 'Funny how he wants to know us now, isn't it?' whispered Ben. But Warren Boyes was already well into his sales spiel. Firstly he thanked Reg for bringing Ben to the attention of his company, Net Gains Ltd. Secondly, he wanted to say that he felt sure a combination of Ben's raw talent and Warren's own all-round experience could go a long way. Quite possibly all the way. The question was, did Ben want to go all the way?

This one, Ken was determined Ben should answer for himself. There was a slight pause. Ben was suddenly serious. 'I want to go all the way, Mr Boyes.' Boyes opened his briefcase. Ben was to be provided with 'a complete tennis environment'. He should regard the club as his second home. Until, that is, he took up a tennis scholarship at one of the leading American universities, thanks to the sponsorship arranged for him by Warren Boyes' own company. Boyes described with enthusiasm a whole host of sports equipment, leisure-wear and health food, all waiting to be associated with a suitable personality. Ben was a nice boy who could be just the well-behaved, clean-cut ambassador the game was looking for, someone the Great British Public would be pleased to invite into their homes. Of course, Warren couldn't go from door to door introducing Ben personally . . . therefore he had to project Ben's image to as many people as possible by the most effective means. That afternoon Ben was to appear on the Centre Court at Wimbledon . . . as a ballboy. That would make good copy for Ken as well, even if Ken didn't agree with it. But first, as a way of sealing the deal, the makers of a new high-energy sports drink would like to know what Ben thought of it. Warren opened his briefcase and took out a small, lucozade-type bottle of purple liquid. Ken felt he'd just been beaten in straight sets . . . by Mammon.

'This isn't like you . . . ' Russell remonstrated with a moody-looking Ken over the strawberries in the Press Marquee. 'Come on, tuck in.'

'Sorry. I've just spent the morning seeing my Corinthian ideal being thrown to the lions. If Alf Tupper was around today, I bet he'd be sponsored by the Global Fish and Chip Corporation. Do you know what it feels like to have someone you care about snatched from your grasp by superior forces?'

'Actually yes,' said Russell wistfully. But what he was talking about was once having a bint in Sevenoaks abducted from under his nose by the Kent Second Eleven wicket-keeper. And anyway he'd forgotten it quite quickly. He decided Wordsworth needed cheering up.

'I've arranged for your son to be sent to public school,' he announced. 'I had a long chat with Alison the other day . . . as a result of which I pulled a few strings at my old alma

41

mater and managed to secure him an assisted place at Emanuel, starting in September.'

Before Ken could say anything, Ben Smith appeared on the television screen, at his most polite, being given a special guest interview by Gerald Williams. Ken's reaction was simple and effective. He hurled a spoonful of clotted cream at the television set, put aside his dish of strawberries and cream and strode purposefully towards the Pimms.

Alison broke the news to Charlie about Emanuel that night. She was lying in bed listening to *A Book At Bedtime* and reading the book that was being read at the same time, when Charlie came in to say goodnight. How could she read and listen to the radio at the same time, he asked. She explained that she liked to see how they adapted them.

'Why – are you thinking of doing the Emanuel School Handbook?'

Charlie had found it on the bookshelf in the toilet. The 'secret' was out – taking a breath, Alison explained that they'd got Charlie a place there starting in September. Here was another 'secret'. Who were 'they', Charlie wanted to know. This was sticky ground. Alison thought it best to be honest.

'Mr De Vries very kindly put in a word for you. You see your father's got ideological reservations about paying for education. Not that he couldn't afford to pay . . . Anyway, it doesn't matter now, because you'll be going there on an assisted place.'

Charlie didn't like the sound of being assisted. Would he have to walk round with 'Reduced' stickers on his blazer? If they wanted help with the fees he'd be happy to flog his cello. Still, the school itself sounded OK. There wasn't much point in staying on where he was now Ben was going. Alison had seen Ben being interviewed by Gerald Williams that afternoon. Charlie was chuffed. 'I bet Dad'll be really pleased about that!'

Ken went round to Rupert Smith's flat that evening to

apologize for the chaos the journey to stardom had become. Rupert was in the process of packing all their belongings into tea-chests. They'd found the Smiths a flat nearer the club and they were sending a van round in the morning to pick up their things up. Things certainly moved fast in Ken's world, he remarked. What with the Pimms Numbers 1, 2, 3, 4, 5 and 6 they were spinning round now for Ken as well. He tried to explain his tidal wave of guilt to Rupert. He'd spoilt their single parent's agreement. He'd let it all get out of hand.

Rupert didn't see it like that, somehow. In his eyes Ken had done them a favour getting them out of the neighbourhood. Far from spoiling Ben's natural qualities by turning them into a promotional package, he'd given Ben just the chance he needed to develop those qualities. Of course Rupert was worried about the two of them getting separated and of what might happen to Ben, but he wasn't going to let his prejudices get in the way of their joint future. What Ben needed and what Rupert needed right now were two different things and Rupert wouldn't be a proper father if he got in Ben's way. How would Ken have felt if it had been Charlie? As for Ken's having spoiled Rupert's carpet by being sick on it, that didn't matter either – it was the Council's.

Ken brought up the question of Charlie going to Emanuel, over a game of singles with Alison the following Sunday. If he could be of any assistance with the school-fees . . . Alison gave him a kiss and served for the match. Her ace went flying past Ken. He looked at the service line and then at Alison. There was a pregnant pause. Perhaps a man should acknowledge when he's got a point to concede. 'Fifteen-love,' Ken called to Alison.

DARK HORSES

Ken and Reg Prosser strolled a little unsteadily through a narrow alleyway behind Fleet Street – one of those alleyways that's dark even on the brightest day. They'd been doing some serious lunchtime drinking in The Inkwell. Surely, Ken thought, if two words were ever made for each other, they were 'lunchtime' and 'drinking' . . . the unique pleasure of going out, during the day, on the pop. He now regretted all those years he'd wasted on milk and sandwiches, just because he hadn't wanted to fall asleep at his desk. Down Reg's end of the Street, lunchtime drinking almost constituted an Olympic event! The after-effects even had their own names: there was the 'Tower of Pisa', where you tilted to one side; the 'Hibernating Mole', where you buried your head in your arms . . . and the 'Scouse Kiss', which was a head-butt straight onto the desk. Anyway, Ken decided, he was in just the mood for a little nap. And Reg agreed.

But there are naps and naps. The nap Reg was thinking of had nothing at all to do with sleeping. He took The Poet Laureate by the arm and led him into a smoke-filled betting shop, crammed with print workers in overalls, odd businessmen in suits and down-at-heel elderly men talking to themselves as they peered at the sheets of racing form on the walls and looking up at the monitors displaying the odds and the results of the day's racing. Reg made his way purposefully through the crowd to one wall and began scanning a page taken from their own newspaper. A masthead like Ken's at the top of the page showed a handlebarmoustached officer type with his ear up against a horse's head. This, apparently, was Reg's racing correspondent. Ken couldn't help thinking it odd he'd never seen The Brigadier (for this was what he was called, according to the graphics) hanging round the office. Reg, meanwhile, was hard at work studying the day's 'nap'. A real Frank McNab of a headline graced the page: 'Teapot to Steam In'. Other prospective gamblers were studying the page as well. With a readership of four million, The Brigadier's naps obviously had a very powerful effect on the odds. Reg for one was persuaded. He was keen they lay twenty each on the nose. Forty quid at three to one. If Teapot won that made a hundred and twenty quid – well, it would pay for lunch. Ken was more cautious. Teapot, it seemed, had never won over five furlongs before and went better when the ground was on the firm side.

They could hear a Greek waiter laying a hundred on her so the tip was obviously good enough for one loyal punter. The waiter crossed himself, kissed his betting slip, and smiled at Reg and Ken, who sheepishly laid their bets.

The horses came under starters orders and then they were off. Silence fell in the room as everybody listened to the race. The voice on the tannoy remained firm and dispassionate in contrast to the mounting tension in the shop. 'They've covered two furlongs and it's Transflash who leads, a length out in front of Gentle Star and Emergency Plumber, then comes the improving Seven Clubs, with Welsh Noble trying to get on terms . . . past the halfway mark and it's still Transflash . . . ' No sign of Teapot.

'Come on my son,' called Reg to the filly.

' . . . But only a half length clear now of Gentle Star, with Seven Clubs still coming on the outside . . . a furlong and a half to run and it's Transflash now being joined by Gentle Star. Making rapid late headway towards the leaders is . . . ' not Teapot but 'Number 4, Saxham Breck, who goes second as the early leader Transflash weakens and drops out of it . . . inside the final furlong and it's Gentle Star being joined by the fast-finishing Saxham Breck and Seven Clubs who's staying on well. Gentle Star, Saxham Breck, Seven Clubs, coming up towards the line, nothing between these three, they've gone past together . . . photograph . . . photo-finish between Number 4, Saxham Breck, Number 8, Gentle Star and Number 15, Seven Clubs.'

There was a moment of anti-climax, the waiter praying fervently that there might be an objection and all three disqualified. Reg was more philosophical. After all, he also had more power. 'Perhaps I'll sequestrate the Brigadier's salary and get our forty quid back,' he told Ken. The Poet Laureate was ticking him off for not having enough faith in his racing correspondent through thick and thin, and they were taking a look at the next nap, when the tannoy announced the results of the photo finish. Teapot was the unplaced 3 to 1 favourite. The waiter rushed towards the wall, shoving Ken and Reg out of the way, screamed at the masthead above him 'You bloody bastard! I cut your throat!' tore the paper down, screwed it up and stamped on it. Reg and Ken were rather scared and, to tell the truth, a bit embarrassed.

'Say nothing,' whispered Reg. 'We've never even heard of the Brigadier, right.' Once the waiter had gone they could both relax.

'You know what I blame this on,' said Ken, sancti-moniously. 'Lunchtime drinking.'

Ken couldn't get down to work that afternoon, and it wasn't just the alcohol that was affecting him. It had bothered him the way the waiter had reacted. He hadn't seen despair like that since Scotland drew with Iran in 1978. It was yet another example, in his eyes, of people getting worked up about sport – letting it affect their very lives. Reg was far more cynical. For him, that was just another mug punter biting the dust. It didn't have anything to do with sport whatever Ken may think. What they'd witnessed today was gambling, pure and simple.

'Horse-racing wouldn't exist if people couldn't bet on it,' he told Ken.

Ken was incensed. Surely Reg had to agree that racing was part of our national heritage, appealing to all sections of the community, even the Royal Family. And it wasn't just that the Queen Mother was betting mad. The English enjoyed racing for its own sake – for the spectacle, the scenes it furnished of country life. They may have been in a city betting shop, putting money on a horse they couldn't even see, but they were there because they could imagine the race itself . . . Sandown Park . . . a hint of autumn mist in the Surrey air . . . thundering hooves as they hit the rise in the final furlong . . . the crack of whips in the desperate surge to the line . . . they hadn't been betting so much as buying a moment of sporting beauty . . . Plus they'd been drinking, of course.

Reg was rather impressed by Ken's lyricism. He'd better go and write it, he told him. That might even take the readers' minds off the Brigadier and his lousy naps. In fact it might be a good idea if Ken met their racing correspondent. At this, Reg flicked a switch on a new intercom on his desk and yelled down it, just as loud as he ever had done through the partition, 'Frank, get in here, will you!' His Master's Voice. Not that Frank reacted to this sign of authority from his editor. He ambled in as normal. The Brigadier, he grumbled, wasn't easy to pin down – almost as elusive as his winners. The last number they'd had for him had been a phone-box outside Newmarket. All they could do was to wait till he phoned in his copy, then bribe him with a champagne and seafood breakfast at The Inkwell the next day.

When Frank gathered what the meeting was for, he looked cynical. 'Are you sure you wouldn't rather entrust this onerous task to a more educated member of the sports desk?' he asked. Ken decided to wind him up. 'We were just reminiscing about emotional sporting moments, Frank,' he explained. 'The 1978 World Cup'. Frank looked suspicious. 'That night Scotland failed to beat Iran, Frank . . . you must have been a wee bit choked.' Ken winked at Reg. Here was sport affecting the lives of ordinary people all right. But apparently Frank hadn't seen it like that. The boys had done him proud, he explained. He'd had fifty quid on the draw at 8 to 1.

'Now there,' crowed Reg as Frank went out, 'is a *true* sportsman.'

Charlie dropped in to see his father that night at the flat. Ken was just tucking in to a convenience food meal which he'd inconveniently neglected to take the lid off in heating up, plus a can of beer and a coffee. Charlie was wearing his new school uniform, which didn't, Ken noticed, bear the sponsor's name (his). He was just off to the Albert Hall. Not, as Ken assumed, to see some boxing, but to listen to a cello concerto Alison thought he ought to hear. Ken offered him some moussaka. 'It's lasagne, isn't it?' Charlie eyed it suspiciously. Ken felt a bit narked at his son's fancy public-school ways, particularly when Charlie informed him he'd had coq au vin and lemon meringue pie before he'd come out – on separate plates.

The single life wasn't all it was cracked up to be, Ken couldn't help thinking. To cover up in front of his son, he explained he was only eating this junk because he was going out himself soon and was pushed for time – it was a toss up between Brentford against Bolton or Wimbledon Speedway. Never a dull moment in a sportswriter's life. Except tonight possibly. Still, he wouldn't want to embarrass Alison by turning up at the Albert Hall. Charlie, it turned out, though, was going alone. Alison was apparently having someone round for dinner that night.

Ken couldn't help speculating on who the lucky man might be. Probably one of her classmates from the Open University. Charlie looked scornful.

'They don't have classes, Dad – the only people she sees are some gink on the telly and the postman . . . '

'What does he do, this postman?' enquired Ken casually through a mouthful of pasta. Charlie wasn't fooled by the apparently uninterested tone.

'It isn't him – he only screws her in the morning.'

'Charlie!'

'Well that's what you want to know, isn't it? That's what you're fishing for . . . you're both as nosy as each other. And she's never going to believe me when I say you've spent the night at Wimbledon Speedway . . . '

'She'd be right . . . I have got other plans actually.' Ken liked to keep himself shrouded in mystery, especially where Alison was concerned.

'I don't want to know them,' said Charlie, covering his ears. 'I'm not her mole and I'm not going to be yours either . . . ' Ken couldn't help admiring his son's integrity. He got it from the Wordsworth side of course.

When Ken arrived with Reg in The Inkwell the next day to find that it was empty apart from the one drunk who was always in there and a dapper ex-public-school type in his early thirties tucking into scrambled eggs, smoked salmon and champagne, he assumed they hadn't been able to get through to The Brigadier. But this young man was none other than Reg's racing correspondent. It seemed the handlebar and nom-de-plume had been Reg's idea, rather like Ken's being dubbed 'the Poet of Laureate of Sport' and having to put up with 'where's your quill pen, Ken?'

The Brigadier had joined the sports desk straight out of Cambridge and they'd felt it necessary to create a bit of instant seniority for him, so that the readers opened their pages and saw a wise, whiskery old buffer smiling out at them instead of some sharp-eyed young smoothie you wouldn't buy a charity flag off. Let alone a dodgy Teapot.

While Reg was explaining all this to Ken, The Brigadier began to get the scent of the reason for his summons. He started into a lengthy explanation of what he called the 'extenuating circumstances' the day before. The downpour at lunchtime had made the going soft and Teapot couldn't act on that surface. After all The Brigadier couldn't be expected to predict acts of God as well. Reg reassured him; he hadn't invited him here to tell him off. He wanted to introduce him to Ken and to get The Brigadier in his turn to introduce Ken to the secret mysteries of racing. Reg himself was more interested in the secret mysteries of Ruby, he explained, leaving them to it.

Ken was rather surprised at this admission from Reg. Surely he must be chasing a loser himself with Ruby? To his surprise, The Brigadier began voicing his thoughts on the subject. He talks about me chasing losers. That's been going on two or three years now, ever since Ruby inherited The Inkwell from her father. Trouble is, her father's due out in six months. He was sent down for running this place as a disorderly house . . . and for trying to blackmail the judge . . . but all good things come to an end.'

Now that they'd broken the ice, Ken got The Brigadier

rhapsodizing about racing with unbridled enthusiasm. 'I think even you, Ken, might have been tempted by the prospect of seeing one of the greatest horses ever to grace the turf . . . whose name I am proud to call my own . . . No, not Red Rum . . . Brigadier Gerard. Winner of seventeen out of his eighteen races. including the Two Thousand Guineas, and beaten only by the 1972 Derby winner, Roberto . . . ' Ken felt more confident that Reg The Stud was wrong, that racing wasn't just about winning money. Then The Brigadier suggested he take Ken down to see a friend of his who happened to be rather beautiful, and who might also be of some help to him. How could a racing enthusiast like Ken refuse?

Which is why, later that same morning, Ken and The Brigadier stood by a track looking at three horses approaching a trot. Here, announced the Brigadier, was his friend. The one in the lead. Baloney. The four year old. Ken was a bit disappointed; nice legs, shame about the face. But while The Brigadier gazed dotingly at his beautiful Baloney, Ken found himself looking at Baloney's jockey who took off his helmet to reveal he was a girl. The Brigadier introduced them. This was Sally Hartley, the trainer's daughter. What was more, when Sally learned that she was shaking hands with Ken Wordsworth, The Poet Laureate of Sport, she launched into a great homily about Ken's ability as a journalist. Well, after that, Ken couldn't refuse her invitation to lunch. As Sally led Baloney off to the stables Ken tried to explain his confusion to The Brigadier.

'First I meet a Brigadier who isn't . . . then I think I'm going to meet a woman who turns out to be a horse . . . and finally I meet a woman who I thought was a man . . . '

'Well, when your head's stopped swimming,' said his companion, 'I've got a proposition for you. How would you like a little piece of Baloney.'

But Ken was still confused. Or was he? 'No . . . bread and cheese'll do me,' he said.

* * *

On the face of it, a share in Baloney didn't look like a very good deal. Ken didn't know much about form, but he could tell that Baloney was no champion. But The Brigadier began talking over lunch of the hours of pleasure Ken could expect from owning a horse – exciting sport and good companionship . . . the perfect background for his feature. And all for a mere 750 – guineas, of course, not pounds – the rich man's VAT. Ken doubted whether he could afford this, but then got distracted when Sally came in, dressed in normal gear. If it wasn't for that, he'd never have agreed. As it was, he found himself signing a cheque to Tommy Hartley for two hundred and seventy five pounds (three months' stabling Baloney and eight nights' stabling The Brigadier who apparently stopped over occasionally for Sally to do his laundry) and giving The Brigadier the balance – in cash. The Brigadier wouldn't take a cheque. Thanks to his losing streak, Reg's racing correspondent had been having a little contretemps with Coutts and Co.

Still, at least, as Ken announced to The Brigadier as they walked across the Hartley's yard together, 'I gotta horse.' It looked as if he might be in with a sporting chance with Sally as well. He'd thought, from the way they'd been talking that Sally didn't only iron shirts for The Brigadier, but The Brigadier assured him that Sally would never be interested in a feckless ne'er-do-well like himself. She had, however, genuinely liked Ken, as well as his writing. Where there's a quill, there's a way . . . As he stroked the horse's neck thoughtfully, Ken listened to The Brigadier explaining why he wouldn't be tipping Baloney the following week at Kempton Park – she wasn't expected to win, and only taking part in the race because she 'needed the outing'.

Charlie was just in the process of trying to get Alison to let him have the afternoon off school to go to the races, and Alison was just explaining that it cost a lot to send Charlie to his new school and he couldn't just skip double Physics, and Charlie was just saying that far from thinking him a skiver, the other boys would be really impressed that *his* father was a famous sports journalist and not something boring like an accountant or a stockbroker or a Euro-MP, and Alison was just saying that being a sportswriter made Ken not so much famous as infamous – when the front door bell rang. It was Russell de Vries with an enormous bunch of flowers – to thank Alison for the previous night's feast. Alison avoided Charlie's look and went off to put the flowers in water.

'So how are you finding life at a proper school, young man?' asked Russell. His normal pompous self.

'It's all right . . . except I can't get time off to go to a sporting event next week . . . '

'That isn't like them,' commiserated Russell. 'In my day it was very much a case of "mens sana in corpore sano" . . . a sound mind in a healthy body . . . '

Charlie looked at him. He didn't need a translation. 'Mum's the one that doesn't understand Latin – that's why she won't let me go.'

'Let me enter a plea on your behalf.' Alison came in with the flowers. 'Alison – Charlie and I have been chewing the fat, and we both think it's important that he sees as much sport as possible during these formative years.'

Alison nearly dropped the vase. 'Sport!? He wants to spend the day at the races with Ken.'

'Ah.' Russell scowled in Charlie's direction. 'That rather alters things.'

'OK, I give in,' Charlie said. 'I'll phone Dad, Mum – and tell him you and Russell have both said no . . . '

As it turned out, it was that which rather altered things. Alison and Russell looked at each other, alarmed.

'Well, I've got to call him. He wants to know what's happening,' Charlie continued. 'So I'll tell him.'

As he was walking to the phone, Alison called sweetly: 'Charlie . . . '

Ken felt a certain thrill at his and Charlie's being allowed into the owners' enclosure at Kempton Park. He had in a sense broken through the class barrier. Seven hundred and fifty guineas' worth of instant status. Horse-racing was, after

52

all, a metaphor for English society – it's breeding that counts, but if you've got a few bob you can still get into the magic circle. He couldn't help thinking, as he pondered on this, that these reflections would translate very well to the printed page.

Charlie, however, was more concerned that Ken and he weren't appearing on television. He didn't want to be beamed live to the staff-room when he'd said he was going to the dentist.

In the paddock, Ken and Charlie met up with Tommy Hartley and The Brigadier who had ensured the defeat that day not of Baloney but of Cape Horn, the favourite. Charlie decided to back a horse called Charlie's Uncle. Then Sally dismounted, and came over to them to receive a good luck kiss from Ken, looking very impressive in her bright red colours – especially chosen, so she said, to pay tribute to The Brigadier's bank account. Charlie noticed this kiss but kept quiet.

As they weaved in and out of the racecourse bookies, Ken thought it part of his son's education to explain to him how the betting worked. 'That "20" doesn't mean that twenty people think it's going to win, it means that *nobody* thinks it's going to win. It's what you call the odds – if I put a pound on and Baloney wins, I get twenty back. The bigger the odds, the less chance the bookies think the horse has got of winning. Of course, they don't know what's going to win, but they're right more often than we are . . . that's why they've all got Caribbean suntans.' And Ken was managing to exercise true parental restraint, not putting any money on Baloney, when The Brigadier mentioned that he'd seen someone offering it at thirty-threes . . .

But in fact it was Charlie's Uncle that won the race that day and it was Charlie that had backed him . . . at sixteen to one, in honour of his own new 'uncle'. Russell de Vries.

Somehow Ken ended up having The Brigadier to stay at the flat that night. While Ken finished off his article The Brigadier ate him out of house and home, leaving a few wrinkled tomatoes at the bottom of the fridge, and then proceeded to polish off all the beers. He was always ravenous, he said, after a good day's racing. Fresh air was so stimulating. Except when it was in Ken's wallet, Ken remarked. But The Brigadier was unabashed. The way he saw it Kempton Park had sown the seeds of an historic victory. Ken took this as The Brigadier's usual unrealistic optimism in the face of adversity and wondered if he'd had any relatives at The Charge of the Light Brigade.

The Brigadier didn't think much of Ken's piece. He didn't understand its lyricism at all. In fact Ken sounded as if he was in love with Baloney even more than with Sally. 'Galloping gamely up to the line, even when all hope was lost, bless her. Surely a promise of things to come . . . ' After all, The Brigadier explained, there would be legions of blind punters out there seeking a guiding light. They'd clutch at anything – a name they overheard in a bus queue . . . any horse called 'Royal' or 'Princess' . . . something the weatherman said that sounded like a horse, such as 'Isobar' . . . or even an owner they knew, like Ken himself, even if Baloney *had* finished fifteenth at Kempton Park.

Still, at least Reg seemed pleased with the piece. Or quite pleased. He was really much more interested in picking Ken's brains on what Ken thought of the races as a stylish day out. It seemed Reg had been making a bit of headway with Ruby. It was too early to tell, of course. He'd only been after her for three years. Still, it would be nice if it all worked out. Drink and how's-your-father all under one roof . . . he wouldn't need to go home at all then. Ken promised Reg that his secret was safe with him.

'You what?' cried the Editor. 'Listen, mate, if Reg Prosser can pull a twenty-three-year old barmaid, he wants the whole world to know about it.'

But, yet again, it was the betting not the racing that coloured the day out for Reg and Ruby at Ascot the next afternoon. The Brigadier gave six tips . . . all of them duds.

When Reg walked into the Ascot press room with Ruby on his arm the two of them were met with a gale of laughter. Reg had even thought for a moment that his flies were undone. By now Reg and his team were not so much bottom of the *Sporting Life* naps table as underneath it. While the front end of the paper was trying to give the readers a million pounds, the back end was trying to take it away from them! And the way Reg saw it, that was entirely The Brigadier's fault. Worst of all, though, was the fact that Reg's pride had been wounded that afternoon. And Reg was a proud man. It was no use The Brigadier's again making the excuse, later that evening when the two bumped into each other, that there were 'extenuating circumstances'. Reg had been extremely extenuated. Reg was also a decisive man. He gave The Brigadier an ultimatum: if The Brigadier's nap didn't win the next day, then The Brigadier would be out on his arse. As a gambling man, The Brigadier would appreciate the piquancy of the situation. If, however, the next day's chosen horse won, The Brigadier could keep his job . . . call it an Incentive Scheme. As it happened, the next day's meeting was at Hereford. And the runners included Baloney.

Ken, meanwhile, was mucking out his flat after The Brigadier, unaware of these events. He was wandering around, trailing a black rubbish bag behind him and emptying into it random bits of detritus – full ashtrays, old newspapers, wire coat-hangers with dry cleaners' bits of cardboard and cellophane attached, screwed-up typing paper, empty beer cans and the mouldering tray of unfinished lasagne from the other night – when his entryphone buzzed.

'It's the apple-cheeked English rose here, up from the shires,' announced the voice. Ken was baffled. 'Don't you read your own paper?' said the voice. He twigged.

'I can't afford to buy it now I've got a horse,' he replied, buzzing to let Sally in. In the few seconds it took her to come up the stairs from the street to the front door of his flat he took all the rubbish out of the sack and spread it back around the room. He then shoved the plastic bag into the fridge.

'Sorry. I've had The Brigadier staying,' he explained, 'and my little woman hasn't been in today . . . or for the last six months, come to that.'

Sally explained why she was here. She'd been up before the Jockey Club that day for 'Improper use of the whip'. They'd let her off with a warning, so she thought she and Ken might celebrate. As for finding him, she'd seen Ken's address on the back of the cheque he'd written her father. And so here she was with a bottle of champagne. Well, the sitting room was far too messy to celebrate in, and it seemed silly to go down the boozer and leave the champagne to go to waste. So they ended up in bed together.

As they lay there, Ken began explaining what had caused the break-up with Alison. He didn't, he said, want to get bitter about it, even though he had had the bum's rush, and Alison had got Charlie and the house and a fat allowance, index-linked. To be honest, he explained to Sally, that was why he had changed jobs. Bigger money for shorter words. Sally twinkled: 'It doesn't matter how short they are, if they're effective.'

'Shouldn't I be lighting up two cigars or something?' he laughed, kissing her.

'Not for me . . . I've got a big day ahead tomorrow. It's a big day for all of us. Didn't Briggers tell you? Baloney's running again, of course . . . and what's more she's going to win.'

'No.' Ken was suspicious. 'Why didn't he?'

Sally shook her head. 'He and Daddy *are* awful, really – wanting to keep it all under their hats. I wasn't trying very hard on Baloney last time, you see. Just giving her a decent gallop without making her look too good.'

'You mean you pulled her?'

'She was never going to win anyway,' Sally pouted, 'but now we've placed her in a race we know she *can* win . . . '

' . . . So her connections can clean her up by backing her at a big price?'

'Why not? It'll help keep the stable in business for another year. A lot of us have to do it, Ken . . . otherwise the Baloneys of this world would end up in tins of cat food. Besides, isn't that what you say you've done? Compromised yourself because you need the money?'

Ken drove Sally back to the stables that night. It was, he thought drily, his time to take *her* for a ride. Reluctantly, he agreed to come in for a drink before his drive back. Crossing the yard, they passed a flashy-looking Ford Escort XR3 parked there. A pair of furry dice hung from the driving mirror and a green sunstrip across the windscreen carried the name 'Steve' over the driver's seat and 'Steve's Bird' over the other. They obviously had visitors. Classy ones. 'That's Baloney's other owner,' Sally explained.

At the kitchen table sat Tommy Hartley and none other than Steve Stevens, Ken's sleeping partner. Spread out in front of them was a heap of money in five and ten pound notes. They were busy dividing the money into £55 piles adding blank betting slips, and putting rubber bands around them. Ken felt as if he'd just had a bucket of cold water thrown over him. First Sally's revelation, then this. Steve Stevens! If he'd known that toe-rag was part of the deal he'd never have got involved with any of them.

Steve leered. 'We're gonna have a nice little tickle tomorrow, Ken. With a bit of luck we'll cop for more in three minutes than either of our rags pays us in three months. You like writing, don't you? Help fill in a few of these betting slips, old son. Here you go . . . Hereford 1.15 – fifty pound win Baloney, plus five pound tax. See, Ken, the trick is to leave it as late as you can before the off, so you don't bring down the odds. If we're clever, we can hold her at twenty-fives. You can do the betting shops with The Brigadier.'

'I've got a better idea, Steve. Why don't you give Seb Coe a ring? He could get round half the bookies in London before they realized what was happening . . . Or stick The Brigadier on one of your horses . . . assuming he's not been nobbled of course . . . '

'I knew this bloke'd have the wrong attitude,' Tommy sneered.

Steve smiled greasily at Ken. 'Look, mate. Face reality. Your Sport of Kings is the Sport of King Eddies nowadays.' Steve flicked a bundle of money at Ken, but Ken was already heading for the door. He'd be in touch with Tommy Hartley, he said, to let him know what he could do with his share of the horse.

In her loose box was Baloney herself. Ken went over to stroke her. 'This is what you do tomorrow, Baloney. Get out in front, and then when you're five yards from the line, dump your jockey. It's what we humans call a moral victory.'

Alison had Russell round for dinner again that night. Afterwards they sat drinking brandy in the sitting-room, listening to Dvorak's Cello Concerto. Alison felt contented for the first time in ages. The dinner had been good, and she was beginning to like Russell more and more. He was, she felt, just what she needed to help her forget all about Ken. And the music was beautiful.

'Who's playing?' Russell interrupted the silence.

Alison decided to help him guess. She jumped up, giggling, and started performing a charade. There were twelve letters – she held up twelve fingers. The first two syllables sound like . . . she began to mime climbing onto something. Russell was enjoying this.

'Climbing . . . climbing something . . . climbing a mountain? . . . *Stepping* onto something . . . ? Calling for help . . . stepping onto a window-ledge and calling for help.' Alison shook her head. 'No? Try again . . . I know. Climbing the stairs and stepping onto a bed – a water-bed, that's only half full . . . Am I close? Am I getting closer?' Russell stood up. He was indeed getting closer . . . and closer.

'Rostropovich,' announced a voice behind them. There was Charlie in his pyjamas. The spell was broken.

'Rostropovich!' grumbled Russell. 'Then what was all this climbing and stepping routine about?' he asked irritably.

'She was climbing onto a conductor's *rostrum* . . . That's all you meant, wasn't it, Mum?'

'Charlie! What are you doing up?'

'I woke up – I was having a nightmare . . . Dad was killed in a car crash . . . There was this other driver coming towards him, on his side of the road . . . '

Russell thought he'd better be going.

'Drive carefully,' Charlie told him.

'You don't have to go.' Alison didn't want Charlie to have ruined everything.

'I know, but I ought to – I'm due on the first tee at Wentworth at 7.30 ack-emma.'

'Who are you caddying for?' Russell laughed hollowly at Charlie's joke. As they went out, Charlie clasped his hands above his head in silent triumph. He sat down on the sofa.

Alison came back in. 'I did wake up, Mum, honest.'

'You'd better get used to a few sleepless nights then, Charlie, because Russell will be coming back.'

Charlie's face crumpled. Alison sat down next to him and lifted his head. There were tears in his eyes.

'Hey, come on, Charlie. It might be a bit of a shock now, but you'll see, in a few months you won't know what you were crying about. And he isn't going to be living with us – it'll still be just you and me.'

It wasn't really that Charlie was upset about. It was just that the chances of his parents getting back together again now seemed further away than ever. It might be boring, but that was what he wanted. For her part Alison was touched. 'You never know,' she told Charlie. 'Nothing's impossible. I must say since your father's got his new job he's become a bit more responsible and a lot less chaotic.' Charlie couldn't help thinking the odds were still about sixteen to one.

Despite Alison's testimonial, Ken arrived in The Inkwell the next morning, unshaven, and still wearing the same clothes he'd worn the night before. He'd reacted in time-honoured fashion to the night's events by getting plastered. On the bar was a huge bunch of red roses. The Brigadier

59

had given them to Ruby, though no doubt Ken was paying for them. And there, hiding behind a copy of the *Sporting Life* was The Brigadier himself. He lowered his paper cheerily.

'Ken! I was hoping to bump into you . . . Today's the day to put the family silver on Baloney.'

'Really.' Ken took a folded tabloid, open at the racing page, out of his pocket. 'Then why haven't you told the readers that, instead of tipping another horse? I'll tell you why not. Because if today's nap was Baloney that'd bring the price down, wouldn't it? Where would that leave the little betting coup? And I thought you actually liked racing . . .'

'I do,' the Brigadier protested. 'I like it all. And that includes the gambling. But don't look on me as the villain, Ken – the bookies are the enemy. They're the ones who've turned it into a bearpit . . . they're the ones who stand with their backs to the race . . . they're the ones I owe five thousand pounds to . . .'

Ken stared at him. 'If you're in debt, why didn't you ask Reg for an advance on your salary – instead of resorting to this?'

'*Reg.*' The Brigadier laughed. 'The same Reg who'll sack me tonight if my nap doesn't beat Baloney. There you have it, Ken – either I keep my job or I get out of debt. I can't lose – but I can't win either . . .'

Now Ken knew why they called it a mug's game.

Ken saw Steve Stevens making his way towards them, carrying a plastic bag bulging with bundles of notes. Steve smiled at the two of them and handed The Brigadier the bag. This was for The Brigadier to do some 'shopping' with. Thirty pieces of family silver, as it were. For himself, Steve was more concerned to find somewhere for a good piss-up in Hereford. Where did the SAS go after a mission? Ken got up. He'd better go and wash off these country smells he said. Steve for once looked anxious.

' 'Ere, Ken – you haven't written anything about this, have you?'

Ken smiled. 'Don't worry, Steve – I wouldn't waste the ink.'

* * *

Ken did have some sort of revenge, however. He went home, changed, and at one o'clock arrived back in the betting shop near The Inkwell. Sure enough, there were the same faces, including the Greek waiter, studying the page which carried the racing cards and The Brigadier's tips. Ken saw him look at the nap and start to scribble out a betting slip.

'Er, don't do that mate. I happen to know that horse has got no chance against Baloney . . . '

'How you know?'

'I know Baloney's owner. He told me it can't lose.'

'But Brigadier say Harsmold *he* can't lose.'

'Yes, I know the Brigadier too – so put your money on Baloney.'

The waiter thought nervously for a moment, looked from Ken to The Brigadier, then back to Ken again. 'I never trust Brigadier's face anyway.' He turned and headed to the window. 'Two hundred pounds win Baloney at 25 to 1.' Ken winced then quickly smiled as the waiter turned to him, holding up his slip. Casually, Ken made for the exit.

He made his way to the churchyard looking down on the betting shop, and said a silent prayer. A few minutes later the door burst open and the waiter emerged, whooping and cavorting, clutching two large bundles of money. He fell on his knees, laughing and crying, kissing the notes he held in his hand. Ken turned and walked away, smiling as he went and singing to himself:

'Even though the darkest clouds are in the sky,
When things go wrong you mustn't sigh,
Spread a little happiness as you go by . . . !'

Reg might have been right that racing was more about betting than about galloping hooves and spongy turf – but there is some glory even in betting. Provided you pick the right horse . . .

OLD PARTNERS

Ken and Steve were arguing one night at an end-of-season cricketing dinner in the Surrey Tavern Bar. Russell stood listening.

'Are you seriously telling me, Steve, that the current England cricket team could take on and beat a team containing the likes of Denis Compton, Len Hutton, Freddie Trueman?'

'Yeah! And what's more *we* could! With you opening the bowling, Ken!'

'I bet you a million pounds they couldn't.'

Russell intervened. 'Has it occurred to you that there are no means of proving it either way?'

Ken looked at him witheringly. 'We're talking sport here, not logic. That's your trouble – not enough imagination.'

Steve challenged him to pick his team. 'Right. Opening the batting I'd have Sir Jack Hobbs and W.G. Grace.'

Steve cackled. 'Fine – and they're both dead – they're going to pose a big threat to my young lads, aren't they?'

'Very imaginative of you, Steve,' smiled Russell. 'That's a million pounds you owe Steve, Ken.'

'And I don't want it in old fivers, neither.'

Ken looked at Russell. 'These junior hacks, eh, Russell. They've got no respect for nostalgia at all.'

' 'Course I have,' grinned Steve. 'What do you think I'm doing here. *Paying* my respects to these clapped-out old geezers.'

Over the brandy and cigars Ken pointed out one of the clapped out old geezers to Steve. 'You know, Steve, when I was a kid I used to go and watch that man clout the cherry all over Yorkshire.'

'Doug Stout? He didn't play cricket did he? I thought he just rabbited about it on telly . . . in between advertising double-glazing.' Doug Stout was preparing to speak.

Waitresses moved among the tables clearing away the remains of the meal and pouring more brandies. A very drunken elderly journalist, Percy Vitterling, had fallen asleep at Ken's side and was slumped half under the table. Ken and Russell looked at Doug Stout in admiration, Ken remembering how he'd collected tea-cards with pictures of cricketers on them. He'd once emptied six packets onto the kitchen table looking for Number 49 – Doug Stout. If only Brooke Bond had been able to pick the team as well as the tea. D.B. Stout had been one of the finest middle-order batsmen never to play for England.

Doug Stout tapped the microphone and proposed the loyal toast. Everyone got to their feet apart from Percy. 'The Queen'. By this time Percy too was on his feet. 'The King'. Everyone sat down, followed by Percy, who promptly fell asleep again. Everyone, that is, apart from Doug, who began his speech: 'Now then – you all know I'm a man of few words . . . specially when I'm not being paid for them! Because charity's the name of the game tonight – providing concrete cricket pitches for the Third World. A very worthy cause I think you'll all agree . . . and I speak as someone who was brought up on a concrete pitch – Armitage Terrace it were called . . . And as a prelude to tomorrow's fixture, the Old Buffers versus the Young Buggers . . . I have here an assortment of cricketing junk, which I am going to auction at exorbitant prices you wouldn't dream of paying if you weren't so drunk! And I'll start the ball rolling as it were with Lot Number 1 – this is the beast with which yours truly used to terrify house-holders within a two-mile radius of Bramall Lane. Aye, I twatted a few corkies through a few windows with this – one of the reasons why I became so popular with a certain double-glazing company.' Roars of laughter and applause.

As Doug started the bidding Russell drained his glass, stubbed out his cigar and put his napkin on the table prior to slipping out at a tactful moment.

Steve was surprised. 'You offski? Can't you stand the excitement?'

'I'm a bit bushed actually,' Russell told him through a yawn, 'and I have to finish a piece for the *Listener*.'

'Do you have to write it in Braille?'

Russell ignored this. 'Are you staying, Ken?' But Ken was far too involved in the bidding to leave at a moment like this.

Ken and Russell looked at Doug Stout in fascination, remembering how he'd collected his winner's gold medal at

Alison had a bit of difficulty getting Charlie off to bed in time. There was something Charlie wanted to watch on television, he said. Alison explained she had a friend popping round for a nightcap.

'Yes, but it's a programme on Nicaragua – won't Russell be impressed if he finds us watching it?'

Alison wondered how he had guessed it was Russell, but as Charlie pointed out, she wouldn't have put make-up on for any of the neighbours. Eventually Charlie went off, complaining loudly and threatening to leave his door open in case Russell wanted to come and tuck him in.

Ken had succeeded in outbidding everyone else for the cricket bat. He ran across Doug Stout later on in the gents. Leaning the bat respectfully against the wall, Ken went and stood at an adjacent pissoir to his hero. As a gambit, he started reminiscing about having been in the crowd the day Doug had put on 278 against the Australians with Maurice Gibbons. He was immediately put right. It was 288. Of course it was. When Doug was out, Ken had wanted to run and get his autograph, but of course you kept off the field in those days. Doug took this to mean that Ken wanted his autograph now instead and moved towards the cricket bat.

'That'd be gradely,' Ken said in his best Yorkshire accent. As Doug signed, Ken told how he'd once had a trial for Yorkshire colts, but had been found guilty of being born in Manchester! Still, at least he now had a genuine Doug Stout bat, even if it had cost him a hundred and fifty pounds. 'Must be worth a hundred and sixty now, wouldn't you say?' said Doug. Ken smiled, and handed over a tenner. Some corner of a foreign field would now be forever concrete.

'Do you see Maurice, ever?' he asked.

'Who?'

'Maurice – your partner of yesteryear! Gibbons and Stout.'

'Stout and Gibbons? No. I haven't seen him for twenty year or more. He always did keep himself to himself, did Maurice. Anyroad, enjoy the game.'

As Doug opened the door, Percy lurched in, his hand over his mouth. He cannoned off Doug and collided with Ken, who caught him and swivelled him round. A case of pointing Percy at the porcelain . . .

Reg and Ken had breakfast together the next morning in The Inkwell. Ken ate heartily, mopping up his plate with bread contentedly, intent on soaking up last night's ale. Finally he pushed his plate away. He hadn't heard a splash on swallowing that last chunk of bread. Reg, however, was hardly eating a thing. Ken wondered if he might be lovesick. But no. Reg explained with a wink that he had no appetite because this was the second time he had had breakfast with Ruby that morning. It hadn't been easy to pull it off, he had to admit. He'd had to lay on a dinner-for-two at the poshest restaurant he could find and then book a room at the Ritz! Nearly two hundred quid. This could prove to be an expensive relationship. Still, what was money? He'd only fritter it away. Ken couldn't help agreeing, thinking of what he'd just spent on a cricket bat. 'I hope it knows as many strokes as Ruby,' said Reg, laughing a locker-room laugh.

Reg knew all about D.B. Stout. He was a good boy – big drinker, great storyteller, terrific personality. If he wasn't a Yorkshireman he'd be perfect. Reg remembered seeing him once – God he was on form that day – had the crowd eating out of his hand . . . 'Course he had the perfect partner.

'I know,' agreed Ken. 'I used to watch them bat together. Maurice Gibbons.'

'No – Nookie Bear! This was a Lords Taverner piss-up, they were doing a pornographic version of 'On Ilkley Moor Baht 'At' . . . I can still remember the words if you want to brighten up your piece about the match.' Ken declined.

'Fair enough. By the way, as far as the lads at the office are concerned, I'll be at the match with you this afternoon. But I won't be, if you see what I mean.'

Unlike Reg's, Ken's day wasn't exactly action-packed. Steady rain slanted across the Oval Cricket Ground, dripping off the pavilion roof and the covers pulled across the pitch. One or two spectators huddled beneath umbrellas and under the stands, vainly waiting for the rain to let up. Clouds hung low over the gasometer and in the distance could be heard the roll of thunder. The Press Box was deserted apart from Percy, who was sitting staring blankly at the rain when Ken squelched in, a sodden newspaper over his head. 'It's all very well working for a tabloid, Percy,' he confided, making his way towards him along the rows of wooden seating. 'They pay more but you get far less coverage.'

Percy smiled. 'Ah, you can't beat the old *Telegraph*, Ken. It's such an absorbing newspaper.' Percy was feeling a little the worse for wear after the night before and thanked Ken for rallying round. It was always the spirits that derailed him, he explained. Ever since Gubby Allen's tour of the Windies in '48: somebody had mixed him the most fearful rum cocktail and he had spent the rest of the week limbo-dancing under lavatory doors.

It didn't look as if the rain was going to stop. The day stretched bleakly before them. It was, remarked Ken, a pity they didn't have one of those concrete pitches. The prospects of getting a story out of the day's event were so bad that Percy found himself reduced to asking if he could borrow that line for his report. The way things were going he would be struggling for even a hundred words. Ken didn't see it quite like that. He was looking forward to the stories about the good old days. When two or three ex-cricketers are gathered together, it's always an excuse for a wallow in the good old days. All Ken was planning on doing was sitting back and then writing it up . . . money for old rope. Percy's despair only increased. Old rope was right as far as Doug Stout was concerned. The hot air he would be likely to generate over the next few days with all his yarns would be enough to fill the gasometer. Clearly it wasn't the spirits that had got to Percy the night before, it was the Stout.

At this low point, Steve Stevens bounced in carrying a dripping golfing umbrella. 'Bad news, lads. They're breaking up the sightscreens and building an Ark!' Ken was surprised to see Steve again. Cricket wasn't his usual territory. He'd assumed Steve's match report would only have extended as far as the dinner. Steve, however, was in the process of conducting a little survey based on his discussion with Ken the night before – 'What the Old Dogs think of the Young Pups.' If he could get them at it, snarling at each other a bit, it would make a good midweek filler. Talking of which, did either Ken or Percy fancy a pie and a pint? Ken got up. Rain Starts Play. Was Percy coming? But Percy decided to stay in the press box in case anything happened.

Doug Stout was holding court in the Press Bar, attended by half a dozen journalists from the night before. Ken listened, enthralled; Steve headed for the hot food cabinet and got stuck into a pie. Doug began acting out one of his stories: ' . . . anyroad, we see this cocky young sod striding out to the wicket, twirling his bat like, so I says to Fred, "We'll have him, shall we." So we go back to our positions, Jimmy behind his stumps of course, and Fred's taking this bloody long walk back for his run-up. So the lad's taking guard and I said, "Looks like Fred's been saving one up for you, Montmorency" . . . "I take that as a compliment. Not as a threat," he minces. ' 'Course, what he doesn't know is that Fred hasn't got the ball – it's already in Jimmy's gloves! So Fred runs in as usual, smoke coming out of his nostrils . . . over comes his arm, he thumps down his front foot, Jimmy slaps his gloves together and holds up the ball. 'There you are,' I shout as the lad looks round agape. 'I told you he were fast!' The audience laughed dutifully. 'But the best bit was the umpire hadn't seen it either and gave the bugger out, caught behind.' There was more laughter as people turned to the bar to top up their drinks.

67

'That was a great story, Doug,' enthused Ken. 'Mind if I reduce your after-dinner repertoire by one?' He introduced himself, but Doug remembered his face – 'The bloke who bought the bat.' Doug had a bundle of money out to pay for the drinks and, as they shook hands, he slipped a tenner to Ken.

'I owe you this for last night. You see, what with the auction and what have you, I forgot to hand it over to the organizers. So you might as well have it back. I mean, if you wrote in your paper that you paid an extra ten quid to have the bat autographed, and the organizers read that and thought "Hang on, we didn't see owt of that" . . . it wouldn't look very good, would it?'

Obviously journalists were people Doug thought it important to keep on the right side of. Well, Ken didn't blame him, sports journalism being what it was. It was probably an oversight on Doug's part. And anyway there was no damage done. He bought the old bugger a pint. 'Any other stories I can help you with, Ken?' Doug resumed. 'Did you ever hear about the Gentlemen versus Players match when we broke into the Gents' changing room and put itching powder into their boxes?'

Ken laughed along with him. 'Must have been a scratch idea, I suppose . . . Did Maurice ever bat with you for the Players?' Doug's laughter drew to an abrupt halt. 'After all,' continued Ken, 'the end of the season's always a good time for looking back – warm memories to last through the winter . . . Your partnership made a big impact on my early life. For other kids it was Bill and Ben or the Lone Ranger and Tonto. For me it was always Gibbons and Stout . . . '

'Stout and Gibbons . . . '

'Of course – the other way's like saying "Ben and Bill", isn't it . . . '

'Yeah, I can see how it must have looked to a young 'un. But there weren't that much to it, really – just two blokes doing a job . . . '

'You can carry modesty too far, Doug.'

'I know – it's one of my faults. But listen, Ken – that's long gone. You don't want to live in the past . . . ' His face lit up as he launched into yet another anecdote, but he was interrupted by Steve Stevens, who wanted to discuss a small business proposition with him.

Ken was thoughtful as he made his way through the rain towards the Press Box. He might be onto something. However, it would be worth checking with old Percy first. Percy was still there with his plastic lunch box and his flask, but he'd been joined by Russell de Vries. They were doing *The Times* 'Portfolio' together, didn't notice Ken come in, and were irritated when he shouted 'Bingo!' behind them. There was nothing else to do,' Percy explained. Russell had already finished *The Times* crossword when he got there. Russell wasn't the sort of man to let a chance like that slip by.

'Under ten minutes this morning,' he mentioned casually. 'Not bad.'

'That's nothing,' Ken retaliated. 'I did ours in thirty seconds flat the other day. It would have been less but I couldn't get "egg on" – five letters.'

'Impel,' said Russell promptly.

Ken shook his head. 'Toast.' Leaving Russell to puzzle this out for himself, Ken turned to Percy with a brain-teaser for him. 'Why is Doug Stout happy to talk about anything to do with cricket, except his old partner?'

Percy couldn't puzzle it out either. Maurice had always been a bit of a sourpuss, while Doug had been the life and soul. That was all that he could think it was. Ken was just gleaning from him that Maurice hadn't turned up in the Obituary pages of Wisden yet so he must be around somewhere, when an announcement came over the P.A. system that there would be no play that day. Ken made to leave.

'Are you going back into town, Ken?' asked Russell.

'Yes, do you want a lift?'

'Er, no thanks – on second thoughts I'd better stay and talk to the Chairman of the Selectors, try and mark his card for the winter tour . . .'

'He does Portfolio as well, does he?' asked Ken, as he left.

As soon as he was out of earshot Russell turned to Percy: 'Toast?'

Frank had been left in charge of the office in Reg's absence. Sitting self-importantly in Reg's chair, he leaned forward and spoke into Reg's intercom: 'Hello, Frank? This is Frank . . . Give yourself a pay rise, Frank.' He glared at Ken as the Poet Laureate wandered in in his raincoat and started rooting through the Wisden Almanacks from the nineteen fifties to get some background on Maurice

'I didn't hear you knock, Wordsworth,' said the Acting Sports Editor. 'I like my door to be knocked upon.'

'Oh leave it out, Frank. I haven't got time to pratt around – I'll be going up north if I can find out where Maurice Gibbons is . . . '

'That's another thing. All travelling expenses must be cleared in advance with the Acting Sports Editor. I run a tight ship.'

'That's not the only thing that's tight. Is it power that's gone to your head, or just twelve-year-old malt?'

'Get out, Wordsworth – you're fired.'

Ken sighed, and went out. After a moment there was a knock on the door as Ken tried again. 'Sorry to disturb you, Mr McNab.' This time Frank was a bit more friendly. He even suggested that Ken ring the club. Ken explained it might be nothing, but on the other hand it might be the tip of an iceberg.

'Ah . . . you know what "Iceberg" means, don't you, Ken,' Frank looked reverent. 'The Titanic. That ship should be decorated for services to journalism. If ever you're stuck without a fancy phrase, it's always there to come to your rescue . . . "Like being offered the job of the captain of the Titanic . . . ", "a bit like rearranging the deckchairs on the Titanic . . . " God bless her, Ken.'

Ken was just off when it suddenly occurred to Frank that if Ken was back from the cricket it was odd the gaffer wasn't too. Ken had to think fast. Reg was, he explained, having a few well chosen words with the Chairman of the Selectors . . .

* * *

Alison had arranged for Charlie to go round to Ken's for his supper and Russell had made sure Ken was bound for Grub Street that afternoon, but they still felt rather furtive about being in bed together. Russell tried to talk himself and Alison into being more self-assured about it. 'It's rather like playing a long innings. You open cautiously, establishing yourself, getting used to the conditions then gradually you gain confidence in yourself and your partner and the whole thing blossoms.'

'Unless you get caught out,' commented Alison, neurotically.

They imagined the scenario. Russell would take Ken out to lunch eventually and put it to him man to man over the port and cigars – the English way of doing things. Alison, meanwhile, would summon Charlie to the library one night after dinner, stand him in front of the great fire, beneath the family motto – 'Death Before Dishonour', offer him the pearl-handed revolver and point it at her breast. The trouble was, knowing Charlie, he'd probably pull the trigger.

That evening Ken and Charlie looked through Ken's various tea chests to find anything on Maurice Gibbons in the faded yellow Wisdens. Ken had found his 1970 England World Cup Single of 'Back Home' and was playing it to Charlie. His appetite was whetted by the entry in Wisden which said that Maurice Gibbons played in the Roses match and was out for a duck and that he never played again. He hadn't even batted in the second innings – 'Absent Ill'. It wasn't as if the game was governed by psychological claptrap like 'fear factors' in those days. There weren't any helmets or thigh-protectors, or shin-guards on your arm. You just went out and played the game. But Maurice hadn't. Charlie was more troubled by the single on the record-player. 'Did they play like they sang?'

'In the quarter-final they did . . . Careful. That's a valuable piece of my past you're tossing around . . . yours too, come to think of it. Shortly after this record was made, your Mum and I made you . . . Labour had just lost the election . . . England had just been knocked out of the

World Cup . . . there didn't seem to be a lot else to live for.'

'Oh, great. So I'm a sort of walking suicide note . . . '

'No, you were the best thing that could have happened to us. If it hadn't been for you we wouldn't have stayed together as long as we did. Still, all that's consigned to the tea chest of history now . . . '

'It looks a bit that way – back home.' Charlie looked at Ken meaningfully. 'Mum's got a new boyfriend. Your favourite pratt and mine.'

'Russell? Your mother's gallivanting around with Russell de Vries?'

'Sorry, dad.'

'That's all right. It's not your fault. It's just that it's . . . well, it's not cricket, that's all . . . '

'Don't worry,' Charlie said with a grin, 'I don't think he's had his thigh-protectors off yet . . . '

The next day Ken drove up to Yorkshire. It was like going home. He found the little town Maurice lived in, a few miles outside Barnsley, and parked his car in front of a parade of small shops. One particular hardware shop at the end was shabbier than the rest. There was a sign above its grimy window: 'Gibbons Corner Shop.' Ken smiled to himself and made his way inside. It was as if he was recapturing a part of his childhood. Behind the counter, between the glass cases of tools, stood a small man in his late fifties in a brown warehouseman's coat. He was sorting out a heap of screws on the counter, separating them into different sizes and putting them into a plastic partitioned box. He looked up as Ken stopped, dramatically, halfway from the door to where the man was standing. 'The last time I saw your head bowed like that it was over the crease – taking middle-and-leg at the Scarborough Festival, in nineteen fifty . . . '

The man interrupted. 'You want Maurice.' He turned and shouted into the back room. 'Maurice! That bloke from London's here.'

Ken felt rather sheepish as the real Maurice Gibbons emerged. He tried to be brave about it. 'But you see what I mean – you could be brothers.'

'We *are* brothers.' Ken had obviously made an enemy. 'Not too long, eh Maurice . . . And finish these screws off while you're yacking.' He disappeared into the back of the shop. Ken approached Maurice with his hand outstretched and Maurice wiped his on his coat.

'Don't do that on my account, Maurice.'

'How do . . . Can you keep it short please, Mr Wordsworth?' murmured Maurice. 'It's our Cedric's shop and I musn't eat into his time . . . What sort of articles are you going to be writing then?'

'Oh I dunno . . . a trip down Memory Lane, I suppose – revisit some of my boyhood heroes, of which you're one, and see how they're getting on.'

'Heroes?'

'Oh yes. That 142 not out against the Australians at Bramall Lane – I think I can remember every stroke . . . '

'More than I can . . . I've even forgotten how I reached me hundred . . . '

'A square cut off the leg-spinner wasn't it?' said Ken, aware that Maurice's sharp eyes were on him. 'From the Football Stand End . . . '

'Aye, that's right! He came down the wicket to shake me by the hand and then called me a pommie ponce . . . '

'It's because they come from Down Under – they can't stand not being on top.'

Maurice was put more at ease by this. He even smiled. 'I never thought of that.'

Ken was encouraged. 'I ran into your old partner the other day – Doug Stout. He sends his regards, wonders how you're keeping . . . '

Maurice's smile vanished. 'Does he now.'

'I'm surprised you haven't kept in touch.'

Maurice paused. He looked at Ken for a long moment, weighing him up. 'Well – I'll tell you this, Mr Wordsworth. If Doug Stout were on fire, I wouldn't piss him out!'

There was another pause. Finally Ken thought it best to be frank. 'That's the trouble with moving South, Maurice – I've lost my Yorkshire subtlety. This is what I've really come to ask you about – your relationship with Doug. Do you mind?'

'You'll be the first one I've spoken to,' pondered Maurice, 'but you seem all right . . . He were the meanest bugger ever to walk this earth. Do you know, when we were staying in digs, he used to give landladies personalized cheques with his picture on, knowing full well they'd keep 'em as souvenirs rather than cash 'em. Did you ever ask for his autograph when you were a lad?'

'Not till the other night,' Ken replied truthfully.

'How much did he charge you? Oh no, you'd have got it free because you're a press man. Got to keep them sweet.'

Ken didn't look at him. 'I suppose it's a way of making the odd ten quid here and there . . . cricket can't have paid very much when you were playing.'

'That's true – not unless you try and grab the main chance when it comes along . . . even if it isn't yours by rights.' Ken looked at him expectantly. 'You won't remember the last time I played . . . '

'Roses match, wasn't it?'

'Remember anything else about it?'

'Yes,' Ken tried to be as delicate as possible. 'You . . . er, didn't bat in the second innings.'

'Stop being so bloody tactful – I didn't bat in the first innings either! I was out first ball. And that one nought's taken a few hundred others off my earnings since then. Some important people were watching that day.'

'The Test selectors?'

'More important than that – the directors of Steel City Glass. They were about to go into the double-glazing market, and wanted a local figurehead to promote their product. Apparently it was a toss-up between me and Doug who got the job, and that Saturday they were having a last look at us before deciding.'

'Did you know you were on trial?'

'*I* didn't – I was framed, as they say in double-glazing circles.'

'What did Doug do – put itching powder in your box?'

'You're warm – he hid me bat.'

'What?'

'It might not sound much, but when you've been using the same one for years you can't do without it just like that.

74

So I got a duck-egg, Doug went out and gave it some clog and that were that. I've had to look at his gob grinning out of home-improvement catalogues ever since . . . '

'But are you sure it was Doug who did it?'

'He came back into the dressing room singing "On Ilkley Moor Baht *Bat*" . . . so there was a bit of fisticuffs. I came out second-best in that too . . . '

' "Absent Ill" . . . '

'Aye. Two black eyes and a broken heart . . . '

They were interrupted by the inimitable Cedric. 'You two still at it? Maurice, there's a pile of screws here wants sorting.'

Ken was about to leave when he suddenly thought of something. 'What was it like, this bat of yours. Just a bit of background detail, for when I put the record straight . . . '

That evening in The Inkwell, Frank was anxious to find out what his boss had been doing at the Oval, considering the match had been called off six hours before. Reg held forth about doing a bit of delving behind the scenes, talking to the Chairman of the Selectors. He was an interesting bloke with a lot of thoughts to confide about the game – at editorial level, of course. He wouldn't have talked to riff-raff like Steve Stevens for example. Frank paused for effect and then produced a copy of Steve's piece – 'From the luxury of his Barbados hotel, where I managed to track him down . . . ' Steve had apparently opened up a lively debate about standards in the game today. Doug Stout said the modern lot were rubbish . . . they said Doug and his generation were rubbish . . . and the Chairman of the Selectors – speaking from his Barbados hotel, said they were all rubbish.

'That Stevens has got a nerve, passing this off as a day's work,' said Reg, weakly.

Frank was brimming with righteous indignation. One of their two men at the Oval had been chasing round trying to recapture his lost youth . . .

'Yeah? What about the other?' Reg challenged.

'Ken was up in Yorkshire.'

There was a pause. 'One of the points the Chairman of the Selectors stressed to me, Frank, was the importance of loyalty in a team. They may not always appreciate what the captain's up to, because he moves in a mysterious way. But they have to trust him. Otherwise, they'll find themselves back subbing shinty results in the Scottish edition. Still, it's better to have these suspicions laid to rest before they fester and poison a good partnership.'

Frank got the message, and was just apologizing when Ruby, having heard the word loyalty, came over to say how glad she was that Reg had told Frank about them, and that it was now out in the open . . .

Back at the Oval the next day, Ken caught up with Doug Stout at the practice nets. It had finally stopped raining and he was batting against several younger cricketers, taunting them as he played. 'It sells papers,' he told Ken referring to his "interview" with Steve. Ken felt glad Doug was the sort of man who thought that the more people that saw a piece about him the better. And he could safely say that Doug would be featuring prominently in his next piece.

He thought it best to be straight to the point, so he told him. 'I went up to see Maurice yesterday and he told me about the time you hid his bat.' Doug was disconcerted enough to lose concentration on the bowling, but he covered it up. He looked at Ken. Ken wasn't to believe anything that cry baby told him, he said. Doug quickly sent the other players away though. Maurice had been looking for someone to blame for having blown it on a big day, ever since it happened, he said. 'There's some who can take the pressure and there's some who can't. One bat's like any other bat, they're only bits of wood. It's a poor workman who blames his tools.' Ken felt on safe ground now. Maurice had described his bat to him, he said, and it corresponded exactly to the bat Ken had bought.

'Listen, clever-bollocks – you want to come round to my house sometime . . . not that you'll ever be invited . . . I've got fifty bats hanging on the wall, just like that one. And they've all done valiant service. So if you ever print anything about me pinching Maurice Gibbons' bat – I'll take you and your rag to the cleaners . . . '

Ken tossed him a 20p piece to buy a copy of the next day's paper. He could keep the change. As Ken walked away Doug shouted after him 'I don't ever want to talk to you again – unless it's about double-glazing.'

Ken intimated to Steve that he had some poison in his nib that evening. Steve, it turned out, had only had to give Doug a thousand to get the story about how the game wasn't what it had been, out of him. If this had been football Steve'd have been talking about five, plus a couple for his agent. Not that Steve and Ken could celebrate their respective good fortunes. After three days' rain the press bar was bone dry.

Back in the flat, Ken sat at his desk, struggling to write his piece, staring at a half-completed page in his typewriter. Was Doug right? Was Maurice just crying wolf? Was there a story here? He scratched his head, then reached for a battered scrapbook. Opening it at a yellowed cutting, he stared at a photograph from the fifties showing a younger Doug Stout and Maurice Gibbons walking out together to bat, a pavilion behind them. Both were smiling at the camera and above them the headline read 'D.B. Stout and M.H. Gibbons – a Couple of Reet Good Tykes!' Ken shut the scrapbook with a sigh and looked back at his typing. After a moment he opened a copy of Wisden at a marked page, began searching for a cross-reference and then another and then sighed again.

He was still unsatisfied. He tore out the sheet and screwed it up. It joined several others littered around his feet. He stood up and began prowling moodily round the room, finally taking Doug Stout's bat from the tea-chest and hitting the balls of paper with exaggeratedly elegant strokes. After a moment he stopped to study the bat, idly picking at a piece of loose binding at the top of the handle. He noticed something and began picking away curiously at the tape until the strip was unwound. Underneath, inked in to the top of the handle, were the faded initials: 'M.H.G.'. Ken laid the bat carefully down, returned to his desk, wound a fresh sheet of paper into the machine and started typing with a will.

'It's dynamite,' was Reg's verdict. 'We can really go to town with this – a big blow-up of the incriminating bat, sworn testimonies from the old bats in the boarding houses he so ruthlessly conned . . . '

'I want the back page!'

'Take it with my compliments, Ken. I'll even get you in a box on the front page – where d'you want to go? Above or below the naughty knickers?'

'Below, I think, looking up.'

It was then that Frank sunk the Titanic with three words: 'Doug Stout's dead.' Reg didn't realize at first. 'He is now . . . Frank, I want you to set up a 96-point headline for the back page . . . "The Yorkshire Rip-Off".'

'No, he's really dead . . . Collapsed on the pitch at the Oval this afternoon . . . '

And that was that. Protocol, as Reg put it. When he'd read the piece for himself, Frank was keen they should still print it. After all, the fact the man had snuffed it was just an unfortunate coincidence. And he'd collapsed after showing off to the young players, so it wasn't in any way Ken's fault. This was great journalism, after all. Reg was adamant; you can't speak ill of the dead. Frank must remember his loyalty to the captain. Frank couldn't help thinking the captain was spending too much time in the long grass, becoming a big, soft jessie, and said so.

Ken got it into his head that he could rewrite it in a modified version, a sort of obituary code, like when 'he didn't suffer fools gladly' meant 'he was a cantankerous old sod'. But, as Reg put it, you can't rewrite history. From now on Doug Stout would be remembered as a wonderful old Yorkshire character with a fund of stories, who carried on playing the game right to the end. Ken might as well write his obituary, excluding anything about his treatment of Gibbons. After all, Ken was one of the last people to talk to him – he must have had some famous last words. Ken could remember them exactly: 'I don't ever want to talk to you again unless it's about double-glazing'. As for the piece Ken had already written, Reg thought they might be able to use it in a couple of years' time . . . if Ken hadn't gone into advertising by then.

Ken went back to the Oval as a sort of tribute. As he walked to the pitch he began to compose the obituary in his mind: ' . . . The passing of a cricket season is always a time for regret. Each one carries you a little further from the summer of innocent childhood, and nearer to the winter of disillusioned old age. But today was especially sad – when Father Time lifted the bails from Doug Stout's wicket, the golden memory of a hero was suddenly turned to clay . . . ' There, glinting in the sun, lay his twenty pence piece. He smiled sadly, put the coin in his pocket and walked slowly back to the press box.

Alison and Russell had a disastrous afternoon. They were about to go to bed together when they came across a grotesque six-inch, 'Master of the Universe' doll tucked into the bed on Russell's side. It was a 'message' from Charlie. Russell was puzzled.

'What do you think it means? Voodoo or something?'

'Worse – he knows what's going on.'

The trouble was, if Charlie knew, then Ken must undoubtedly know too. As they were pondering the implications of this, Alison's alarm went off. She'd set it in case they'd dozed off. As she leaned across to switch it off she switched the radio on at the same time. ' . . . And finally some sad sports news – the cricketer Doug Stout collapsed and died this afternoon while playing in a charity match at the Oval.' Russell looked suitably sad. 'Eheu fugaces,' he mused.

'The Oval? Isn't that where you're supposed to be?' asked Alison.

'Shit a brick!' yelled Russell, diving out from the duvet.

* * *

The Press Box at the Oval was now alive with activity as journalists typed and chattered. Percy typed on an old portable while Ken wrote in longhand. Steve Stevens was on the phone and covered the mouthpiece to ask everybody what Doug had had for lunch. Getting no answer, he invented something – veal-and-ham pie and cling peaches. Percy was now full of admiration for Doug. A showman to the end. He'd made sure the charity match got a write up even if he had to die to do it!

Percy would have dearly loved to include in his report that when Doug had first collapsed the umpire had given him out 'hit wicket'. Still, he couldn't do that for fear Doug might come back to haunt him with his stories. Mind you, perhaps then he could write a 'ghosted column'! Ken was puzzled, and a little hurt by Percy's attitude.

'Aren't you sorry to lose another colleague from the good old days?'

'Can I let you into a little secret?' Percy whispered. 'They weren't that good . . . they were just old. In another thirty years you'll be calling *these* the good old days.'

'So I was wrong to look up to Doug and Maurice Gibbons, and to go and see them whenever I could?' Ken felt defensive.

'No – but what you were watching was a couple of good county pros. They weren't that special . . . As I remember the only special thing about Doug Stout was his pictorial cheques – I've still got one somewhere, that I didn't cash. It ought to be worth a few bob now.'

Ken was just on his way out, depressed, when he bumped into Russell, flying breathlessly in, the flap of his shirt sticking out of his trousers. Russell looked very embarrassed. He had been taking tea with the Chairman of the Selectors, he said. Ken thought it a pity Russell didn't read the popular press. Then he'd have known the Chairman of the Selectors was in Barbados.

'Let's face it, Russell – you've been caught with your trousers down.' Russell started tucking in his shirt.

'Now look here, Ken – I think it's time we had a calm

discussion about this, man to man.' But Ken wasn't in the mood.

Alison came round to the flat that evening to talk things over. Ken was cleaning Maurice's bat, trying to remove Doug Stout's autograph with meths which Alison immediately thought he was drinking as a way of drowning his sorrows. After all, that was his usual emotional response to a crisis.

'Crisis, Alison?'

'You know – this afternoon.'

'Well, yes, I was pretty cut up about Doug Stout dying.'

'You know who I'm talking about.' Alison was adamant. 'Russell.'

'Russell your lover? Well, if he ruts like he writes you're in for a big disappointment.'

'There you are, I knew you'd be upset.'

'Of course I am! Wouldn't you be upset if *I* went to bed with Russell de Vries? Alison, how could you fall for such a bad writer?'

Alison had him there. 'Because he cares more about life than sport.'

Ken thought for a moment. 'Why am I like this, Alison? Why does the death of that cricketer get to me more than you and Russell? How come I can lay my hand on any Sheffield Wednesday programme from the sixties but I'm buggered if I can remember where our wedding photos are? Why, whenever sport kicks me in the teeth, do I keep going back for more?'

'You've never really grown up, Ken. You look like an adult, but inside you're still wearing a bobble hat, rattle in hand, hanging onto your dad's arm as he takes you through the turnstiles.'

'Under the turnstiles, actually. He never paid when he could help it. But that's what it does to me – when it's right, there's nothing like sport to give you that sense of wonder you had when you were a kid . . . before it got corrupted by sex, and drink, and relationships . . . '

'And responsibilities,' said Alison significantly. 'Ken, I

really want Charlie to grow up to be a proper kid, not some pervert. You should have seen what he left in my bed. I want you to come to dinner sometime with Russell. It'll show Charlie that it's all right, that you don't mind. I'm asking you not as my ex-husband but as Charlie's father. How about tomorrow?'

'Sorry.' Ken smiled. 'Tomorrow I've got a date with *my* childhood.'

'He got away with it, didn't he,' said Maurice Gibbons the moment Ken walked through the door of the hardware shop the next day. Ken smiled. 'Happen . . . but I did speak to him beforehand.' From behind his back he produced Maurice's bat and laid it on the counter. Maurice gasped. 'Bring me my bow of burning gold,' said Ken. 'Doug asked me to give it to you. They might even have been his last words . . . '

Maurice looked up at the bat lovingly, then picked it up and essayed a delicate late cut. 'How can I ever repay you, Mr Wordsworth?' Sheepishly, Ken fetched out of his pocket an old autograph-book with a taped-up spine. As Maurice was signing his name, Cedric appeared.

'This doesn't look much like work to me, Maurice.'

Maurice didn't even look up. 'I'm just giving this youngster me autograph, Cedric – so get knotted.'

There were some children playing on a derelict building site just by Gibbons' Hardware Store. A nostalgic smile lit up Ken's face. 'Now then, lads,' he told them, taking the bat. 'A quid if you can get me out.'

'Make it a fiver.'

Ken had forgotten he was back in Yorkshire. Taking off his jacket, he agreed. He took guard. One of the boys bowled. Ken ran down the wicket, took a great swipe and was clean-bowled. The bowler advanced on him with open palm outstretched.

TWO TRIBES

Going to Rugby League matches on a winter Saturday had been part of Ken's childhood. Of course, things were a bit different down in London. It wasn't so easy to find a Rugby League game for a start. Occasionally he'd take Charlie to Fulham where you could just about see a game through the 'Keep the GLC Working for London' advertisements. He was there one December afternoon with his son, screaming in delight as the hulking players grappled in the mud.

'You dirty git! Have him off, ref! Sin-bin! Sin-bin! Sin-bin!'

Charlie, meanwhile, died of embarrassment. The crowd was very thin and everyone was staring at his father, who was on his feet, his long black and white scarf wound round his neck yelling at the referee. Charlie huddled in his seat, trying to keep warm as well as trying to make himself invisible.

Ken carried on, oblivious. 'He nearly had his head off! Go on, ref – send him for an early bath! Early bath, early bath!'

'Dad . . . everybody's looking,' tried Charlie.

'Yeah – everybody but the bloody referee! He should have had an early bath for that!' It was obvious that Charlie didn't even know what an early bath meant. 'When a player gets sent off – as that bloke should have been – he's the first one into the team bath, isn't he?'

'Sounds like a reward, not a punishment.'

Ken shook his head. Fancy young Charlie not knowing that.

'Early jacuzzi, we'd call it at school,' Charlie added insult to injury.

'Sometimes I wonder what they teach you there,' Ken said in despair.

The answer was simple. Rugby Union.

Ken felt he'd better explain to Charlie the poetry of

Rugby League so he didn't go through life with the normal Southerner's hang-up about how Rugby Union was superior. Rugby League, after all, was one of the finest team games ever invented – a delicate balance between grace and strength, quickness of hand and . . . but at that moment he broke off to leap to his feet and yell at the ref again.

'He's punching him in the kidneys. Look at him!'

Charlie thought journalists weren't supposed to take sides.

'When I'm off duty I can. I'm free to behave like a human being, instead of bottling it all up in the press box. I've been waiting months to let rip like this . . . You great fairy!'

'Do you feel better now, Dad?'

'Certainly. It's therapy, Charlie; a very underestimated facet of sport. The opportunity of paying two pounds fifty for hurling abuse without getting punched in return.' But it looked as if Ken might have been talking a bit too soon. A beefy, mud-spattered player was making his way towards them across the pitch. Glowering at Ken, he stopped on the touchline and yelled up at him, 'Who are you calling a fairy?'

Ken hastily rummaged in his pocket and produced a card: 'It's okay . . . Press.'

At half time Ken and Charlie tucked into Bovril in plastic cups and sausage rolls. Charlie's breath was coming out like steam, it was so cold. 'Is this what it's like up North, Dad?' Ken laughed. This would be classed as a heat-wave. He looked round him in satisfaction at the crowd, stamping their feet and rubbing their mittened hands together. It was very like life back home. Hot Bovril, cold feet, warm hearts . . . and pasties the size of pit ponies. 'Yes, Fulham have done a big favour to exiles like me, bringing God's own game down here.'

Charlie couldn't help speculating on what God would say when he found out that Ken had just finished writing a book on Rugby Union. *Try and Try Again* was the autobiography of the international forward Bob Donnelly, an old friend of

Ken's. As usually happens with these memoirs, Bob had told the stories and Ken had done the actual writing. Only Bob's picture appeared on the book-jacket, though, whereas when Russell de Vries produced one of his three books a year, he always had his picture on it. Charlie knew, because Russell left them lying round the house. He felt rather cheated that his father's face wasn't going to be on Bob's autobiography. Then Charlie could have stuck Ken's book on top of Russell's. Ken was non-committal. Maybe the next one. Typical Russell to leave his books in prominent positions. Still, Alison had always wanted to live in a library . . .

Making his way towards them was Bob Donnelly himself. He was a great hunk of a man. Perhaps there was something in Ken's excuse that there wouldn't be room for both of them on the book cover. Bob was delighted to have found them. He thought they might be at the bar. The talk soon turned to the game.

'You've missed a great first half.'

'Yes, I'm sorry I'm late – I had to come down by train. I'm having a bit of trouble with the car at the moment.'

'That's a bit embarrassing for a fan-belt rep . . . you remember Charlie, don't you, Bob?'

Bob put a huge palm on Charlie's head, as if measuring his height. 'You've shot up since I last saw you'. Charlie was irritated at this platitude.

'That's funny, Uncle Bob – you seem to have shrunk.'

'That's what ten years of international scrumming-down does for you, Charlie,' said Ken. 'Your head disappears into your shoulders.' To illustrate this he started twisting his head round like a ventriloquist's dummy. Once again, other heads turned to look at Ken. Charlie told Bob that Ken was supposedly taking him out for a bit of fun . . . yet how could he enjoy himself with his Dad carrying on like this?

Ken despaired. 'Listen to the little perisher, Bob – he's lived down here so long, he's forgotten what real entertainment's like. He'd sooner spend the afternoon at the NFT watching the Marx Brothers instead of the Fox Brothers.' Charlie was mystified.

'Who?'

Bob stopped laughing to explain. 'The Fox Brothers played for Wakefield Trinity in the Sixties. Before your time.'

'They were the Charlton Brothers of Rugby League,' added Ken.

'All right . . . ' conceded Charlie. 'But who were the Marx Brothers?'

Alison had spent the afternoon baking flapjacks back in Wandsworth and Russell was also there engrossed in *his* new sportsbook, *Victor Ludorum*. Russell was very often round at Alison's nowadays. Alison wondered how much longer the game would last. Russell put down his book with a sigh.

'Let me think – Union's forty minutes per half, with a couple of minutes to change round . . . of course, in League there are only thirteen of the brutes, so they have to take a break at half-time because the poor things are exhausted . . . then of course the crowd must have its ration of pale ale and meat pies . . . say an hour and a half . . . ' It was 4.30. 'I'd say we're good for another half-hour yet . . . What do you have in mind? Rudelbumpfs?' He put his arms round her waist seductively, but Alison was unresponsive.

'Sorry to be suburban,' she said, holding her floury hands up in the air, 'but the flapjacks have got to go in the oven.'

'Couldn't we give them a bit of a roll first?' said Russell, trying to bear her down onto the kitchen table.

'Certainly not . . . stop it.' Amused despite herself, Alison slapped him playfully on the buttocks and pushed him away.

'Oh, come on Alison – it's such fun in flour. Didn't you ever see *The Postman Always Rings Twice*?'

The doorbell rang. 'No, but I think my ex-husband's just rung once.' Alison hurried off to let them in, telling Russell to try not to look too much at home. Russell fished out *Try and Try Again* from the bottom of a pile of books, opened it at random, and posed as if he was reading it. Ken stuck his head round the door hesitantly, then tiptoed in and stood for a moment watching Russell standing in front of the fire pretending to concentrate on the book.

'You can come out now, Russell . . . '

Russell did a wonderful imitation of one surprised. 'The man himself! I say, what a treat – perfect light reading for the hols . . .a rugby stocking-filler.' He chuckled. 'Make yourself at home, Ken.' He realized what he'd just said and changed the subject quickly. 'Er, Alison's been baking like a Trojan all afternoon, especially for the occasion. You've got to hand it to her . . . '

From the two floury hand-prints on the back of Russell's trousers, Ken could see he already had. Russell was just holding forth about the merits of Rugby Union as opposed to Rugby League when Bob wandered in.

'Now *this* is what I call a rugby player,' crowed Russell, taking in Bob's blue England Rugby blazer with its red rose on the breast pocket. 'I've read the book and I think it's absolutely smashing, mate. Would you mind signing it for me?'

Bob obliged. 'Who is it again?'

Russell was humbled. 'Russell de Vries?'

As he signed the book, Bob told Ken how 'Ali' and he had just been having a laugh about that New Year's Eve Fruit-and-Veg party when they all got dressed up as carrots, and Alison had thrown up during 'Auld Lang Syne'. Sick as a Carrot, cracked Ken. Russell felt obliged to join in the laughter. After autographing the book for him, Bob insisted that his co-author sign it too, an opportunity Ken made the most of. Russell stared at what Ken had written in the book in dismay. It would never be worth anything now.

As Alison came in with the tea she was pleased to see Ken and Bob chuckling together. She'd been worried about the effect on both of them of seeing Russell ensconced there – especially as the three of them shared so many memories.

'Now isn't this agreeable,' began Russell. 'Sunday afternoon tea on a winter's day with friends.' Silence fell.

'Mum, can I put the telly on?' said Charlie.

'No you can't. We're having a conversation.' Silence fell again.

87

Russell began once more. 'We didn't anticipate you being home this soon after the rugby. Rugby? Ha! A collection of beer-bellied yahoos indulging in fisticuffs, and they have the nerve to call it sport! The oval ball is a mere innocent bystander. Don't you agree, Bob?'

'I don't actually. I played Rugby League for five years at school. It taught me all I know about running with the ball.'

'You'd have remembered that, Russell . . . if you'd read the first chapter in the book,' added Ken.

Russell ignored this. 'Make sure there are fifteen in your team when you next turn out for Emanuel, Charlie – the Great Unwashed are at the gate.'

'They've probably come for an early bath, eh Dad?' Charlie gave Ken the first crumpet he'd been busy toasting. Alison was annoyed.

'Charlie, guests first!'

'Dad *is* a guest.' There didn't seem any point in arguing about that.

'How are the flapjacks doing, Ali love?' asked Russell.

Alison bristled and Ken and Bob stifled their giggles.

'If there's one thing Alison doesn't like, Russ,' explained Bob, 'it's being addressed as Ali.'

'Isn't that mentioned in Chapter Two, Bob?'

Alison was furious. 'And Russell doesn't much care for "Russ", do you love?' How long are you down for, Bob?'

'Go back in a week I expect – after the book launch.'

Here Russell felt confident he was on safer ground. What had Ken managed to fix up? Any celebrity interviews? Two or three. How many? Two . . . Chiltern Radio and 'Breakfast Time' that Wednesday. When? 7.15. 7.15? Well, Ken had heard a lot of influential people were up at that time. Russell moved in for the kill. He didn't want to brag, but when *Victor Ludorum* was published he'd appeared three times on the telly, done a couple of phone-ins, dozens of interviews and had a whole page to himself in the TLS.

'But you weren't invited to speak to the Emanuel Third Year Modern Studies Group, were you?' Charlie challenged him.

'Really?' goaded Ken. 'And you an Old Boy, Russell?'

'No, but they haven't been either, surely.'

'Yes they have – I'm inviting them now.' Charlie handed
'Russ' the charred remains of a burned crumpet.

After this charade, Ken and Bob felt in need of several
pints. Back at Ken's flat, later that evening, they tucked into
a curry. Bob was amused that Ken knew all the names for
the different bits that went with it – nan and aloo gobi –
now he was a Southerner. London, Ken explained was a
sophisticated place. Bob thought it must be. He didn't think
he could have sat in his front room watching a wife of his
entertaining a berk like Russell. He'd have thumped him. In
the South, though, Ken explained, the right hook was no
match for the barbed comment. Bob had better get used to
that now he was going to be a media personality. Bob took
the idea seriously.

'What?' Ken was genuinely surprised. 'You don't want to
go in for all that, do you? Appearing on quiz shows and
competing in junk sports? Sorry, Bob, I can't see you racing
an Eskimo canoe in the Bahamas.'

'You can make a good living out of it.' Bob looked
wistful.

'No doubt – but you haven't got what it takes – stupidity.
Stick to what you know. Now you've got more time to
spend on the job, you'll be the company's ace salesman.
Area manager before you know it.'

There was a pause. 'You know that trouble I was having
with my car . . . what I meant was, I haven't got it any
more. Haven't got the job either. They only gave it me in
the first place because I was "Bob Donnelly. England
Rugby Forward". Now I'm just Bob Donnelly it's not good
enough apparently.'

Ken gave the sophisticated point of view. 'What a shower
of bastards.' There was going to be a lot hanging on *Try
and Try Again*.

Reg's reaction to *Try and Try Again* wasn't altogether
favourable. It hadn't got any songs in it, he complained.
You couldn't have a rugby book without songs, in Reg's

eyes; that was the only thing that sold them. He didn't think much of the cover either. What they needed was a bird in a scrum-cap, draped round Bob's feet, with Bob holding a pint. Ken could imagine it – entitled *Get Your Twickers Off*. It was a bit too late to change it now, though. It was being published the next day. Reg didn't see any problem – they might give Ruby a bell at The Inkwell and ask her if she'd come round to do a bit of tasteful disrobing. Books weren't like newspapers, Ken explained. This had gone to press six months ago. Well, publishing was a mystery to Reg. He didn't think any of the sports desk had ever written a book before. Or read one, come to that.

Ken took an embossed card out of his jacket and gave it to Reg. Could Reg do him a favour and get someone to give the book a plug? More for Bob's sake than Ken's? All they had to do was come along to the launch at The President's Club. And there was a piss-up there as well. Reg was impressed. Ken, meanwhile, was off to have a literary lunch with his other editor to discuss the next book.

'Yeah, well,' Reg looked knowing, 'You can tell him from me to give it more balls. And a few tits if possible.'

Ken could just see it – *The Everyday Story of an East German Lady Shot-Putter* . . .

Ken had expected at the very least a three-course lunch with cheese, port and brandy-and-cigars. Wasn't that what publishing was all about? Instead, Belinda Potter, his editor, took him to a stripped pine vegetarian cafe in a cramped cellar. They wandered round the bare wooden booths, full of students wrapped up against the cold, and eventually found somewhere to sit. Ken cleared away their trays as Belinda took off her Barbour and draped her Hermes scarf round her neck. Ken thought he'd better not take off his coat. Looking at the stuff on his plate, he wasn't so sure it wouldn't eat wool. He pulled a face as he downed a fruit juice. His system was simply immune to health food.

Still, perhaps it was a good idea to have a brief respite before the next day's excesses. Belinda put him right on that count. They weren't going to be too excessive. The powers-that-be had restricted them to two cases of wine. Ken couldn't believe it. Two cases for a party of journalists and sports people was like trying to launch a ship on dry land!

'It won't be *that* big a party, Ken . . . because it's not that big a book. I mean it's very well-written and jolly interesting if you like rugby . . . but it's never going to be a bestseller.'

Ken couldn't see why not, but Belinda put him right. Apparently they were only even printing four thousand copies. Ken couldn't hide his anger. Seventy thousand people turned out to watch Bob play rugby for England. At this rate, sixty-six thousand of them wouldn't even have the chance to buy the book. Belinda looked agitated.

'Don't blame me, blame the powers-that-be,' she said, lamely.

'They won't put their hands in their pockets until they know the book's got legs. It's a chicken-and egg situation.'

'No love – it's a chicken-and-rooster situation, and Bob and I are the chicken!'

It wasn't himself that Ken was worried about. What would Bob say? It was obvious Ken would have to provide the drink himself. Would Belinda mind if they went to the pub he asked. Ken's treat? Belinda looked round for the receipt but judging by what he'd just eaten, Ken couldn't help thinking he might have swallowed it.

Ken broke the news to Bob on the way to Emanuel that afternoon. Once they'd knocked off the hire of the President's Club and paid for most of the catering and shared out the royalties, Bob wouldn't be left with that much. He'd better take the bus home rather than the train. Still, someone might pick up the film rights. The sensitive story of a shy, working-class lad who achieves international sporting fame on the rugby field. Bob might even star in it – *Conan and the Barbarians*.

They locked the car and made their way up the school drive, which took them past the school's rugby fields. A Rugby Union game was in progress, two teams being refereed by an older boy. Bob stopped to watch the scrappy scrum. The ball came out of the back to the scrum-half who passed it back to the fly-half, who immediately kicked it into touch, ignoring the line of wing three-quarters. The ball bounced towards Bob, who retrieved it with one hand and strode off in the direction of the straggly line-out which had formed on the touchline.

'Look, son – you had good early possessions there, the three-quarters outside you, full-back ready to come into the line . . . so give them the ball! That's the trouble with the game today – everybody wants to kick instead of running with the ball.' The boy apologized. Bob turned back to Ken, who'd been watching all this with interest.

The Modern Studies class turned out to be a lot grittier than Ken and Bob had expected. A fair-haired, blue-eyed Aryan-looking boy called Beesley grilled them. Why hadn't Bob wanted to go on the Lions' tour of South Africa, he wanted to know. Bob had obviously preferred the company of fan-belts to that of fans of the veldt. Beesley's classmates groaned. Bob checked with the schoolmaster, Malcolm Sadler, who was with Ken and Bob at the front of the class, that it was all right to answer this question.

'Yes, I do object,' he explained. 'I think apartheid stinks.'

' . . . But I'm sure you'd go on a tour of the Soviet Union – despite Afghanistan?' continued Beesley. The class groaned again.

Ken stepped in. 'I think it's up to the individual conscience, Beesley, and what it finds more objectionable – external aggression or internal oppression. I mean, which would *you* dislike more – a thump on the nose from Mr Sadler or one from me?' The boys sniggered, Malcolm Sadler smiled and Beesley glowered.

'Anyway, there's a good reason for playing rugby in Russia,' Bob continued. 'They're about the only country we could beat these days.'

Then Charlie asked a question. Would Mr Wordsworth be writing another book? It was funny Wordsworth should ask that, mused Ken. From the research he'd been doing, he thought there was definitely a gap in the market for *The Topless Vegetarian's Rugby Song Book*.

The bell rang for the end of the lesson. Malcolm thanked Ken and Bob for coming along, and all the boys applauded, with the exception of Beesley, who stalked out clutching his briefcase. Bob was surrounded by the others demanding autographs.

Ken cornered Charlie.

'Was that all right?'

'You were great, Dad.'

'No, I mean really? Your chums won't hang you upside down in the toilet because your Dad's a pleb?'

'No, I think the bogs are booked for Beesley – why do you think he did a runner? I'll see you at the party.'

Malcolm came over to apologize for Beesley as well. Ken said he thought Beesley must have been rehearsing his address for the following year's Tory Party Conference, but apparently he'd already spoken at this year's, on the return of capital punishment.

Malcolm was very complimentary about Bob, and Ken suddenly had an idea. What if Bob were to do some coaching here? Naturally he wouldn't want to squeeze anybody out, but surely a school like Emanuel could afford the additional services of a top-class England International – and author. Malcolm saw what Ken meant. He'd bring it up at the staff meeting that afternoon he promised. Ken surreptitiously handed him a card for the President's Club. Then Malcolm could tell him how it went.

Christmas was in the air, and The Inkwell was full of early-evening journalists using this as an excuse to get more drunk more often. Ruby was trying to hang up decorations whenever she got a spare moment. Reg blew her a kiss as he made his way to Frank at the end of the bar. Frank was staring morosely at the festivities over his pint. Bloody Christmas got earlier every year. All it meant to Frank was more white space to fill when all the fixtures were called off because of the weather. Reg was obliged to spend Christmas at home with the wife, so he was having to make an extra effort with Ruby. He'd promised to take her to *Cats* that night, but he couldn't get any tickets, so he was taking her to the dogs instead. Same thing, really – you just needed more chocolates for the intervals. Anyway, Frank would have to hold the fort, but Reg reassured him that most of the donkey-work had already been done.

He'd put the Arsenal transfer rumour in as the lead and the transfer rumour denial on the inside-back. Frank just had to watch out that Steve Stevens's comic didn't lead with the denial, in which case he'd have to *deny* the denial, but then stick the rumour on the inside-back to be on the safe side. Frank nodded. It did look like a quiet night.

Reg had one more job for his Deputy Sports Editor – a review of *Try and Try Again*. Frank wasn't very impressed with the title. 'Is that supposed to be clever?' Had he been doing this in the firm's time? Reg assured him Ken had got it under his belt before the momentous day he joined them and became a proper journalist. Frank didn't have to read it, all he had to do was to be nice to it. He might even get invited to the Press Launch. Once he heard this bit of news even the title began to grow on Frank.

The President's Club Do went much better than Ken had imagined. An assortment of journalists together with several older rugby types turned up to imbibe the atmosphere of the wood panelled room, drink the ample supply of wine and eat the sausage rolls and stuffed mushrooms. And some of them even looked at the book. Alison, Charlie and Russell came to give moral support to Bob. Belinda plied everybody with drink, and even Reg, Frank and Ruby turned up, Ruby in her new fur coat, all feeling – and looking – rather out of place.

Steve Stevens arrived early, collared the butler and got stuck into the vol-au-vents, using *Try and Try Again* as a makeshift tray. He was, he told Ken, really impressed. He'd always thought publishers were a bit stingy. They were obviously very pleased with the book. Had the serial rights gone yet? Because his paper might be interested. Of course they didn't cover rugby normally, but they *un*covered it.

When that Erika Roe streaked at Twickenham they had done a double-page spread. One on each page! Did Erika get a mention in the book? 'Where Are *They* Now?' Ken put him right. Erika wasn't mentioned but the match was; Bob had scored a try.

'A what?'

Ken was clearly being too technical. Steve was more interested in the sex-in-the-showers angle. Nor was he excited by Ken's offer of money-in-the-boots being featured – supposedly amateur players being slipped back-handers. That was just Mickey Mouse to the likes of Steve. He wanted wide-screen corruption. Little 'Naughty Fidos' fouling those corridors of power.

Ken left Steve to go and make peace with Russell, who was holding forth to Charlie about how after the previous year's Varsity match Johnny Sinclair's fish-knife had done serious damage to the walls of the President's Club. It was, he explained, always the same when the Old Blues got together. Russell, it appeared, had got a Half Blue for Rugby Fives at Oxford. Perhaps Charlie would get one there too. For playing the cello, added Alison darkly. She kissed Ken in congratulations. Ken offered his cheek to be kissed by Russell too, but Russell recoiled. Russell thought it better to get on to safe ground.

'I don't know about Half Blues but I'm half-green with envy, Ken – I've now had time to read the book, and I think it's marvellous.'

'He does, really,' Alison added. 'He finished it last night – and you should have heard him, grinding his teeth in his sleep.'

Ken took this in his stride. 'Well, thank you Russell – I've always believed that irritation was the sincerest form of flattery.'

'My pleasure. And the book deserves a distinguished gathering such as this . . . with one or two exceptions. I mean who are *they*? Distinctly League rather than Union, I'd say . . .'

Ken realized in horror that Russell was pointing at the three other most important people in his life, his editor, his deputy editor and the barmaid of The Inkwell. And it looked as if Reg, Frank and Ruby had heard his remarks as they were making their way towards the door. Ken felt hurt.

'You're not leaving already are you? Come on, Frank – I'm relying on you to see off that table of booze.'

'Not me,' Frank apologized. 'I've always been more grain than grape.' Nor would Ruby stay to be waited on. This was the second duff night she'd had in a row. She had thought Hackney was bad, but they had made her feel welcome there . . . and at least the greyhounds had circulated. Reg felt disgruntled too. He'd rubbed shoulders with Toffdom in his time but he hadn't been given a cold one such as this since he fed the ducks with sliced bread at Henley Regatta. They couldn't even be persuaded with the promise that in half an hour all those stiff upper lips would be warbling to the chorus from 'Four and Twenty Virgins'. Ruby wasn't keen on hymn-singing. As Ken showed them to the door, he thanked Frank for the nice review of the book. It had been no trouble, Frank assured him. He'd got it all from the blurb on the jacket.

Ken gloomily poured himself a glass of wine, knocked it back, poured himself another and was about to drink it when he saw Malcolm Sadler come into the room. He went over to greet him. Apparently there was some good news for Bob. There might be a vacancy for him at the school. The Headmaster was very keen on the idea. Ken was delighted and suggested Malcolm go and tell Bob. If he asked, the Bob-A-Job idea had been Malcolm's, not Ken's.

Ken smiled benignly at Malcolm making his way over to Bob, then turned to Belinda, who was offering him more wine. Belinda might as well open another case he told her. The party had already eaten into Ken's royalties, so why not let it drink into them as well.

After the party was over, Belinda helped Ken carry the unused cases back to his flat. They lurched up the stairs singing 'Four and Twenty Virgins Came Down from Inverness' and slumped onto the sofa together.

' "Balls to your father . . . " ' sang Belinda. 'Why Inverness, for God's sake? My Aunt lives there – it's the last place on earth you'd find virgins . . . apart from my aunt, that is . . . Wasn't it clever of me, by the way, salvaging so much plonk?'

'Yeah, and this isn't going to the powers-that-be either.'

Ken reached into the case, fetching out a bottle. 'This is for us.'

Belinda declined. She really must go.

'You don't have to, you know.'

'Ah, I was afraid you might say that.'

'Well, when you said you'd come in, I thought . . . '

'All I did was help you upstairs with the booze. Is that supposed to be body language for "I want some nookie"?'

'Among certain primitive Northern tribes, yes.'

'Look, Ken I'm very . . . '

Ken couldn't bear it. He stopped her saying, 'I'm very fond of you, but I hardly know you' or 'Can't we just be friends . . . ' Couldn't she just say 'I don't fancy you, you drunken old slob'?

Belinda smiled. 'What I was *going* to say was "Look, Ken, I'm very attracted to you, but I don't sleep with my authors".'

'I'll change publishers then.' But he couldn't even do that. They'd already got an option on his next book. Now his sex life was being controlled by the powers-that-be. He'd gone to the effort of giving Bob fifty quid to put up at a nearby hotel as well.

'I'm sorry, Belinda – it's just been a big day for me – my first book's been published, a lot of nice things have been said about it. I didn't want the evening to end with a whimper, but with a bang.'

As he realized what he'd said, they both laughed. He gave her a friendly kiss and she made her way to the door.

'You'd better get some sleep – you're on national telly in less than four hours,' Belinda reminded him.

Ken looked round at the empty flat. Empty except for the wine bottles. 'It's a quarter to three . . . there's no one in the place, 'cept you and me,' he sang, contentedly to them.

'Welcome back . . . it's just coming up to 7.15,'

announced Nick Ross on *Breakfast Time* the next day, 'and today sees that annual encounter between Oxford and Cambridge at Twickenham, the Varsity Rugby Match. An appropriate time, then, to look at a new book about the sport which is published this week. It's by the former England forward, Bob Donnelly, and Bob's with us this morning, as you can see from the way the sofa's listing to port, together with his collaborator on the book, sports columnist, Ken Wordsworth.' The camera cut to a single shot of Ken, sleepy, unshaven, dishevelled and still in the clothes he'd worn the night before, semi-sprawled on the couch, not taking a lot of notice. Nick Ross hurried on. 'Tell me, Bob, because it's something I always wonder about books by sports personalities – how much of it did *you* actually write, and how much of it was, er, Ken?' He looked across at Ken apprehensively, but the camera didn't follow his gaze.

Bob tried to soldier on. 'It was a mixture really, Nick . . . Sometimes Ken would come up and talk to me, then I'd go down and see him . . . up and down, up and down, until it was done – isn't that right, Ken?'

The ups and downs had been making Ken feel increasingly queasy. He didn't dare to reply to Bob's question as panic began to show on his face. There was an ominous silence.

'How do you feel about rugby, Debbie?' asked Nick.

Debbie Greenwood had been sensing that a volcano was about to erupt on her other side, and the question took her off-guard. 'I've only been through it on the train, so I don't really know . . . ' she said sweetly.

By now Ken was masking his mouth with his hand. 'Would you like a cup of coffee, Ken?' Ken shook his head as gently as he could, but it was too late. There was nothing to do except twist round and lean over the back of the sofa. The camera cut away hastily to Nick, talking desperately to Bob in an attempt to save the conversation and not draw attention to what was happening next to them. Strange noises punctuated what they were saying.

'I see that when you were a schoolboy you played Rugby League . . . '

'That's right – and I've still got a lot of time for the old up-and-under game.' An unfortunate phrase in the circumstances.

'I'm terribly sorry,' mumbled Ken, off-camera. 'Was that a new dress?'

Charlie, horrified in front of the television at home, quickly switched off as Alison came in in her dressing-gown.

'You're too late – you've missed him.'

'What was he like?'

'Brilliant,' improvised Charlie. 'He made a big impression on Debbie Greenwood.'

'Oh, did he? I always knew he fancied her.'

'There was real chemistry going on between them.'

Alison began rewinding the videotape as Charlie looked on in dismay. 'This I've got to see,' she chuckled.

'Wouldn't you rather watch Roland Rat?'

Ken spent most of that day lying on the sofa in his flat sleeping off the nightmare. He stirred as Bob unlocked the front door and let himself in. Bob looked rather depressed. He made his way over to the window and drew the curtains.

'Come on, Ken – do you know what time it is?'

'Of course I do – I can still see little blue clocks in front of my eyes.' He declined Bob's offer of a cup of coffee as it gradually came back what had happened to the last person who'd suggested that to him.

'Oh, God – did I really do what I think I did?'

'Yes – on TV too.'

'Perhaps everybody'll think it was nerves . . . No they won't – I've made a real idiot of myself this time.'

Bob took off his blazer and sat down. 'Join the club,' he said dolefully. 'I've just walked into Emanuel to see when I was going to start, and instead I was told I'd already finished. The Headmaster was very keen to take me on initially, but since then he's been advised he shouldn't – because apparently by writing that bloody book I'm making money out of rugby, which means I can't be allowed near an amateur game.'

'What money? Haven't they seen our drinks bill from last night? And who are "they" anyway?'

'I don't know – but whoever they are they run Rugby Union.' Bob looked despondent.

Ken didn't feel sick any more. 'Come on, Bob – we're not going to take this lying down.' He sat up. 'We'll fight this injustice in the highest court in the land . . . The Inkwell – His Honour Judge Reg Prosser presiding. We'll see what the power of the press can achieve.' Bob didn't have much faith in the printed word at that particular moment, so he left Ken to appeal in The Inkwell and made his way off to the Job Centre.

Reg and Ken were just getting into the swing of things in The Inkwell, condemning people who pontificated about what Bob Donnelly could and couldn't earn from the game, confident in the cosy amateurism of the well-to-do, and planning how the Poet Laureate would put the boot into rugby, when they were interrupted by the sound of raucous singing and shouting from the street outside. Perhaps it was the printers spending their Christmas bonus? No, it wasn't. Ruby looked alarmed as half a dozen middle-aged hearties in sheepskin coats and dark blue Oxford scarves made their way down the steps into The Inkwell. They conga-ed round the tables, singing their own obscene version of 'Old Macdonald Had a Farm'. Ken noticed in horror that Russell was among them.

'I say, Ken, I hope you don't mind, but we've got some time to kill before our dinner, so I thought we might avail ourselves of your excellent facilities. Do you know what? We drew with Cambridge! Ten-six!'

The others were becoming more and more boisterous. One of them jumped up and tried to swing on one of Ruby's paper chains, which broke. Another took baubles off the Christmas tree and juggled with them, smashing them as they each fell on to the floor. Things were getting nasty.

It was obvious Ken would have to get rid of them. 'I'm sorry. It's members only.'

'But we *are* members . . . ' trilled Russell. 'Tony's a

Member of Parliament, Tiger's a member of Lloyds and Johnny's a Member of the Stock Exchange!'

'We've all *got* members too,' added one ruddy-faced individual. The others laughed raucously and one man barged into the Christmas tree, knocking it over. Ken was angrier now, 'Come on – get out.'

Russell got defensive. 'You can't talk to him like that, you know – he's a very important man. Aren't you Buzzer? He's on the committee – you can't talk like that to Buzzer Beeesley . . .'

By now some of them were helping themselves to the contents of the bar. One was even sprawled across the counter, trying to get his mouth under a lager tap. Suddenly even Reg lost his temper.

'Now that is well out of order! Okay lads,' he called to the other journalists. 'Let's heave 'em out.' The rugger buggers realized they were outnumbered and made a hasty exit.

'Everybody follow Buzzer to the President's Club!' called Russell weakly. He was momentarily distracted by Ruby. 'I say who's this beguiling creature? Why don't you come and have dinner with some real men? We'll show you a good time – All of us . . .' Ken threatened to give Alison a ring and tell her Russell wouldn't be home that night. Reg had turned white with anger.

'Now you see what Bob Donnelly's up against, Reg,' said Ken. 'The Buzzer Beesleys of this world.' A sudden thought struck him. 'Beesley?' There couldn't be too many obnoxious Beesleys in the Home Counties.

Reg was fuming. 'I don't care how you do it, Ken – I want 'em nailed. It doesn't matter if we're done for libel, the damages'll be worth it. Just Exocet 'em!'

Ken would see what he could manage. Maybe even get somebody else to do his dirty work for him. He gave Steve Stevens a ring.

Russell and his friends enjoyed a hearty dinner at The President's Club. A butler clearing away the dessert was tipped by Buzzer and told he could leave. He should just see that the guests weren't disturbed. The butler went out. But outside he was offered an even bigger tip to leave the door unlocked. Inside, Buzzer had laid on a little entertainment for his chums. This was an annual treat of theirs. He opened a side door to reveal a veiled belly-dancer who plugged a portable cassette recorder into the wall and began gyrating round the room. Meanwhile, Buzzer and his friends prepared their 'ammo' – dollops of trifle. Steve Stevens poked his head round the door, smiled to himself and closed it again. By now the girl was removing her veils. Russell was transfixed. 'My God – if the England centres could swing their hips like this we'd win the Grand Slam.' Eventually, led by Buzzer, they started chanting.

'I Ziggy Zumba Zumba Zumba, I Ziggy Zumba Zumba Zay . . . Haul him down, you Zulu warriors, haul him down, you Zulu Chief! Chief! Chief!'

'On each 'Chief!' the men picked up large dollops of trifle and flicked it at the girl's bare midriff. In the middle of the fun, Steve Stevens appeared again and opened the door wide. They didn't notice him.

'Excuse me, Gentlemen,' announced Steve, 'I think your goose is cooked.' Buzzer, Russell and Co whirled round. A flash photographer appeared in the doorway and started taking rapid pictures of the scene.

Next morning Alison and Charlie scanned the papers anxiously for any betrayal of Ken's fate on *Breakfast Time*, just in case Charlie couldn't go to school or Alison to the library out of shame. Alison had by now recorded over the videotape – an episode of *Cheers*, which they both felt was rather appropriate. It was then that they came across the photo in Steve's rag. Russell was prominently displayed along with Buzzer Beesley looking in alarm at the camera, with the trifle-covered belly-dancer between them.

As they were still staring at it, Russell walked in in his dressing gown, yawning and dishevelled. He noticed the pile of newspapers in front of them. He'd better play it cool.

'Morning! Anything in the papers?'

Alison and Charlie nodded slowly in unison.

* * *

Ken went down to the country the same morning to sing 'Old Man Beesley Had a Farm' to Buzzer himself.

'Wordsworth . . . aren't you something to do with that Donnelly book?'

'Donnelly . . . didn't you have something to do with ruining his career? ''With a phone call here and a phone call there . . . '', ''I say, Pater – guess what? They're going to appoint some horrible lefty as our rugby coach.'' '

'You've been tapping my phone.'

'I didn't need to – but I wouldn't mind hearing what you've got to say.'

'Of course – I think it's a great pity that Bob's talents will be lost to the game – but he does know the rules about writing books. Standards must be maintained.'

'Well, the public already knows about *your* standards.'

'I don't see what the fuss has been about – it was a harmless bit of fun. High jinks. The girl was well paid for her services.'

'Oh, so *she* wasn't an amateur, then?'

'That's another thing – I gather from your book that Bob once flirted with Rugby League. He does seem to make the *most* unfortunate associations.'

'So you'd say that you're in favour of sporting links with South Africa, but not with the North of England.'

'I couldn't have put it better myself!'

'Okay, thanks for the interview, Buzzer – it should make a nice follow-up to this morning's picture-show.'

'I do hope so – I'll be dining out on all this till the next Varsity Match! Now would you mind getting off my land?'

Young Beesley didn't have much of a day either. All the boys in his class hurled cream buns and pieces of cake at him, for some reason. Most of the shots were accurate.

Bob received a generous cheque for seventeen pounds sixty pence for appearing on 'Breakfast Time'. But by now he didn't care. He'd decided to join Fulham Rugby League team. After all, if you can't beat the amateurs you might as well join the professionals.

Ken went to watch him the next Sunday.

'You great fairy, Donnelly! Call yourself a rugby player! Get back to selling fan-belts . . . !'

Bob gave him a 'V' sign as he made his way back into the fray.

RUNNING FEUDS

Reg and a staff photographer made their way through the crowd towards the Arrivals Gate at Heathrow airport. The plane had just landed and it was vital they met it. There, coming towards them, was the man they had come to meet and photograph . . . Ken Wordsworth. Ken was ambling along, in the middle of a crowd of other passengers, carrying a plastic bag of duty-free drink in one hand, looking slightly more suntanned than normal but in every other respect his normal self. So he couldn't understand why, as he reached the end of a corridor by the mobile walkways, Reg should have beckoned to Harry the photographer to start taking pictures. He even looked behind him to see there wasn't a celebrity on his tail, but there wasn't. Reg breezed towards him and started shaking him fervently by the hand while Harry snapped away at this as well. Ken was beginning to get suspicious.

'What's all this, Reg? It's not the *Golden* Handshake, is it? "Sports Editor seen wishing Columnist all the best on his early retirement"?'

Reg chuckled. 'Not likely, Ken – you've filed some of the best cricket copy our subs have ever had the privilege of mangling . . . That's enough "Arriving" stuff, Harry.'

'Oh, so it's a bonus – that's what this is in aid of.'

'No.' Reg paused for effect. 'The news is, Ken – while you've been away, you've been selected to carry out a mission of the highest importance and prestige to this newspaper.'

Ken quickly set off back down the corridor. He was sure he'd left something on the plane . . . but Reg restrained him.

'You haven't even heard what it is yet, Ken . . . You, my son, are going to be our representative in this year's London Marathon.'

Ken didn't mean to be rude, but he couldn't help nearly falling over with laughter. 'The Marathon? Me, run twenty-six miles? I've got a stitch just saying it, Reg!'

Reg was getting carried away with the notion. 'Twenty-six miles. Twenty-six great Ken Wordsworth columns charting your progress from an average slob-in-the-street to a shining example of what makes Britain great!'

'It'll be twenty-*seven* columns, Reg – you forgot my obituary.'

'It's too late to think about dying now – you're all signed up . . . and your fitness programme starts here . . . ' He relieved Ken of his duty-free bag. 'Harry, come and get some action shots of Ken jogging up the escalator.'

Harry looked anxious. 'Eh? I only do VIPs getting on and off planes, Reg – I've forgotten how to do anything else! This is more my line – Angie Phillips.' He nipped off to photograph a glamorous, busty model in her early twenties who was coming along the corridor, and who enjoyed his attentions more than Ken had done. Ken hadn't recognized her with her clothes on.

Reg saw an opportunity as he followed Ken's gaze. 'You know, Ken – after a few weeks training you'll be fighting off birds like her. She'll invite you to appear on her calendar.'

But Ken was adamant. 'Never in a month of Sundays. I'm not doing it, Reg. See you tomorrow, when you've got over your jet-lag.' He turned, came back, and retrieved his plastic bag off Ken – 'Excuse me, baggage reclaim' – then stepped onto the mobile walkway. After a few seconds he became aware that Reg was level with him on an adjacent walkway, jogging through the oncoming traffic of passengers like a mouse on a treadmill and beaming at him.

'See, Ken?' Reg was incorrigible. 'Nothing to it.'

The pressure didn't ease off the next day when Ken got into the office. Reg summoned Ken into his office and brandished a sheaf of officially-headed papers at him.

'Here we go – sift through this lot. Arthritis Research, British Heart Foundation, Lifeboats – you can raise money for all of 'em by running in the Marathon. But no, you won't – you're spurning 'em.'

Ken felt harassed. 'But if I took part I'd end up with half these diseases!'

'There's a picture of a kid in a wheelchair somewhere here . . . How's that able-bodied young son of yours doing?'

'Still walking, thank you very much.' This was ridiculous. 'I'm all for charities benefiting from marathon runners, Reg – but why choose a wreck like me?'

'You just said it! You're the perfect physical specimen to pull in the sympathy vote. And you don't have to win it.'

'That's very generous of you.'

'I know it is – I'm giving you the chance to write some magnificent first-hand stuff – the preparation . . . the pain . . . the "Loneliness of the Long-Distance Runner" – it's all there for you on a plate.'

'*My* plates!' But Ken was beginning to be won round. 'I suppose it would be my last chance to take part in a major sports event . . . Not that I'm agreeing, but say I did want to start training?'

Reg beamed and produced a plastic folder containing typewritten sheets – a high-energy diet drawn up by a top Harley Street doctor. Ken looked at them, then handed Reg the clanking bag of booze: his first donation to charity.

His flat would have to be cleared of alcohol as well. Charlie had come round to welcome him back and watched in amazement as his father wandered round the flat, collecting all the full and half-empty bottles of vodka, wine, whisky and gin from the cupboards and the fridge and under the bed, and put them all into a plastic 'Cold-box'. He couldn't help thinking it must be a joke, but Ken was dead serious. He would have a lot of writing to do about this marathon, so he was determined to do things properly. No half-measures. Charlie wondered if Ken could put him down for the TV set in his will, but instead Ken got him to sponsor him at fifty pence a mile, payable to the National Society for the Protection of Cruelty to Children.

Charlie gave him twenty-five pence then and there. He could give him back the change after the race. Ken felt incensed. Charlie had obviously never heard of Emil Zatopek, who was still winning medals in his thirties. But, as Charlie pointed out, Ken was forty-two. He'd noticed it in Ken's passport. Ken looked even older in the photo. It had been taken before he went to Munich in 1972. Not the Olympics of course – the Beer Festival. Still, all that was behind him now. His month in the sun had given him a new lease of life and he was ready to face anything. Except, that is, the news that Alison wanted Russell to marry her . . .

Alison had got *her* tactics all worked out. While Charlie was off with Ken, she was determined to have a little word with Russell. She put on one of her better dresses and waited for him. He'd said he'd drop by on the way to a cold afternoon's sports reporting. When he arrived, they kissed companionably.

'Bit snazzy for a Saturday morning, aren't we? Bound for Sainsburys rather than Tescos by the look of it.'

'No. I got all the shopping out of the way last night. Coffee and a calvados?'

'Smashing. I can't stay too long, though – I'm doing Queens Park Rangers this afternoon.'

Alison decided to adopt the direct approach. 'I hope you've got time for a little chat – about the future . . . '

Russell felt suddenly nervous for some unaccountable reason. 'Yes, well, I still don't think that plastic pitch of theirs will catch on – I give it another year at the most.'

'Not QPR's future, Russell – ours.'

Russell poured himself a drink. 'I must say I've enjoyed Ken's stuff on the cricket tour – you can always tell when a man's relishing his work. Mind you, I suppose the endless round of cocktail parties and embassy receptions helped . . . the jammy old bugger.'

'Finished?'

'Yes.' Russell looked sheepish. 'So you really want to talk about the situaggers do you?'

'The thing is, Russell, we're practically living together

already, so what's wrong with taking it a step further?'

Russell couldn't think of any concrete reasons why not, so he resorted to the abstract. 'Yes, but there are steps and steps . . . a step on the moon, for example . . . '

'All I'm suggesting is getting married – we don't have to have children immediately.'

'Children? Sprogging? Alison, we hardly know each other!'

'Charlie'll have kids of his own before he gets a brother and sister,' said Alison in exasperation.

Talking of the devil, Charlie walked in. He could see they'd been having words. He'd obviously come back too early. Or was it too late? He handed Alison a cold-box full of Ken's bottles as a peace-offering, informed them of Ken's decision to run in the marathon and showed them the miniature cricket-bat Ken had given him as a present.

'It's signed by both the teams, look, and their drug-dealers . . . '

Alison and Russell's reactions differed considerably over the news about Ken. For Alison, it was just another of his schoolboy fantasies; that was the trouble with sportswriters – old enough to drink but not to be adults. Russell, on the other hand, saw it as rather a brave thing to do; a really good wheeze. Besides, he was grateful to Charlie for getting him out of a tight spot. Would Charlie like a game of indoor cricket before *Football Focus* he wondered. Alison glowered and walked out.

Reg really went to town over Ken's marathon preparation. He took Ken on a shopping spree himself and got him kitted out with an all-weather tracksuit and krypton-padded motion-control running shoes. And he arranged for him to undergo training at Jack Mells' Coaching Clinic. Jack Mells was the original Marathon Man, reputed to have run enough miles to have covered the globe twice. For a moment, Ken thought he was expected to run all the way to Epping Forest to the clinic as well, but Reg had arranged a car for that. First, though, they had to stop off at The Inkwell, for a last bit of organizing.

Ruby was just serving Frank his first pint of lager of the

day when Reg and Ken arrived. Reg relieved him of his pint and gave it to Ruby.

'Pour this down the sink please. From now on you're drinking orange juice, Frank. Don't touch any more of that.'

'Come on, Reg.' Ken looked anxious. 'I don't mind people drinking round me. Let the man have his pint.' Frank was staring at Reg. He'd gone white with shock. 'Look,' added Ken. 'You've cut off his life-support system.'

Reg was adamant. 'No, Ken – if you're making sacrifices on behalf of the paper, then the least we can do is back you up. Ruby, as from now my Sports Desk is declared an alcohol-free zone. Not one drop is to pass their lips until the Marathon has started.'

Frank looked at Ken in horror. 'What have you done?'

'Honestly, Frank, this wasn't my idea. I feel bad about this, Reg, damaging the social fabric of The Inkwell.'

But Reg was not to be moved. 'Good! The guiltier you feel, the harder you'll try in the race. So we're all happy,' he announced to the three miserable faces around him.

'Right, I'm taking my custom elsewhere,' announced Frank.

Now it was Ruby's turn to look shocked. 'Oh, thanks a bunch, Reg! All the pubs round here are going to do very well out of me.'

'No they won't . . . because Frank and the boys will be doing no drinking whatsoever. Not in pubs, or in the office, or at home, or in the toilets, or on the bus . . . Ken may be doing the running, but this Marathon's a team effort. And if you don't want to be part of that team, then I'll enter you for the Sack Race, Frank. Understand?'

There was a miserable silence. Frank exhaled deeply and, probably for the first time in his life, ordered a Barbican.

Reg left Ken with Jack Mells for some expert training. After a quick warm-up, Jack took Ken out for a run in Epping Forest. Despite his silver-coloured 'Gore-Tex' track-suit and chic thick-soled running-shoes, Ken felt exhausted embarrassingly soon and had to collapse against a tree to get his breath back. If this were an Olympic Marathon he was running, Jack informed him, looking at his stopwatch, he'd have just about left the stadium. Jack helped poor Ken to breathe properly, taking the air through his nose, holding it for four seconds then letting it out through his mouth.

'Did you ever feel bad, during a race, Jack?'

'Oh yes – after about twenty miles, usually. You feel like you've just eaten a bowl of Vick. Of course, they call it "The Wall" or something nowadays.'

'But that's just an accumulation of phlegm, isn't it?'

'That's about the strength of it . . . but you can't call it that. It's not nice. You have to use the right jargon. Do you know what anti-pronation means?'

Ken could see some good material here for his articles. 'Stopping yourself falling arse over tip?'

'Right. Don't laugh; try putting that in an advert for running shoes and see how many you sell. It's these bloody Californians I blame. Running used to be just that till they got hold of it. Now it's become a fashion-parade, a lot of herberts got up in fancy tracksuits . . .' He stopped to look at Ken. 'Oh, sorry Ken – I didn't mean you.'

'I am serious about it, Jack. But if taking me on's going to be embarrassing to you . . .'

'Don't be stupid – I earn enough out of the London Marathon contestants to keep me going all year! Now come on – a quick half-mile sprint and you're finished for the afternoon.'

Ken watched him hare off. 'Hang on,' he shouted after the disappearing figure. 'I think I'm in a nascent-knackered situation.'

One of Russell's little treats was to have lunch at a particularly smart wine bar off Fleet Street and read the day's international newspapers, starting with the *Corriera Della Sera* and working through to *L'Equipe*. He was tucking into a bottle of wine there one day when Steve Stevens stumbled across him and made a characteristically rude remark about Russell's pretending he was in Paris again. Not that Steve thought Russell so pretentious as to stop him from sitting and talking to him for a while, and taking a glass of the 'Fleurie Liquid' Russell didn't offer him.

Steve was clearly rather flummoxed by Ken's training for the Marathon. Forget the training – how could he torture his body like that, giving up alcohol? It'd never last. He was determined not to give in to Russell's dig that someone was peeved because someone else had got in first on the marathon bonanza. Boozing was the only thing that kept 'em going on Reg's sports desk, Steve claimed. It helped them forget how well Steve himself was doing. Anyway *he* was considering doing a little survey on 'Sex during the Marathon' to follow his last year's 'Sex Before' feature. All those people in skimpy shorts crammed together – there must be some of 'em at it. Besides, had Russell seen the state of Ken's colleagues? Frank was apparently wandering round every pub in the street trying to get a drink. Reg had put the word out and they were all banned. Steve hadn't bought him one, of course – The Bad Samaritan. Just showed how seriously Reg was taking it all. Russell raised his glass to Reg's success. 'I've a feeling this one will run and run . . . '

Ken's training was going well. One night he even walked down to the Arab off-licence instead of taking a taxi as normal. Then, of course, he turned back and jogged all the way home. What was more, he'd captured the popular imagination in a way he couldn't remember having done since he described someone 'setting a new record in the Pope-vault'. They were inundated at the paper, on the one hand with worthy causes, and on the other with offers of help from the Great British Public. Put them together and what had they got? As Reg put it, 'Ken Wordsworth – Poet Laureate and Saint!'

It rather appealed to Ken to feature a few names on his running vest. He wouldn't say no to being a sandwich board for charity. But Reg was adamant. The front of his vest was to be reserved for the name of the paper – Ken's sponsors – and the back – well, the back was reserved for the holiday firm. What holiday firm? Ken wondered. Tours of the North Sea by lifeboat? It seemed a certain firm was offering a load of money to support Ken plus two free weeks in Eilat. Ken began to fantasize about two weeks' free recuperation, but they were already spoken for. Reg had decided to take Ruby there to make up for all the aggro The Inkwell had been suffering. After all, charity begins at home. Especially when it gets you away from your own.

Alison wished Russell would show a bit more charity in the direction of her home at the moment. He'd stopped coming round. She'd be all set for him and then he'd telephone at the last minute and put her off and say he couldn't make it the next night, even for supper. The night Russell phoned up to say he'd been called upon at the last moment to cover a fight in Leicester Square and that on Wednesday night he had to do his VAT, Charlie tried to give some platonic advice to his mother. He'd got the drift of things. 'Thursday night I bet he'll be washing his hair.'

'Do you think I'm frightening him off?' asked Alison.

'Dunno – I thought I was doing that . . . '

'Of course you aren't, Charlie – Russell likes you very much. He thinks you're terrific.'

'Oh good. It *must* be you then.'

'He *is* two weeks late with his VAT. Oh, shit.'

'Don't worry, Mum.'

'I can't help it, love – I got it wrong with your dad by giving him too much rope . . . and it looks as if I'm getting it wrong again giving Russell too little.'

'Well, he gets plenty of rope judging by the noises coming from your bedroom!'

Alison half-smiled. 'You're still not too big to get clocked round the ear.' Well, she thought to herself philosophically, she'd better make the most of Charlie in the two years left to her before he went off to University. Charlie for his part couldn't help thinking if Russell didn't realize how great Alison was, he must be daft.

* * *

By now Ken had got into the swing of going down to Jack Mells' coaching clinic every afternoon for work on his hamstrings, pelvic circles for hours on end and interval running, accompanied by his class of fellow Marathon trainees. One in particular, a solemn young man called Philip Spreckley, was a wonderful source for Ken's columns. Spreckley called interval running 'Fartlek', much to Jack's annoyance. When he first heard this Ken felt like setting off on foot immediately to tell Frank. The headline possibilities were mind-boggling.

Jack was giving his class instructions on a new exercise one afternoon – 'Just follow what I do . . . hands on hips, gently circle round like this . . . get those groins nice and loose . . . ' – when into the gymnasium walked Steve Stevens accompanied by Angie Phillips, the model from the airport, dressed in a track suit. Ken stopped exercising and looked at them in horror.

'Sweet little action there, Ken.' Leered Steve.

Jack didn't understand what was going on. 'Who's this?'

'One's "The Top Voice in Sport", the other's a topless model.'

Jack looked at Angie and at Steve, who was wearing a shirt, open to the waist, and gold pendant. Jack wasn't sure which was which.

'I've brought Angie to train for the Marathon, haven't I? As recommended in the Press.'

Angie was keen to get on with it. 'Do I take my tracksuit off yet?'

Jack could see the coaching clinic was about to turn into a madhouse. He told Spreckley to lead the others off down the road.

'A bit low-rent this, isn't it Steve? Getting a woman to do your stunts for you?' said Ken.

'Makes sense, Ken – who wants to see me run in a race – or you, come to that – when they can see Angie breasting the tape? The Nation's favourite girl-next-door!'

Jack was alarmed. Had Angie ever actually done any running before?

'Yeah, actually I jog twice round Hyde Park before

breakfast every day . . . or Central Park, if I'm in New York. And I do an hour's aerobics every afternoon. And I never touch alcohol, only fruit juices.'

'And if she wins,' added Steve, 'she'd like to open a donkey sanctuary and work for the good of mankind.'

Jack thought a moment. The money for coaching Angie would always come in useful. He agreed, provided he had cash in advance. Steve started peeling off notes from a big bankroll. Would Jack mind posing with Angie for a photographer? Another twenty quid? Sort of 'Beauty and the Beast'.

'I should go for fifty after an insult like that, Jack,' sighed Ken as he jogged out the door.

Russell invited Ken to have lunch with him at the wine bar. 'I do admire you,' he began over his bottle of red, and Ken's Perrier water, 'having the will power to forgo one of life's great pleasures – wasn't it Aristotle who said "A day without wine is a day without sunshine"?'

'No, but it's up on the wall at Aristotle's Restaurant in Camden Town.'

'Perhaps that's where I read it.' Russell took a long swig of wine.

'I take it this prolonged heatwave means you aren't going in for the race, Russell.'

'I'm completely the wrong build for it, old love. Didn't you see our "classical marathon physique" profile?'

'I saw the picture of the Greek statue in leg-warmers, but I didn't read any further.'

'Well, if you had you'd realize that an endormorph like me has only a thirty-six per cent chance of completing the course. You're in clover, Ken – you're an ectomorph!'

'Never mind, Russell – I'm sure there are plenty of compensations. You endomorphs probably stay other courses better . . . like marriage for example.'

They looked at each other a long moment. Russell took another swig of his Chateauneuf du Pape.

'You're probably wondering why I asked you to lunch, Ken.'

'No I'm not – I know exactly why. To ask for my ex-wife's hand in marriage.'

'Why? Has Alison been on to *you* about it?'

'No, Charlie told me. But if he doesn't mind, I don't mind.'

'Ken, you're missing the point – *I* mind! A hell of a lot! *That's* what all this is for. To ask what you think I should do!'

'Sorry Russell . . . The drink must be slowing me up . . . are you saying you don't want to marry Alison?'

'I just don't know. In many ways she's the ideal partner. She's a superb cook, she looks up to me intellectually, we have a wonderful time between the sheets . . . '

'Very glad to hear it. So what's the problem?'

'The sense of impending claustrophobia, Ken. You know the sportswriter's lifestyle – it's so important to hang onto the feeling of freedom, to know that you can take off with a typewriter and roam the world!'

'And if you *are* going to be cooped up – let it be in the press box at a Third Division football ground.'

'But you know what I mean, Ken – how many of our colleagues actually live in a state of domestic bliss?'

Ken racked his brains while Russell finished the wine. He couldn't think of anybody.

'Exactly! It's the nature of the beast, Ken. The free spirit in me wanted to enter for the marathon like you, but I couldn't because of Alison.'

And what could Ken say except he thought Russell might be wrong about Alison. 'When we were married she gave me all the freedom I wanted but all I did was abuse it. And my body. And my brain.'

Russell looked pensive. 'Anyway, I must shoot, Ken. Overdue VAT returns.'

Ken smiled at him. 'Go ride that tiger, Russell.'

Alison arranged a meeting with Ken as well – at his flat, which she hardly recognized, it was so tidy. She'd had to bring her own wine, in the cold-box he'd given her.

'How long have you been off it now, Ken?'

116

'I've almost stopped counting – ten days, three hours, perhaps.' Alison felt peculiarly hurt that Ken could give up drinking for a marathon when he hadn't been able to for her. Obviously the solution had been at her fingertips all the time. Instead of 'What time do you call this?' she should have said, 'Why don't you go out for a run?' She did remember once telling him to take a flying poke at a doughnut; that was vaguely athletic. Not that his drunkenness had been very funny; all those occasions she'd had to help him up the stairs or found him slumped in the porch or force-fed him an omelette at three in the morning. Perhaps they were best forgotten.

'So – what did Russell say?'

'Well – he told me how good your sex-life was . . .'

'He's right.'

'But . . . ?'

'But.' Alison tried to imagine what Russell could have said. 'That's all there is to it as far as he's concerned?' She looked genuinely anxious.

'What? No, what I meant was, "But it wasn't a patch on *our* sex life, Ken" – that's what you were supposed to say! No, no – he thinks the world of you, Alison. He's just a bit worried about this marriage business. He's not sure if he's quite ready for it yet. After all, he's only forty. To his credit, he is thinking of you as much as himself . . . you know what Lady Bracknell would have said – "To marry one sportswriter is unfortunate enough but to marry *two . . .*"'

' . . . is asking for trouble. But I know what I'm doing, Ken. I know what the pitfalls are.'

'Good – just walk around a bit before you stumble into them. It's a bit like marathon running, Alison – there are periods of the race where you can make rapid progress, and there are others when you just consolidate your position. It should be like that with you and Russell.'

'Fartlek.'

'You've been reading me. I'm touched.'

'So you really wouldn't mind if it did happen?'

'I'd be very happy for you, love. You know I think he's a pratt but he is a decent pratt.'

'Thanks very much, Ken. We shall have to see. Of course, if I did marry Russell, I wouldn't be a financial burden to you any more.'

'My God – I never thought of that! Get me a priest!'

The Inkwell just wasn't what it used to be. When Reg asked Ruby for a 'St Clements' and she didn't know what it was and he started to sing 'Oranges and lemons say the bells of St Clements', for a wonderful moment she thought he'd cracked and was ordering a Bells. But he wasn't. It was costing her a packet, all this malarkey. Since Reg imposed his ban her takings had gone down by about half. Reg for his part couldn't hide his satisfaction in his team. He wondered if it was affecting the pound. Ruby was most worried of all about Frank, who was a shadow of his former self, not that his former self was up to much. She was giving Reg a piece of her mind when Frank wandered in carrying the first editions.

He passed various soft-drinking colleagues, who exchanged long-suffering looks and raised their glasses in ironic sympathy. Reg, however, gestured to a police intoximeter, a plastic box with a mouthpiece and a scale, which was standing on the bar like part of the furniture. He couldn't control the pubs in town, so this was his security. Blow – or go. Frank dutifully breathed and Reg checked the reading. One more test. Frank had to say 'The Leith Police Dismisseth Us'. Reg could hardly get his tongue round that one, so they let it drop.

'Suffering Ada!' Reg looked at the sorry sight of his Deputy Sports Editor's work. 'What do you call this for a headline, Frank? "Marathon Man"? I'm asleep already! Oh, no, I don't believe it . . . the best you could do, and here's Ken talking about "Fartlek training"? It was an open goal! What happened to "Second Wind" or something? And that's without even thinking! "Marathon Man" . . . '

'It's not my fault, Reg – what do you expect from a car without petrol?'

It was then that Reg caught sight of Steve Stevens' spread. Covering most of one page was a picture of Angie

118

Phillips wearing tiny shorts and a T-shirt, getting a piggyback from an embarrassed-looking Jack Mells. Above it was a huge headline; 'Marathon Woman!! Sexy Angie Joins Our Big-Race Team. How Far Will She Go?'

Jack took Ken out for a bit of individual tuition the next afternoon. Ken was trying to encourage Jack to take part in the marathon himself, rather than just coaching for it. Show the fun-runners what a real athlete can do. As Jack explained, however, you can't just join in. The closing date for entries had been several months before. Ken didn't dare ask how people like himself and Angie Phillips had been able to sneak in at such short notice. Obviously The Showbiz Eleven were always free to jump on the band-wagon.

Jack and Ken were jogging along together over a hill both breathing easily, when they ran into some trouble. Below them, in a hollow, Angie Phillips was standing topless, with two men in bear-suits cavorting around her, while a photo-grapher took shots of the tableau from various angles. Standing to one side, supervising the proceedings, was Steve Stevens. Ken could see the headline now: 'When she ran down to the woods today, Angie Phillips was in for a big surprise!' Ken and Jack were just about to run on when Steve spotted them.

'This is just a bit of fun for the build-up,' he shouted. 'Mummy Bear, Daddy Bear and Angie Bare!'

Angie had seen them by now. 'Hello, Jack – can I book one last session with you?' Jack couldn't believe his ears. He liked a laugh of course and he liked being paid money, but there was a limit to even his endurance. He didn't mind training people for the London Marathon, but he was not going to do it for the Last Night of the Proms.

'Listen Grandad,' Steve was getting vicious. 'Marathon running is a very boring sport. I mean, I'd rather watch two flies going up a wall. It's only people like me and Ken who put it and you on the map.'

Ken objected to being classed along with Steve and said so.

119

'Why? You weren't even in it till Reg Prosser thought it'd be a good stunt to boost your flagging circulation!'

Jack looked at Ken accusingly. 'When *did* you enter?'

'About four weeks ago.' This was too much for Jack. He turned and ran off. Ken stood watching him disappear and turned back to Steve.

'Oh dear – have I just put my paw in it?' Steve chortled.

Of course Ken was short of material from then on – Jack Mells wouldn't give him the talks he had promised on marathon tactics. When Reg heard Ken had been present at The Teddy Bear's Picnic he thought he should have had Steve Stevens banged up for indecent exposure. Then he was struck by a thought:

'You know the only way we're gonna beat 'em now, don't you? By your coming last in this race.'

There was a long pause. 'You're joking aren't you? . . . You're not joking.'

'It's worth thinking about, Ken – you're not going to win, are you, so how else do we get any decent publicity? . . . Night falling, search parties sent out, a hero's welcome as you stagger over the line sometime on Monday afternoon.'

Ken felt that if this were to happen he'd then stagger back up Fleet Street and with his last ounce of strength would personally strangle his boss. 'What do you think all this training's been about, Reg? I could have come last the way I was!'

Reg didn't have time to argue about it now. Frank had gone AWOL, so Reg was having to do two men's work.

'Poor old Frank – over three weeks without a drink. He's probably suffering withdrawal symptoms.' Ken sympathized.

'Yeah, so am I, courtesy of Ruby. Bloody marathon, I'll be gladd when it's all over.' Reg was just wandering out of his office when the phone rang. 'Get that will you, Ken. Tell 'em I'll be back in ten minutes . . . unless it's the wife, in which case I'll be back in ten days.'

It was Harry, the photographer, at the airport. He'd

come across Frank, who had gone up to Scotland on the shuttle that morning, saying he was homesick and wanted to gaze on the waters of the Clyde. He'd been able to drink all day and had now flown back, by the sound of it without the plane.

By the time Ken got there Frank was sitting on the rotating luggage carousel, signing 'But There's Something the Matter with Glasgow, 'Cos It's Going Round and Round', clutching a bag full of bottles and swigging whisky. A uniformed guard stood nearby.

'No photographs, Harry,' warned Ken. Harry went to turn off the carousel and Ken approached his friend gingerly.

'Ken! What are you doing in Glasgow?'

'I've come to see you, Frank.'

Frank was duly touched by this and was about to offer Ken some whisky when he found the carousel was taking him away from him. To humour Frank, Ken jogged along with it. Ken did his level best to try and explain why Frank should come home with him. After all, Frank knew what would happen if Reg found out.

'Reg? That evil machinating sassenach methodist bastard!'

'Well, that's one point of view – let's discuss it on the way home shall we?' The carousel stopped and Harry and Ken took an arm and a leg each – Harry careful to take the side furthest from him so he could keep away from Frank's right hook. He'd had plenty of experience of being punched at airports.

The last straw for Frank had been when Ruby had refused to serve him the Dish of the Day at The Inkwell, 'Coq au Vin'. Frank always got nearly all his meals there. He had a little oven by his bed and on a Sunday morning he'd occasionally have a lie in and cook breakfast at the same time, but normally he'd go straight down The Inkwell. He quite simply couldn't survive without it.

Somehow Ken managed to get him back to his flat. He stopped off on the way on the pretext of buying an early edition and phoned Alison, who was asleep. Funny how he often went crying back to her, he thought. But he couldn't manage this one on his own. While he was waiting for her, he set to work force-feeding Frank an omelette. What with trying to grab the whisky bottle off Frank and give him the omelette, it slipped off its plate and fell onto the floor. Just at that moment Alison marched in.

'Did you do this?' She pointed a finger accusingly at Frank who looked sheepish, and then at the mess on the carpet.

'No, Ken made it.'

'Don't try to be clever with me. God, if there's one thing worse than a drunk, it's a messy drunk.' Ken was astonished. He'd never seen Alison quite so forceful before.

'Who's this?' Frank asked. 'Your cleaning lady?'

'I'll tell you who I am,' said Alison, taking the bull by the horns. 'I used to be married to this person when *he* was a lush. So I know how to deal with bums like you.' She seized the bottle from Frank's grasp. Frank cowered. Alison went across to the sink and started calmly pouring its contents down the plughole. She turned back to smile at Frank. Ken by this time was busying himself with a brush and dustpan, sweeping up the omelette, keeping out of the way.

'Right, my lad, there's nothing left for you to do now but sleep. What you'd better do, Ken, if he's still after a drink in the morning is get on the phone to Alcoholics Anonymous.'

'They wouldn't be in the book, though, would they?' argued Frank.

Alison whipped round. 'See? You stop drinking and already you're getting your sense of humour back! With a bit of luck they may yet be able to turn you into a useful member of the human race!'

Frank was soon snoring away. Ken had been astounded by Alison's successful tactics, and told her so. Obviously the 'softly softly' approach she'd always adopted with him had been the wrong one. The Wrath of Grapes. After all, this was the logical outcome of all Russell's guff about the sportswriter's free spirit . . . it ends up *in* spirits. He could see it all so clearly now he was a reformed character. They said running clears the brain. Or was he just a bit too sanctimonious, he wondered. He'd probably return to his normal self once the big day was over. And of course the big day was tomorrow.

As he bent down to lift Frank's feet onto the couch he felt a sudden shooting pain in his neck: 'Pre-Marathon Twinge'.

Which is why Jack Mells ran in the London Marathon that year after all. Jack was just telling his trainees that they shouldn't feel embarrassed about dropping out if they got into trouble, and Philip Spreckley was explaining that he'd have to keep going whatever happened because he'd be doing Operation Raleigh the next year so he couldn't re-enter, when Ken walked in wearing a neck-brace. Jack looked sceptical.

'What's this, another press stunt?'

'Displaced vertebrae . . .'

'How did you do it – lifting a drink?'

'Lifting a drunk, actually.'

Jack looked a bit dubious at first when Ken put his plan of action before him. They'd never know that it was Jack instead of Ken who ran . . . or at least not till after the race. Couldn't Jack do it for the hell of it? For the old days! Pre-Pain Barrier, Pre-Sponsorship . . . Well, Ken would donate ten quid a mile to Alcoholic Anonymous for personal reasons. Jack couldn't turn down an offer like that.

Everyone at The Inkwell was crowded round the television set watching the runners massing as they waited for the sound of the starting cannon. Ruby beamed as she lined up the pints and shorts again while Reg played Mein Host to the various drinkers, patting them on the back.

He smiled at Frank. 'All I'm saying is – next time your granny's going to die suddenly, try and give me a bit of notice, eh?' Frank decided not drinking wasn't going to bring his granny back anyway and tucked into a pint of lager. He'd have to be getting his drinking cap on for some headlines to flow again. They peered at the screen to see if they could see Ken. The runners were off. Someone said they thought they'd spotted him twenty-five down and ten across. Ruby giggled as it was announced on the telly that a Ken Wordsworth had collided with Angie Phillips and knocked her out of the race. Frank was already inspired. 'How about "Angie Boobs"?' he chortled.

Reg was brimming with pride. 'Storming back to form, Frank. Fancy tripping that tart up – what a great team I've got!'

Reg raised a celebratory pint to his lips. Suddenly he froze. Coming down the stairs in his neck brace was Ken. In disbelief he followed Ken's progress across the room towards him.

'How am I doing?'

There was an immediate stewards' enquiry.

Russell, Alison and Charlie nearly died of exposure waiting for Ken to pass by the 'Cutty Sark'. They decided Ken must have hit The Wall at a very early stage. Russell suggested they go and have a wander round the ship but Charlie sneered at this suggestion. On a Sunday it'd be full of kids with one of their divorced parents. Alison gave Russell a meaningful look. For her part she was worried about Ken. She had this vision of him, distressed, gasping for air, staggering along, his legs like jelly.

In fact, Alison's description wasn't too far off. The only thing she'd got wrong was Ken's distress. After a quick enquiry Reg had dismissed the case, and he, Frank and Ken had got down to some serious alcoholism . . .

JOBS FOR THE GIRLS

Every June the whole of the sports journalism world comes to a halt while the Sportswriters' Golfing Tournament takes place. This year was no exception. There was, however, a slight change in the rules: instead of putting pairs together from the same newspaper it had been decided to pair players at random, regardless of which newspaper they worked for, which is how Reg Prosser came to be playing with Steve Stevens and Ken with, of all people, Russell de Vries.

Things weren't going too well for Ken and Russell. They had lost the first round, looked as if they were going to lose the next against Colin Nuttall and Pip Hamilton, and would then have to win their third round if they were to stay in the tournament at all. Russell took all this terribly seriously. Ken was plain embarrassed by the sight of his partner, dressed to the nines, positioning himself with exaggerated delicacy for a two-foot putt. Russell crouched behind the ball to squint at the hole, picked up bits of grass between the ball and the hole and, finally, settled down to his putt. Ken by this time was getting impatient and said so, which delayed Russell all the more. Ken, Russell felt, was the last person to be telling him that he could blow it in from where he was. After all, somebody had to try and win the game for them, and it wasn't going to be Ken. Russell resumed his putting stance, wiggling his legs professionally. Colin and Pip glanced at each other and smirked. Russell looked as if he was trying to lay the shot rather than play it. Finally, after a few minutes' more deliberation, he sank the putt without difficulty.

'Shot, de Vries – probably the most impressive eighteen-inch putt I've ever seen,' said Pip.

This was an excuse to hold forth about comparative shots in the '67 Ryder Cup. Russell made it clear there was no comparison at all. After all, he explained, removing the ball from the hole, this was a pressure putt. 'It's all down to you now, partner.'

Ken had already clouted the ball, though. It shot past the hole and stopped at the other end of the green. As soon as he had hit it, Ken set off enthusiastically in pursuit. He was, he felt, taking this tournament in the right spirit. He gave the ball another swipe. It's the taking part that counts, not the winning. Russell didn't see it that way. He casually picked up Ken's ball as it was rolling past him and tossed it back to Ken. Ken was irritated, to put it mildly. He eyeballed Russell, tossing the offending ball up and down menacingly: 'Oi – d'you frow that?'

It was clear Russell de Vries and his partner, The Laughing Cavalier, had lost the first hole. Colin produced a hip-flask. This called for a drink, he said. Ken, however, refused, atypically.

'Not for me, Colin . . . I'm driving.'

The joking was interrupted by a young lady golfer, dressed in jeans and a track-suit top in contrast to the men's proper gear, who was standing about a hundred yards away in the middle of the fairway. Seeing them chattering by the flag, she called out to them. Unlike them, she had no time to waste.

'Excuse me! Do you mind if I play through?'

She returned to her ball while the four men stood by the hole watching her. Ken mentioned that it might be a good idea if they got off the green, but the others disagreed.

'Oh, I don't know – being next to the hole we're probably in the safest place,' drawled Russell.

Colin offered a side-bet on how many it took the girl to get down, and Pip offered a tenner. At this, the girl cried 'Fore!' The ball came flying in their direction, forcing them to scatter, and landed impressively near the flag. They all looked at it, astounded. Russell was the first to recover and concede her the hole. As he bent down to pick the ball up, the girl yelled at him not to touch it. Russell recoiled. Ken was amused that she could put him down so successfully. She putted the ball in calmly and went on to the next hole, leaving the four sportswriters bemused. Ken wished he were playing a round with her, so to speak.

'I dunno,' moaned Russell. 'The golf course used to be the only sanctuary we blokes had from women . . . come on chaps.'

They got over it in the bar over three Bloody Marys, two gin and tonics, four pints and a pernod. Each. Reg and Steve ambled in, delighted with each other's company. Ken offered Reg a drink.

'Never mind me, Ken – attend to this young man here . . . Steve Stevens – the most devious, underhand, unsporting bastard it's ever been my privilege to play golf with!'

'Leave it out, Reg.' Steve shrugged modestly. 'I don't want to make a fuss . . . I'll just have a glass of champagne.'

Apparently on the field of play all rivalry had been dispelled. They were all brothers. Clearly Cain and Abel had won. Ken enquired how much by.

'Six and two,' leered Steve.

'You wouldn't know this, Steve, 'cos you're only a sportswriter – but you can't actually win "six and two" . . . six and five, yes – six holes up with five holes to play.'

'Not six holes, Ken,' Reg explained to this amateur in Sportswriters' Golfing Trophy technique, 'Six balls! We had four more than they did! So every time we go into the rough, he slides a new one down his trouser leg onto a prime position on the fairway!'

'Sweet,' as Steve put it, 'as a nut.'

It had been such a good day for the Sports Desk, Reg thought Ken should perhaps telephone a couple of paragraphs on it through to the Acting Sports Editor, Frank McNab. That way they could make the news and write about it. Ken groaned. It was just his luck. He hadn't covered small time golf matches since his early days doing Rotary Club reports. 'Tell me, Mr Prosser – how did you feel when your ball in the bush was worth two in his hand?' Not that he could take the mickey too much. Steve Stevens was evidently keen to write it for Reg himself. 'In fact,' he confided in Reg, topping up his glass. 'You can take me on full-time if you make me the right offer.' Ken resolved to step into line and quickly ask the right questions of Reg Prosser, 38.

The Acting Sports Editor hadn't been having a very good day. Centre-stage in front of an empty house. Nothing had happened in that great wide world of sport; nothing he could flex his muscles on. As compensation he was having a quiet pint with Ruby, chewing over the possibilities of a story at Ipswich Speedway. Ruby only knew about Ipswich because her father was in prison near there. That set Frank wondering if they might by any chance have a football match on there that night. Indoor league. Ruby didn't think so. Thursdays they all watched *Tomorrow's World* so they'd be able to cope when they got out. Frank was fantasising about a streaker at Ipswich speedway causing a major pile-up when Ken phoned through the golfing report. He'd tried the office first of all, he explained, but had realized his mistake, so he'd put a call through directly to The Inkwell. Frank took the news fairly calmly, even if he did puzzle Ken at the other end with his suggestion for the headline – 'Putt Out'.

Ken put down the receiver and was making his way back into the bar when he saw emerging from the Ladies lavatory (which was called the 'Birdies', as opposed to the 'Eagles'), none other than the woman golfer of earlier in the day, a full jerry can in one hand. She made her way to the exit, but Ken intercepted her.

'Can I get you a scotch and ice to go with the water?' He marvelled at his own enthusiasm for anything in a skirt, when he'd been feeling so unenthusiastic about life a moment before.

'Despite appearances, I don't drink.' Well, that squashed that one.

'I thought I'd better offer,' he explained, 'to try and make up for the behaviour of my playing partners this afternoon.'

She seemed quite matter-of-fact about all that. 'That's all

128

right, I couldn't hear any of the comments, just the – what were they called? – Wolf-whistles?'

'That's my generation, I'm afraid . . . it's a quaint predecessor of ''Hello Darlin' ''.'

'Anyway – it isn't ''darlin' '' – it's Laura Fox.'

'Ken Wordsworth.' They shook hands. 'Got a bit of trouble with the sink?'

'Yes – why, are you a plumber?'

'Only when I can get the work . . . the rest of the time I scrape by as a sportswriter. Do you live locally?'

'I do at the moment.' The oddness of that remark didn't strike Ken till later.

'So, you'd be, er, free to have a drink? A soft one.'

Having a drink wasn't such a good idea after all. They were met by wolf-whistles as they entered the bar.

'Hey, look lads!' Colin whooped. 'Kenneth's pulled already!'

Laura made it clear she didn't approve and left quickly to get on with her plumbing. Ken was obliged to return to the table alone.

'Thanks a bunch, fellers – that's the second time you've made her play through today.'

'Aw, shame,' Steve commiserated. 'Did we give her a headache?'

'Anyway, you know the rules, Wordsworth – dinner first, crumpet later!'

Not that there was much crumpet in Dorking, as Russell pointed out. A strange remark, Ken felt, coming from someone who had said that the whole reason for a golfing holiday was to get away from women. As far as Reg was concerned, they were there for the sport and the good fellowship. The only pinks getting potted there tonight, he announced, with what he felt to be a quiet dignity, were those on the billiard table. With this, he led the way into the dining room where they tucked into prawn cocktails, steak and chips and Black Forest Gateau, accompanied by House Red and much raucousness.

After dinner Reg, Colin, Ken and Russell returned to the

bar, bleary eyed, and Colin called on Eric the Barman, Chairman of the Bar Committee to make the draw. Reg read out the slips of paper Eric drew out of an empty champagne bucket.

'Number Three. Nuttall and Hamilton . . . '

As secretary, Russell dutifully wrote this down.

' . . . will play number six . . .Brighton and Hove Albion . . . Sorry, Austin and Williams. Number Four . . . Callard and Bowser . . . who can't play for toffee . . . ' They collapsed into paroxysms of silly giggles, then pulled themselves together. This draw was going to be very important to the others when they staggered back from town after chasing the local talent. Probably a wild goose chase in Dorking, but they had to be respected for trying. Some of the older contestants who'd stayed behind would have willingly settled for any sort of goose, but as married men they felt they were doing the right thing by going to bed alone and preparing themselves for the next day's golf.

' . . . Number Four, Stevens and Prosser will play . . . ' But Reg didn't get to learn that night who was barring his path from the trophy. A small voice came from the other end of the bar.

'Reg . . . ' There was Ruby, clutching a weekend case. Reg whirled round and she gave him a shy smile and a wave. 'I just happened to be in the area,' she said by way of explanation. Reg was already heading towards the door, oblivious to the challenge of who he would be playing the next day.

'Tell me in the morning . . . '

Ruby was having her own problems. 'Am I an "Eagle" or a "Birdie" Reg? Cos I'm dying to go.'

Colin decided to turn in as well. Ken and Russell looked round and found they were the only people left in the bar.

'Isn't that the barmaid from The Inkwell?' mused Russell. 'Yes, I thought I recognized her. She has a striking Edith Piaf quality about her.'

It suddenly struck them it would be interesting to find out who Stevens and Prosser were playing after all. 'Wordsworth and de Vries', announced the piece of paper.

They looked at each other. The prospect of another day's defeat loomed ahead, not to mention a lonely night. They were, after all, at an awkward age, too old to go out on the razz with the Steves and the Pips but still young enough to hope that two little ravers might walk through the door to the bar at any minute. Not that two little ravers did walk through the door. And not that Ken would have allowed Russell to be unfaithful to Ken's ex-wife.

In desperation, Russell put a call through to Ken's ex-wife herself, back in Wandsworth. Alison and Charlie were, he told her, the only two little ravers he cared about. Alison was amused. There's nothing like a bleak night out with the lads to make you appreciate what you've got at home, she thought. She contemplated getting him to agree to marry her there and then, but decided against it. Instead, she broke some other news to him. Helping Frank come off the bottle had had a profound effect on her. She found that she had really enjoyed being able to help someone for once. And after all, she had more time on her hands nowadays . . . She'd seen an advertisement in The Guardian Public Appointments page for counsellors for a charity called 'Alcohol Anxiety'. When Charlie had returned from a hard day's O Level Revision at Emanuel, he'd found her bent over a little portable typewriter, composing an application. It meant that Charlie had had to get his own supper for once – oven chips and fish fingers which he cheekily suggested he might wash down with a bottle of white wine. Nevertheless it might be no bad thing his learning to take care of himself, if he wasn't going to take any O Levels in useful subjects like Domestic Science. She told Russell so on the phone that night as well. It might be good for him to have to take a bit more care of himself too. The prospect of life without Alison's cooking made Russell somewhat emotional.

Alison was hard at work typing her application up the next morning over breakfast. Charlie had had to do his own catering again.

'Morning, Mum. There you are, look, all my own work.' He held up a doorstep of a sandwich.

Alison didn't even look up. 'Very good, Charlie – you must let me have the recipe.'

'It's easy – you get a pound of butter . . . '

'Not now, love – I'm trying to concentrate . . . Er, would you mind checking the spelling for me? And don't get your breakfast all over it. They're anxious about alcohol, not marmalade.'

Charlie scrutinized it. The typing was a bit faint.

'Well this is twenty years old, this typewriter. I bought it for your dad when he got his first job in journalism.'

Some of the letters were a bit uneven as well.

'It's never been quite the same since I threw it out of the window one night . . . '

Charlie pondered over this information. 'Well the spelling's okay . . . but are you sure you're the right person to go into social work?'

The day stretched bleakly before Ken as he loaded his luggage into the back of his car. He and Russell obviously weren't going to win, which meant they'd be out of the tournament, so he thought he might save time by getting everything ready to go beforehand.

Next to Ken's Renault was Steve's orange monstrosity with its 'Steve/Steve's Bird' sunstrip, and beyond that was a small 'motorhome'. Ken was taking his golfing shoes out of the boot and putting them on when he saw Laura Fox emerging from a side-door of the motorhome. She saw him and came across.

'I didn't know you lived *that* locally,' Ken told her, gesturing in the direction of the van.

'Nice, isn't it?' smiled Laura. 'I won it in a hole-in-one competition . . . A *home*-in one. It's handy for getting me round the circuit.'

'Does that mean you're an electrician?' Ken asked, deliberately being as obtuse as possible – a tactic which sometimes worked.

Laura laughed. 'Its difficult for most men to get their heads round the idea that I'm a golf pro,' she told him. 'Even the polite ones . . .'

Ken leaped to his own defence. 'Well, I did recognize talent when I saw it – the way you scorched round the course while the rest of us just got lit up.'

Laura made as if to go. 'Oh well – nice to have met you.'

But Ken was keen for her to stay and give him a few quick professional tips on the day's play.

'Yes, I wish I had the time . . . but I've got to go to work.'

'Shouldn't you be going in the other direction? The golf course is this way.'

'No, this is my morning to work in the pro shop – got to keep the wolf from the dormobile.'

Ken had a flash of inspiration for a good golfing angle.

He quizzed Russell on the way to the first tee. Russell had never heard of Laura Fox, nor had Pip and he was one of the best golf writers in the business.

'Therefore she doesn't exist . . . I suppose it must be a battle for women to be taken seriously,' said Ken.

Russell had been informed of this over the phone by Alison in the wee small hours of that morning. He had to agree, it was a man's world.

'Ah yes – I sense another Wordsworth campaign on behalf of the underdogs and losers . . .'

They were met at the first tee by the confident, grinning faces of Reg and Steve. Steve was so sure of success he hadn't even bothered to put on golfing gear.

'Don't scoff at losers,' Ken cautioned his partner. 'I think *we're* about to join them. Morning Reg – how's the back?'

'Nicely relaxed, thank you, Ken.'

Steve gave them his normal leer. 'Hello playmates.'

Ken didn't answer but went straight for the pockets of Steve's blouson jacket instead and produced two handsfuls of 'spare' golf balls, like a conjuror.

Russell was full of admiration for once. 'Well played, partner.'

133

Of course, they lost anyway. Ken wandered in to the golfing shop to ask Laura if she wanted to buy a set of scarcely used clubs.

'That bad, was it?'

'Worse – they beat us fair and square. Haven't you ever felt like giving up the game, Laura?'

'Is this an interview or what?'

Ken was a bit taken aback by her aggressive attitude. There must be some reason for her defensiveness. Yes, he told her, as it happened he would be interested in doing a column about her, finding out what made her tick, what it was like dealing with the male establishment.

'How much would I get for talking to you?'

'Ah well – I don't actually go along with chequebook journalism . . . '

'Cash'll be fine.'

'Is it really that much of a struggle?'

Laura tried to explain just how much of a struggle it was. She couldn't afford, for example, to buy any of the stuff they were selling in the shop. She wore what she found at the bottom of her bed and played with a set of clubs her father had thrown out years before. If it hadn't been for one golden shot that won her the van she'd have been camping out in the bunkers.

'But what about sponsorship? Surely, someone who's been voted Rookie of the Year . . . '

Laura coloured. 'You *have* been busy since breakfast-time! Oh yes, I've been taken out for long lecherous lunches by blokes who are pushing hand-cream and crimplene twin-sets – but as I'm not into either that's as far as it gets.'

'So there is such a thing as a free lunch. How do you survive then?'

'I have to win every tournament I enter. But as there aren't that many, I fill in here as the pro's assistant. Two pounds fifty an hour, you know. Still, at least it's an honest penny.'

Ken was quick to offer lunch with him – not that he wanted to build her hopes up too much – but she declined.

She didn't get off till three and then she had to get to practice.

Just at that moment the door opened and Pip sauntered in, carrying a golf club. He acknowledged Ken and ignored Laura.

'The bloody face is coming adrift on my number two wood.'

'I saw that coming yesterday,' Ken told him blandly. 'The way you were dropping your shoulder on those short holes . . . '

'Cobblers, Ken . . . Oh, hello sweetie – now look, I need a bit of technical help . . . is the pro around?'

Laura and Ken exchanged knowing looks.

Ken had a bit of difficulty selling the idea of the story of a lady golfer to his Acting Sports Editor back in Fleet Street. Was she on the bonny side, Frank wanted to know. Ken tried to look aghast. That was neither here nor there, he told Frank sternly. Laura Fox was a very promising golfer who deserved every encouragement she could get . . . He hadn't even looked at her face . . . Or her figure . . .

Frank still wasn't convinced. He was trying to make a bit of impact while Reg was away. Couldn't Ken come up with something more lively about Golf. Ken saw his chance to get Frank to approve the story.

'You see, what interests me about Laura Fox is that here's someone who's talented and hard working, but who doesn't get any of the glory . . . '

'You mean, someone who doesn't get the recognition he . . . she deserves?'

'Exactly – a bit like yourself, Frank, if you don't mind me saying so . . . '

Frank was touched. 'No, I don't mind – thanks. Perhaps we ought to give the lassie a fair crack of the whip – what's her name? Laura Fox?'

'Yes. Fox. That's a Scottish name, isn't it?'

Frank was mulling this over when the phone rang. It was Reg, calling on his cordless phone, direct from the eighteenth green. Reg and Steve had just beaten the crestfallen Colin and Pip, so, while Steve took large amounts of money off

135

the losers, Reg thought he'd give Frank a ring to find out what he'd be reading in his sports pages the next day.

'No, Frank – what I'm going to *read*, not ignore! Well what's Ken got lined up? . . . Dear oh dear – who does he think we run this paper for – women? Use that to follow your little effort on Ipswich Speedway, and you'll be delivering a million readers into the hands of my partner here! Anyway, there's only room for one golf story tonight . . . copy to follow!'

When Reg let slip that Ken had been trying to foist him off with a woman golfer, Steve's ears pricked up. That evening he paid a visit to the dormobile for himself. Laura heard a knock at her door and opened it to find Steve leaning against the bonnet of his car, an unfinished drink in one hand.

'Care for a drink?'

'Sorry?'

'Steve Stevens – sports journalist and amateur golfer . . . I understand you play professionally?'

'Yes, and I've got a full day ahead tomorrow, so if you'll excuse . . . '

Steve gave the motor-home a long look up and down. 'Live in there, do you? Bit small isn't it? I'd have thought someone of your stature would have had something more substantial . . . '

Laura maintained a frosty politeness. 'It suits my purposes for the moment, thank you.'

She went to close the door, but Steve was quick to prevent her. 'I think I can see a way of getting you a bigger one.' The half-closed door opened again.

'How would you do that?'

'Well – being a journalist, I'm interested in people's lives . . . specially people with interesting lives like yours must be . . . all girls together, parties and that . . . I bet that dormobile could tell a few stories.'

'The sort of stories a paper would pay money for?'

'Right! Life in the Passion Wagon! I bet it's seen some action. My little motor has, I can tell you.'

136

'Is that why the sticker on your car isn't too specific?' she asked, indicating 'Steve's Bird'.

'Yeah! Look, as we're getting on so well, why don't we talk some business?'

'Yes,' breathed Laura. 'I think I could use a drink now.'

Russell walked through the front door in Wandsworth and tripped over a metal golf-hole. Charlie, who was revising in the dining-room, heard the yell but didn't look up. He wasn't to be disturbed, he told Russell. With exaggerated delicacy, Russell leaned his rattling golf bag up against the wall.

'Don't see any "goff" trophy. Being engraved is it?' remarked Charlie drily. Russell always called 'golf' 'goff', like Ken always called 'football' 'footy'. Little boys, all of them, as Alison put it.

'It's not being engraved with my name, alas, nor your father's,' Russell told Charlie. 'All that fresh air . . . I'm starving! Where's Mum?'

'*My* Mum's out job hunting . . . don't know where yours is.'

'Ah, so no supper then? Sorry about the noise – my stomach rumbling.'

'Well it's your fault – you shouldn't have encouraged her last night on the phone.'

Here, at last, was an issue on which Russell and Charlie were united. They were all for Alison broadening her horizons, but what with her Open University and now a career, in their opinion she was taking on too much. It might be difficult for her to accept, but she was playing a key supporting role in the lives of two intellectuals. And brainwork needs proper, regular nourishment. As for the immediate crisis, of what nourishment they could get then and there, Russell suggested a takeaway. Charlie was amazed. 'You mean you've heard of 'em?'

'I've *lived* off them for most of my working life! I thought I'd left them behind by moving in here . . . hey ho.'

Charlie disappeared into the kitchen to warm a couple of plates.

137

Reg had turned down the Laura Fox story on the grounds that it was boring. Ken and Frank commiserated with each other in The Inkwell afterwards.

'It's not your idea that's wrong, Ken,' confided Frank. 'It's just Reg playing power-games with me . . . putting me in my place . . . finding fault with every decision I make.'

'Well, here's one decision he can't interfere with – what are you having to drink?'

'Thanks, Ken – I'll have a large . . . ' Out of the corner of his eye Frank caught sight of Alison who was making her way tentatively towards them through groups of curious Inkwell regulars.

'Oh, no – that's the last straw – he's sent *her*! The avenging angel!'

Ken kissed Alison. 'Hello love – what would you like?'

'My underwear back, when that lot have finished undressing me. You might have told me it was a Men Only establishment.'

'It isn't – women just don't want to come in here, that's all . . . '

Alison turned to Frank. 'Hello Frank, remember me?'

Frank was stiff with terror. Alison took in the empty glasses in front of him. 'I see you're back on the drink again.'

'Yes, sorry.'

'Don't apologize to me, it's yourself you'll have to say sorry to.'

'Oh. Right.' Frank put down his two-thirds full lager glass and pushed it away.

Alison smiled in a matronly sort of way. 'You see – you did that of your own free will . . . '

'Aye.' Frank was still intimidated. 'But you took a lot of the credit,' he told her. 'I'll see you back at the office!' he nodded at Ken and headed straight for the exit.

Alison had come to get Ken to write her a reference for 'Alcohol Anxiety', but as Ken pointed out she didn't really need one after that. If they'd videoed her encounter with Frank they could have used it as a training film. The Inkwell would be the first place she'd clear out when she got the job, said Alison. She started making suggestions as to what Ken should write. If they contacted him it would mean they were interested in her – so just sort of general stuff about her potential would be best. He might also put in something about how he felt strongly that her lack of formal qualifications shouldn't be a barrier. Ken agreed to two hundred words of fulsome praise, though he should warn her, he said, that his own confidence in his judgement had been a bit dented over the past few days.

'I wanted to do a column about this woman golfer I'd met, but Reg turned the idea down flat.'

'But she isn't, presumably?'

'Don't be sexist, Alison – it's a good story about a young sportswoman who's being unnecessarily hampered in her career.'

'I'm not surprised he turned it down, there's never anything in the sports pages for women readers,' Alison said. 'And when they do condescend to write about women – if they're pretty enough to photograph, of course – it's usually in terms of what their boyfriend thinks.'

'You wouldn't like to write this down and give it to Reg as a reference, would you?' But Alison was confident Ken didn't need any help from her. In her opinion, he should just go ahead and write the piece. And if he wrote as well as she knew he could, they'd have to print it. After all, when did he ever give up on a story he had really wanted to do? Ken thought for a moment.

'Well, there was that night you threw my typewriter out of the window . . .'

'You've done it, Ken – I never thought you could, but you've convinced me,' Reg told him as he sat in his office finishing off Ken's Laura Fox piece.

'What, that you could read a piece with minority appeal without falling asleep?'

'No, that there was someone on that course almost as

139

impressive as yours truly.' Reg tapped the head of the statuette on top of the golfing trophy that stood before him. Immediately the golfer's club began to swing and it started playing a tinny recording of Bing Crosby's 'Straight Down the Middle'. Ken was about to continue as if nothing was happening but Reg held up his hand for silence until the chorus had finished.

'Anyway, well done Ken . . . I'd like to melt this statuette down and recast it as a pen and present it to you. But I won't – my approval is your reward.'

'My cup runneth over, Reg.'

'There is a problem however . . . ' It turned out Reg was in a bit of a Wisdom-of-Solomon situation, having had a freelance piece submitted to him on exactly the same subject. He handed it to Ken.

' ''Sex Queen of Clubs''?' Ken went white. 'Reg, tell me that doesn't say ''Sex Queen of Clubs'' . . . '

'It's only a working title.'

'What is this shit? ''After a day on the links, it's a night of high jinks for the girl they call 'The Foxy Lady of Golf' . . . sexy Laura Fox (25) who brings a whole new meaning to the word 'mixed foursomes' . . . '' Who wrote this garbage? Sorry, emptied it onto the page?'

'A young journalist who's keen to come and work for a top newspaper.'

'Keen? He must be desperate. And *she* must be desperate – how much has he paid the poor girl to do that?'

'Nothing – unless we print it.'

'What? You must *really* be desperate. Even Steve Stevens' rag wouldn't sink this low!'

'Funny you should mention that, Ken . . . '

There was a long silence as Ken stared at Reg.

'And this is his job application form, is it?'

'Don't panic, Ken – he's not after yours. But you see, I'm like a football manager – always interested in strenghtening my team.'

'Well if I find myself playing in the same game as him, I'll be asking for a transfer, boss,' warned Ken. 'In writing.'

He stormed out. Reg looked at the empty office and at the two rival pieces he was holding.

'But I haven't decided which piece to go with . . . yet,' he said to himself.

When Ken went to check up with Laura Fox about all the stories of three men in her bunk leaving their plus-fours on, and the circus acrobats she met on the road in her 'Passion Wagon', she was her normal direct self. All she had done, she told him, was empty a drink over Steve Stevens' head. He'd wanted to write some kiss-and-tell rubbish about her, so she'd told him to piss off. After the beer shampoo, he did. So now Ken knew the truth. And he knew what to do. The trouble was, standing on a golf course, there wasn't a telephone box in sight.

When Ken had told Reg, and Reg told Frank about the dead dog of a story from Steve Stevens, Frank's reaction was that they should be grateful they had found out in time. It could have been worse than Hitler's diaries. At least Hitler hadn't been able to sue. Just then Steve wandered into The Inkwell, to give Reg a picture of their sexy golf star to go with the article.

'I'm sure it'll be up to your usual high standards,' Reg told him.

Steve was impatient for his next assignment. Had they got anything for him?

'Yes, as it happens. I want you to cover a golf tournament. In America.'

'Good-oh. Where is it?'

'Death Valley.'

'I didn't know they played golf there.'

'They don't – but I'm sure you'll be able to make something up. Put him back in the gutter.'

Frank dutifully obliged. Reg looked at the photo of Laura.

There was a daily ritual which had been established over the breakfast table at Alison's house. Alison always read the

141

Guardian, Russell read *The Times* and Charlie read his father. That morning, however, Alison was more interested in the post. Along with two parking fines for Russell was an official-looking envelope addressed to Ms A. Rathbone. She read it as Russell dished out scrambled eggs and croissants for Charlie and he.

'Le voila!' announced Russell. 'Les Oeufs Brouillés à la de Vries!'

'There were about four mistakes in that, Russell! It's "Les voila", for a start . . . and it's "au de Vries".'

'Careful, Charlie – don't peak too soon. Save it for the exam.'

Alison folded the letter and put it back in the envelope. She hadn't got the job and was trying to put a brave face on it. It wasn't their fault, after all. She should have worked harder when she was at school.

'Well, it's not the end of the world.' Russell commiserated, trying to encourage her. 'I must have written a hundred letters before I got my first job . . . and *that* one wasn't worth having.'

'And there aren't going to be *any* when I get out of school!'

'Thanks boys – you've made me feel much better! But there must be something out there for a woman with no qualifications.'

At this her eyes fell on Ken's Poet Laureate column open by Charlie's plate. Next to it was a huge photograph purporting to be Laura Fox in tight shorts, standing with her bottom to the camera in a saucy Betty Grable type pose, grinning over her shoulder as she swung her golf-club. Above it the headline read – 'Queen of Clubs'. Alison pulled a face. She'd better get on with her ironing in this man's world.

Ken thought it best to go back and apologize.

'Sorry,' he told Laura.

'What for? Why sorry? It wasn't me. Just some model who looked like me.'

'I know. It wasn't *me* either. A little legacy from Steve

Stevens which I'm afraid my editor was happy to inherit.'

'Well there are three firms of stocking-makers who seem to think I've got very good legs now they've seen the photo. They're in play-off for me at the moment!'

'Stockings? That's not really your style, is it? Especially now those faded jeans have been immortalized in print.'

'I look at it like this, Ken,' Laura explained. 'If they're offering me fifteen thousand a year to wear something on legs I haven't got, who's the mugs – me or them?'

'Yes it was a pity to run the column, really.' Ken was feeling defensive, and attack seemed the best way to cope. 'We could have filled the space with another lookalike with better knockers and you could have cleaned up the bra market as well.' Where was the liberated woman he'd been trying to understand over the past few days?

'Now don't be silly.'

'I'm not being silly.' Typical female reaction. 'I'm just a bit confused.' He tried to explain. 'I've been trying to play a line between all these chauvinist sandtraps, and when I fail, through no fault of my own, I'm disappointed that you don't feel as bad as I do.'

'Come off it – you're just disappointed that you didn't get me my big break – and your reward that went with it . . .'

'What reward?'

'Be honest – the only reason you wrote the piece in the first place was because you wanted to get into my knickers!'

There wasn't much Ken could say to that. He'd written the piece and he hadn't. Case dismissed. It was then that Laura mentioned that she would actually like to see him again. The trouble was, Ken was booked up that week going to the Test Match and Laura was off to Scotland the next and then to France and Spain. July was out what with the athletics, more cricket, men's golf . . . There was nothing for it. They'd have to go to bed with each other there and then. In the Passion Wagon . . .

FATHERS, SONS AND LOVERS

'What a Scorcher – Official' read an *Evening Standard*
billboard. It was a sunny July afternoon and Reg and Ken
were conducting an editorial meeting in shirtsleeves and
sunglasses on a bench in front of Dr Johnson's House in
Gough Square, off Fleet Street. They had got to the Diary
Liaison Stage, contemplating what Reg had got lined up for
his leading Sports Feature writer.

'This isn't a diary, Ken, it's a travel brochure. It must be
a sports columnist's dream – Three 'A's at Crystal Palace
. . . Benson and Hedges Final at Lord's . . . with the World
Archery Tournament thrown in as a bonus! *And* you're
getting paid for it!'

'Archery, Reg? Where's that?'

'Ealing.'

'So Crystal Palace, Ealing and St John's Wood. Not so
much a travel brochure, Reg – more a bus map. Look – I've
got a weekend free here which just happens to coincide with
the end of the Tour de France – perhaps I could nip over to
Paris, and . . .'

'Ken, please – how can you entertain such unpatriotic
thoughts, here in the shadow of Doctor Johnson's House?
Your duty should be to the noble English bowman, not a lot
of frogs on bikes, with onions round their necks . . . It's not
for someone as dedicated to sport as you, Ken.' Reg looked
positively insulted.

Ken had just felt like getting about a bit. 'Still, perhaps
the good doctor was right – ''When a man is tired of
London, he is tired of life . . . '' '

'You know, Ken, that could have been me talking.'

' '' . . . For there is in London all that life can afford.''
Or all that the *paper* can afford, anyway.'

Ken should have never had said that. It laid the way open
for Reg to bring up a little project he had in mind for the

Poet Laureate. Ken was to go walkabout. Reg would explain all in The Inkwell.

Ruby was chalking up the day's Special on the blackboard: 'Sallad'. She loved these summer days – no cooking, no tights. Frank McNab, sitting in a dark corner, didn't agree. He liked a quiet pint in the shade. None of that sprawling all over the pavement outside pubs, laughing loudly. Pavements, as Frank saw it, were for walking on and puking on, in the dark of the night. Ruby reckoned he must have been a creature in the bottom of a rock-pool in a previous life . . . Frank McCrab! He should have changed places with Ruby's father, Bryan, who was due out from his dark damp cell in Chelmsford prison the next day. Frank drank to that in silence.

Reg and Ken had overheard this last piece of news.

'I shouldn't worry, Reg,' Ken told him. 'I'm sure Ruby's Dad will be delighted to have you as a son-in-law . . . even if you *are* still married to somebody else . . . '

'Oh, bigamy wouldn't bother Bryan – but the fact that I'm five years older than him might! Maybe *I* should go to the seaside for a few days . . . '

The conversation turned to what Ken would be doing over the next few days. 'You've heard the news then . . . ' Frank remarked dourly. Apparently it was the editor who had decided that his top feature writers should go walkabout to the seaside. The only thing left to be fixed was where Ken should go. All he had to do was pick a resort, find out what sporting activities were going on there and write a week's columns giving the unique flavour of Britain at play! Well, nearly all. The Editor took the view that while they were there it would be a pity not to give the paper a bit of extra publicity. After all, Ken would have to walk from 'A' to 'B' anyway, going about his normal business . . . so he was almost bound to bump into some of his many fans . . .

'Oh God! Not "You are Ken Wordsworth and I claim my five pounds!" '

'Of course not! Ten pounds.'

'But why have *I* got to make a fool of myself?' Ken felt he had to make some sort of stand.

'It's not just you,' wheedled Reg. 'All our star names are mucking in! The theatre critic's going to be strolling up and down the pier at Brighton, waiting to be approached . . . '

'Yes, but he does that every weekend. And maybe he doesn't mind being treated as a cash dispenser. As a writer, I mind very much . . . '

'Come on, Ken – it's just a bit of light-hearted, impromptu summer fun . . . which The Editor insists upon.'

Ken's father was due to visit the Wordsworth family home. It was panic stations.

'They always make one mistake – py-jams under the pillow,' announced Alison, brandishing a pair of Russell's Chinese dragon pyjamas. Russell was trying to close his suitcase, crammed full of shirts, underwear, suits and shoes.

'Who are *they*, Alison?'

'Criminals, leaving the scene of the crime.'

Russell was irritated by this. 'I am not a criminal – I am a consenting adult. We're *both* consenting adults . . . and it isn't as though it's *your* father . . . or even your father-in-*law*, now! You're divorced from Ken – so why this palaver?'

'I know, Russell, but he's an old man – I don't want to hurt his feelings.'

'Well he's going to have to face up to reality one day. What happens if you get married again?'

'Then you won't have to move out for the night, will you?'

'Oh dear – own goal.'

They were clearly going to have to put Wordsworth père first. Alison made a snide remark about there being room in Russell's suitcase for half a dozen of his books as well if they really wanted to eliminate all traces of his existence. Russell thought it best to ignore this, but browsed along the bookshelves to find something suitable to keep him company that night even so. There was nothing quite like one's own words to do that – even if Russell would probably need a double bed to accommodate them all.

'What are you going to do?' asked Alison, peaceably.

'Probably find some sleepy County Championship match to cover, and put up at a country house hotel, with a decent restaurant and a list of fine wines . . . I'd better take the Good Food Guide.'

'Yes, do – Arthur won't be needing it. He thinks a mixed grill's pretty perverted.'

'Mmm – no frills and no frolics. I detect a quaint northern morality. I suppose that's where Ken gets his from.' This, it appeared, was the reason Ken couldn't billet his own father. There had been a bit of feeling between Arthur Wordsworth and his son ever since Ken and Alison split up. Arthur had taken Alison's side and Ken had resented it.

Charlie had been celebrating the end of exams at the Wandsworth Common Tap Room. He swaggered in tipsily and tossed his briefcase onto the floor.

'That's enough of that for six weeks . . . bye bye George Eliot, hello George Michael!

''Wake me up before you go-go
Don't leave me hanging on like a yo-yo!'' '

Russell smiled fondly at him. 'Ah yes, Charlie. Nothing tastes quite so sweet as those first under-age drinks brazenly bought in school uniform . . . '

'I had my first one when I was twelve you know, Russ . . . '

When Alison broke it to him that his Methodist grand-father was arriving for a visit in a couple of hours, the alcohol seemed to evaporate into mid-air. Charlie sat bolt upright and knotted his tie in alarm.

Ken was to pick his father up from St Pancras station. Arthur took control immediately and made his way to Ken's car, leaving Ken to lag behind carrying a suitcase and a heavy, cylindrical leather bag. Arthur waited frostily while Ken opened the hatchback and put the case in.

'No, not that one.' Arthur pointed at the leather bag. 'I'll have it on me lap.'

As he was obviously going to be treated like a taxi-driver, Ken thought he might as well behave like one. 'My mistake guv. Cor blimey, what you got in 'ere?'

'Mind your own business.'

Ken handed him the bag and opened the passenger door. 'Would you rather sit in the back?'

'Makes no odds. I could have found me own way to Alison's, you know.'

'She thought it'd be nice for me to come and meet you. The sentimental old thing. Still, at least we're having a conversation.'

'Foreign job this, isn't it?'

'Well, if you want to go across the road, there's a nice British 77A bus . . . '

'I'm here now.' Ken could see exactly what sort of journey it was going to be.

'You broke your mother's heart, do you know that?' Arthur was off again.

'Dad,' Ken looked wearily at his father. 'She died five years before Alison and I were divorced.'

'Yes, but she could see it coming.' He stared out over the bag at the London streets they were driving through with obvious distaste. 'Moving to London, that's what did it.'

'And that was five years after it stopped "Swinging"'! It was obviously best to change the subject. 'Have you come to play a bit of bowls?' he asked, pointing at the leather bag.

Arthur gave him one of his withering glances. 'No, no – I came to see *you* . . . '

Bryan Pike was paying a visit to his family as well. It was good to be back in The Inkwell again after serving time in Chelmsford. He downed a ceremonial pint, watched by a handful of hard-core regulars including Reg and Frank. 87p seemed a lot of money for one drink. After all, Bryan had only been in three years. Bryan wasn't a great one for well-chosen words at the best of times, but he made it clear he was glad to be home. Nor was he the sort of man to offer Drinks on the House. He made a half-hearted offer of half-price drinks for the next thirty seconds and left it at that. There was a good-humoured rush for the bar, leaving Bryan free to talk to Reg.

It appeared Bryan had been sharing a cell with a journalist for the past three months. The journalist had been in for stealing a body from a grave – his editor must have told him to see what he could dig up! This journalist had apparently heard of The Inkwell, and in particular he'd heard about a bit of what Bryan described to Reg as nonsense involving Ruby and some married geezer. Bryan wasn't too happy with this state of affairs. He wouldn't like to think that any liberties had been taken with his little girl; not while his own liberty had been taken.

'So you haven't heard anything?'

'No, it's true what they say – the editor's always the last one to know,' said Reg, hastily. 'Specially where sport's concerned . . . Not that I'm equating that with what Ruby's involved in – or most likely isn't involved in . . .'

Bryan slapped him on the back. 'Yeah, well thanks for listening, Reg. You've reassured me. But if you do hear of something going on – and you find out who it is – let us know so I can twist his balls off, eh?'

Alison gave Arthur, Ken and Charlie ham-and-egg salad for tea. Charlie wolfed it down but turned his nose up at the sliced white bread-and-butter Alison offered him.

'I don't want that . . . why should I have sliced bread, anyway? *I* haven't got false teeth.'

Alison had hoped it might settle Charlie's stomach. He'd had a bit too much of what, for Arthur's benefit, she called 'apple juice', at his end-of-term party. Ken gave his son a beady look which Charlie missed.

'That's right, Charlie lad,' his grandfather told him. 'You stick to the apple-juice. We don't want you going off the rails like some I could mention . . . your dad, for instance.'

'Don't worry Grandad – I don't even like pubs. There aren't any decent ones round here anyway . . . '

'From what you've heard from the older boys . . . ' Ken prompted. It was obvious it would be best to change the subject. There must be something it was safe to discuss.

'What sort of bowls tournament is this you're going in for, Dad?'

Apparently Arthur didn't want to discuss this topic even if his son did. His reply was brusque. 'The Margate Under-60s Open'; and *he* then changed the subject fast. 'Have you got some more tea there, love.'

Ken, however, wasn't going to let this lie. Arthur had been 63 last birthday and Ken pointed this out. If he was under 60 he'd have been Charlie's age when Ken himself was born.

Arthur looked sour. 'You think you're very clever don't you. I fancied a few days by the sea, taking a few bob off the southerners, and now I've got me Railcard, why not use it?'

'Don't you have to be 65 before you get a Railcard?' Ken was determined to get his pound of flesh.

Alison glared at him. 'Stop trying to cause trouble, Ken.'

'I should think so,' agreed Arthur. 'Are you going to get a holiday this year, Alison, love?'

Ken let out an involuntary yelp of amusement. When was Alison ever not on holiday? The others looked at him. They resumed the conversation.

'You work too hard, that's your trouble. Look, why don't you and the lad come down with me? Change of scenery'll do you good. It'll be like a real, old-fashioned, family holiday. You, me and Charlie all together . . . '

'D'you remember those weeks we used to have in Scarborough? The Wordsworths and the Rathbones – always in the same boarding-house . . . ' Ken rhapsodized, ignoring the snub. 'And somehow we always managed to coincide with the Cricket Festival. That great, grassy amphitheatre, surrounded by brass bands, and marquees, and funfair rides. I can even remember the smells – calamine lotion on sunburned skin and donkey-droppings on the beach . . . I knew they were great days even then.'

'*You're* not coming with us,' his father told him flatly. 'I'll start doing the pots. Come on, Charlie, you can dry.'

'We just leave them on the draining board here, Grandad . . . '

'Not while I'm in the house. Anyway I want to hear about these O levels . . . '

As Charlie reluctantly picked up the plates and followed Arthur out, Ken and Alison let out sighs of relief.

'What brought on the sudden attack of Roy Hattersley?' asked Alison.

'Just limbering up – I've got to create something dynamic out of the following ingredients – sea, sun, sand and sport. Which is why I thought I'd tag along; to see if my Dad playing bowls might work a bit of magic . . . '

'I see – when all else fails, use the family. The last resort of the desperate journalist. Well, I don't mind . . . I suspect Arthur will, though.'

'Oh, don't worry about him.' Ken's eyes twinkled. 'What would an old-fashioned family holiday be without old-fashioned family rows?'

'By the way, thank you for including me in your golden memories just now . . . '

'Well I could hardly mention sex in the Scarborough sand-dunes in front of Charlie, could I?'

Alison giggled. 'Do you think our parents were really fooled by us going off with *The Observer's Book of Butterflies*?'

'I don't like to think about it.' They looked at each other fondly. 'So what have you done with Russell?'

'He's in quarantine.'

'What?'

'Well, Charlie's let his name slip a couple of times, so I told your Dad he was a dog we'd put in kennels.'

'Many a true word, Alison . . . '

Reg gave Ken two hundred pounds in new ten-pound

notes to give to twenty lucky winners. If it got to Tuesday and he was running out he was to stay indoors or put a bag over his head. He must also mind he was strict with the rules. They had to have a copy of the paper in their hands, they had to accost him with the right form of words: 'You are the Poet Laureate of Sport, and ten pounds to give me you Ought' (it had taken Frank three hours to think that up), and last but not least they had to answer the day's simple question before Ken was to hand over a crisp tenner. Ken didn't even look at the typewritten sheet of questions Reg handed him. He could just imagine them: 'Name the current Albanian World Cup Team and their girl-friends . . . '

'Now hop it, Ken and have a good time.' Reg sat down, looking preoccupied. His hands were shaking.

'Are you all right, Reg?'

'No, I'm not. I've got a terrible ache in the lower regions, and it isn't lust, it's fear. Bryan Pike's on the warpath.'

'Oh, I see – "you are the man who ravished my daughter, and break your legs I oughter".'

'Just once it'd be nice to get some sympathy round here.'

'Come on, Reg – I'm sure if you just lie low for a few days and keep your distance it'll all blow over.'

'Oh, sure – here I am relying on the tact and discretion of that crowd in The Inkwell, when most of 'em'd shop their own grandmothers for the price of a pint . . . sorry, half-price. Look at me – I'm more like our theatre critic than the sports editor! Why don't I come straight out with it and tell him? I can always phone him from an airport . . . '

'I wouldn't do that, Reg – the last thing parents want is to find out what their offspring are really up to.'

Their first day in Margate was Ladies Day in the Bowls Tournament. Ken, Arthur and Charlie went down to study the form. Ken and Arthur were getting on better by now. Arthur began discussing tactics.

'If you let it, this game just becomes straight up-and-down bowling. So what you do is make it more complicated. Keep 'em guessing – throw in a few short ends, they don't like that. Let's face it, it's easier for me to adapt to these Southerners' conditions than them to mine . . . ' They were interrupted by Charlie bouncing a football onto the green right into the middle of the game. Charlie followed it and dribbled it back to the edge. Ken looked embarrassed.

'Charlie! You're not on Wandsworth Common now you know – you're on holiday, so behave!'

If this was the level of excitement he was in for, it didn't seem like much of a holiday to Charlie. Arthur announced that they'd better get this young man back to the boarding house.

'I know what the "bored" means in "boarding-house".' Charlie told them as they made their way away from the green. 'No video films, no room service . . . '

'There's a big jug of water and a bowl, what more do you want?'

'But why can't we stay in a hotel, Dad, same as usual?'

'Because I happen to prefer the small scale intimacy of a guest-house, tucked away from the sea-front.'

'Why?'

Arthur pointed at a placard fixed to a nearby lamp post. On it was a large blow-up of Ken's Poet Laureate of Sport logo with the words ' . . . is in town today' printed underneath. 'I think your Dad's got his reasons, Charlie.'

Ken shuddered. 'Oh God – I'll just go on ahead if you don't mind. I'll be in my room, waiting for nightfall.'

Arthur looked disgusted. 'You know, Charlie, I remember a time when that used to be a decent newspaper . . . '

Charlie's boredom hit rock-bottom while they were waiting for dinner. Alison sat on a settee in the 'Television Lounge', reading a novel, and Charlie slumped in an armchair by her side.

'Please can I put the telly on?'

'No. Find something to occupy your mind.'

'That's why I want to watch telly – that'll do it.'

'No it won't – least of all at this time of year. It's either repeats or American rubbish, or worst of all, sport.'

Charlie looked round the long, bay-windowed room divided into two sections, a dining area with half-a-dozen tables each set for four and the 'Television Lounge' made up of bamboo furniture with a bar in the corner festooned with plastic grapes. Canned music played 'Guantanamera' in the background.

'Where are we going for dinner?'

Alison pointed through to the dining room area. 'There.'

'Oh no! Have you seen tonight's menu? Gammon steaks with pineapple rings, or ham salad with pineapple rings! What a dump . . . '

'You're spoilt, that's your trouble, Charlie,' his mother told him. 'I stayed in places like this all the time when I was your age. And it suits your grandad, and we were lucky to get in . . . '

'All right, all right – but what did you and Dad do for fun? There can't have been *any* telly then.'

Alison chose her words carefully. 'Well – we made our own entertainment.'

Just then a pretty, sun-tanned, seventeen-year-old girl in a T-shirt and jeans came into the lounge. She made her way confidently to the empty bar and rang the bell for service. Charlie's eyes followed her across the room. She sat on a bar-stool, waiting, munching peanuts from a dish. Charlie seemed suddenly more cheerful.

'Fancy a drink before dinner, mater?'

'No thanks – but you can have a coke.'

'Right!' He sauntered across to the bar, his hands in his pockets. The girl looked at him. She offered him a peanut. He took one, then another, then another. There was a silence. The girl rang the bell again.

'It takes about ten minutes to get served in this place,' she said. 'The landlady's busy doing the evening meal.'

'Opening all those tins of pineapple.'

The girl laughed. Charlie was encouraged. She pointed to a pineapple-shaped ice bucket. 'There's another one.' More laughter. Then a pause.

'Been here long?' asked Charlie.

'Second week.'

'You're quite brown.'

'Thanks – I'm Mary Dobson.'

'Charlie Wordsworth. Can I get you a drink, Mary? Cider, or something?'

'No, I don't like cider – makes me go all light-headed.'

'Yeah, I know what you mean. I went on a cider binge the other day . . . still got a bit of a hangover, actually . . . ' He raised his voice for the benefit of Alison who was ear-wigging discreetly. 'That's why I'm having a coke. So what goes on in Margate?' He rang the bell.

Ken sauntered in with a couple of tourist leaflets, wandered across to Alison, taking in Charlie at the bar, leaned over the back of Alison's settee and whispered in her ear: 'Charlie seems to have made a friend.'

Alison showed her amusement. 'He's buying her a drink. I hadn't realized chat-up lines were hereditary. Where's your Dad?'

'Curled up in bed with his woods. He daren't let them out of his sight before the big match. I think I'll skip dinner if you don't mind. I've found a holiday camp darts tournament that should provide some decent copy . . . '

Alison was surprised. Ken normally hated darts. Obviously intolerance was fading with age. 'Charlie's looking for some entertainment tonight,' she pointed out. Ken went over.

But Charlie didn't seem too keen.

'Oh, hi, er, – Ken . . . ' He turned to Mary. 'This is Ken – he's my older brother . . . I'm sharing a room with him. This is Mary, Ken.'

Ken was amused. 'Hello, Mary. Charlie, your er, Alison was just wondering . . . '

'That's Ken's girl-friend.'

'If you'd like to come to a darts match with me tonight?'

'Er, no thanks, Ken. I think I'll just have dinner here and a quiet night in . . . '

'I understand. Oh – perhaps if you have a moment, you wouldn't mind tidying your bit of the room . . . our kid? Bye Bye Mary, nice to meet you.'

'See you Ken.'

Ken raised his eyebrows to Alison on the way out. 'You see? Tolerance itself.'

Mary had watched Ken going out. 'How old's your brother?'

'Twenty-seven – he'd just had a bit of a hard life.' Charlie rang the bell again – a louder, cockier ring.

The Darts Tournament took place in a smoke-filled club room, crowded with sun-burned, beer-swilling holiday-makers. A commentator shouted the score through the racket of people cracking bad jokes to each other. Right at the other end of the room from the darts sat Ken, in dark glasses, sipping a pint, his empty notepad before him, keeping a moody silence. A large hand was suddenly plonked on his shoulder and a rolled-up copy of his paper thrust under his nose. Ken flinched, but stared straight ahead of him, ignoring the hand. He could guess what was coming.

'You are the Poet Laureate of Sport, and ten pounds to give me you Ought!' A perspiring pink face grinned at him. He tried to control himself.

'Well done! Now I have to ask you a simple question, don't I?'

'Yeah, and it's Tuesday, so the question is, "Where were the 1968 Mexico Olympics held?" and the answer's "Mexico *City*" . . . '

Ken checked his list. 'Quite right . . . Not so simple after all, was it?' The sarcasm was lost on the man. 'Congratulations Mr . . . '

'A Hooper of Watford. Thanks, Mr . . . what was your name again?'

'Ken Wordsworth.' Ken looked puzzled, but noted down the man's name and turned back to his pint. Immediately another hand tapped him on the shoulder and thrust another tightly rolled tabloid under his nose.

'You are the Poet Laureate of sport and ten pounds to give me you ought! . . . Mexico City . . . '

Ken looked round to see an entire queue of men building up behind him. Right at the end, where A. Hooper of

Watford was exchanging his tenner for a fiver, was Steve Stevens, sitting at a table. Ken gave the second man a tenner and told him to share it with the others.

'Sorry, lads – this gift horse has been withdrawn . . . '

Realizing they had been rumbled, the men dispersed.

Steve grinned. 'Sorry about that, Ken – just a wind-up . . . Tell you what, though – why don't we cut out these middle-men and split the prize money between us? I'll give you a few names and you'll be spared a lot of aggravation.'

'No, I don't need any help with names where you're concerned, Steve Stevens – I've got a list as long as my arm: A. Creep, A. Nuisance, F. Off . . . '

'Now, now – mind your manners or I'll throw you out . . . '

'A bouncer in a holiday camp? You're going up in the world.'

'As it happens, my paper's heavily involved with the running of this tournament – so technically you're my guest, Ken. We've done a little tie-up with the brewery that's sponsoring it. They're placing a major advertising campaign with us, and we're giving these here matches a lot of favourable publicity . . . What's more – we're printing little vouchers that give 5p off one of their pints . . . result? They sell more beer, we sell more papers . . . Makes your 'crisp tenners' look a bit soggy, don't it, Ken?'

Ken got up. 'A brewery, darts and your rag. That's what I call a marriage made in hell.' Still, at least he now had some material for a good solid piece.

'Yeah, don't forget to give us a mention, eh, Ken? Hi-de-hi!'

But as far as Ken was concerned, it was Low-de-low.

Reg was delighted with the knocking copy Ken phoned through: 'By the end of the evening some competitors were so sponsored they could hardly hit the wall, let alone the board – I suppose this is what happens when the grubby hand of commercialism is also on the dart. God help us all if they ever got round to javelins . . . ' Frank wasn't so pleased; the way he saw it, Ken was just giving that shower of Steve's publicity. And Stevens would undoubtedly be out for revenge. Why didn't they put the boot in then and there, while Steve was on the deck? What about supporting an event of their own – like Ken's father's bowls tournament? Something like 'The Francis Drake Memorial Trophy' Beat the Argentinians again! Get all those old guys done up in doublet and hoses. But Reg didn't bite. In Frank's eyes, his boss had lost his bottle ever since Bryan Pike got back. Now Reg even turned down Frank's offer of a jar down The Inkwell, courtesy of Steve's 5p vouchers. It seemed Reg was going straight home to his missus – provided he could remember the way. But at least Reg could still laugh at Frank having a drink on Steve Stevens.

'You know, Frank – I always thought ''The Harlot of Fleet Street'' was a newspaper, till I discovered you.'

The next day Ken, Alison, Charlie and Mary Dobson went to watch Arthur play his first round of bowls. Ken and Alison sat on one bench and Charlie and Mary, discreetly holding hands, sat on another a few benches away. Ken applauded as his father delivered his first bowl towards the 'jack' at the other end, sending the others out of the way into the ditch and leaving his pair to win.

'But he knocked those other two off the pitch,' complained Alison. 'That wasn't very nice.'

'Of course it wasn't, Alison – there's an undercurrent of viciousness in most of the genteel English pastimes, take croquet for example . . . '

'Or marriage . . . '

'Thanks, I'll use that.'

Charlie, meanwhile, was trying to explain away Ken's having called Arthur 'Dad' earlier on. Yes, Arthur *was* Ken and Charlie's father. The Wordsworths were known for starting early and finishing late. Would Mary like a walk?

Arthur had his card checked by the umpire and came across to Ken and Alison, taking a pinch of snuff as he did so. He always took snuff when he was playing bowls. It helped to concentrate the mind.

'Shouldn't that kid have a chaperone?' he asked, pointing at the two disappearing figures.

'No, she's old enough to take care of herself,' Alison reassured him.

'It's Charlie I meant – she's a right little minx. I've seen her in the boarding house, wearing nowt but a T-shirt.'

'Well, I've spoken to Mary's Mum and Dad and they're delighted she's found a pal to play with.'

'Did you get a chance to read my column, Dad?'

'I started it . . . but then it was time to clean me shoes – and I had to put something underneath them, didn't I? And I don't want a hatchet-job done on bowls the way you did on darts.'

'So you did read it!'

'While I was bent down polishing, yes.'

'Have no fears, Dad – you'll come out of this whiter than white.'

Ken gave Alison and Arthur an arm each. 'Come on, let's go for tea . . . now that everything in the Gardens is lovely.'

Not that it was . . . Steve Stevens had been watching them through a telescope further along the clifftop. He raised an eyebrow as he noticed Arthur taking a pinch of snuff.

While Ken sat typing in the boarding-house bedroom Charlie preened in front of the mirror, doing up his tie, then unfastening it to make it look more fashionable.

'Your tie's not done up properly,' Ken told him. 'I remember spending a whole afternoon with you, showing you how to do a Windsor knot.'

'It's meant to be like this, Dad – casual – cas'.'

'What's all this "Dad"? If we're going to be cas', call me Ken.'

'Yeah, sorry about that . . . I didn't want her to think I was on holiday with my parents . . . I thought it might be less embarrassing if I pretended you were my brother. But I did say you were only twenty-seven . . . '

'Oh, well – that's all right, then! So what are we going to

159

do tonight? What's Club 18-30 got lined up for us? A beach barbecue? Strip frisbee and jacket potatoes?'

'Leave it out – I'm only taking her to the pictures.'

'Sorry, Charlie – if the truth be known, I'm jealous.' Charlie couldn't cope with this at all. 'I just remember what it was like to be young on holiday, on a warm summer evening, with a pretty girl for company . . .'

'I thought you were already going out with Mum then?'

'I was! She was pretty . . . she still is. And *I* had to make up a lot of stories to get away from *my* embarrassing dad. But I'm a bit disappointed that you felt *you* had to. I thought we'd got a better relationship than that – more like brothers really . . .'

They looked at each other in the mirror for a moment. There was a knock at the door. It was Mary, coming to pick Charlie up.

'Come in Mary. You're looking very pretty,' said Ken, wistfully.

Charlie closed the door behind her. 'Er, Mary – I told you a bit of a fib before. Ken's not my brother – he's my Dad.'

Mary looked puzzled. 'But if he's only twenty-seven, how old does that make you?'

'Old enough to take you to the pictures, Mary,' Ken reassured her.

'Tell me, what's your surname?'

'Dobson.' Ken made a note on his pad.

'And where are you from?'

'Ilford.' Ken made another note.

'Now say to me – "there are *no* horses in a water-polo team".'

'Eh?'

'Just say it,' urged Charlie who had twigged what was going on.

Mary said it. Ken took a tenner out of his wallet.

'Mary Dobson of Ilford, that earns you a crisp tenner! Take Charlie Wordsworth of Wandsworth for an ice-cream after the flicks.'

Alison spent the evening getting further on in her novel, sitting in the Television Lounge. She had just got to a good bit when someone covered her eyes and a voice from behind her said 'Hush, hush, whisper who dares!' It was Russell. Alison guessed immediately and was not amused. What would Arthur think? It had been an early finish at Russell's cricket, courtesy of Imran Khan who had taken 6 for 72, and as Russell had found himself unexpectedly free he'd thought he would tootle over from Hove to see his beloved. He'd been drinking as well. Not with Imran Khan of course, who was a Muslim. Or, as Russell put it, a Mulsim. To Alison's embarrassment Russell proceeded to slide off the settee onto one knee.

'The fact is, Alison – I've had enough of being one of the lads on the loose . . . country house hotels and good living . . . when all it adds up to . . . is being alone in your room at night typing up some bloody match report or other. Look . . . while I'm down here . . . I want to marry you, Alison.'

Alison looked at him and then at the people who were staring at them.

'All right – now will you go?' But Russell insisted on toasting their betrothal in champagne first. Except that the boarding-house only had Babycham. They might as well start as they meant to go on, thought Alison.

Ruby insisted on giving Reg big, saucy kisses every time Bryan wasn't looking. She gave him one while Bryan was bending down to inspect Ruby's new arrangement of putting the brown ale on the bottom shelf now nobody drank it any more and Reg was trying his hardest to be accommodating to Bryan while taking Ruby's point about moving it.

'You agreeing with her, Reg?'

Reg hastily wiped his mouth to remove any lipstick.

'No, no, Bryan – I was just thinking how there were two sides to every argument . . .'

'Not the way I see it, Reg.' Reg turned white and muttered something about two perhaps pushing it rather.

'By the way, have you heard any more about that how's-your-father with Ruby?' asked Bryan.

'No – that's why I came in, actually – wondered if *you'd* heard any more.'

'No, nothing. I'm thinking about putting up a reward – you know, free beer for a year, or something. See if anyone'll turn supergrass.'

Reg trembled. 'Well I did hear a whisper, from a friend of a friend, about a geezer who took a bit of a shine to Ruby, but then went to work on the Tasmania Herald, fell into a swamp one day and that was the end of him! So what about the reward?' He laughed weakly.

'Sure – when can you produce the body?'

The next day it was Arthur's second game. It was clear to Ken and Alison, who sat watching him, that he was set to win again. Ken watched him taking indulgent pinches of snuff and beamed with satisfaction.

'Look's like Arthur's done it again. Only two more hurdles to jump – well, bend his way round – and he's in the final!'

Alison registered his good mood. 'Yes – actually, I cleared a little hurdle of my own last night.'

'Just a minute, love – the other bloke's calling for a measure.'

'No, I'd better tell you now in case Arthur loses. Russell turned up last night and asked me to marry him . . .'

Ken kept looking straight ahead of him. 'I think he's got it, you know . . .'

'And I accepted.'

On the green the umpire raised both index fingers. 'Yes . . . panic over. Sorry – Russell asked you what?'

'You heard every word.'

Before she could go on, Ken's attention was seized by the appearance of two uniformed policemen who were walking along the edge of the green, surveying the bowlers. As Arthur took another pinch of snuff they pulled up sharp, pointed him out to each other, and unceremoniously marched onto the green towards him. It crossed Ken's mind they might be transport police who had caught up with Arthur over his railcard. But then out of the corner of his eye he saw Steve Stevens standing some way away from them. Steve was signalling to a young photographer who was at a high vantage-point, taking pictures of Arthur and the policemen through a telephoto lens. Ken's eyes narrowed. He gave instructions to Alison to go and give Arthur a hand and made his way across to Steve.

'Hello Ken, turned out nice again, hasn't it?'

'I take it you've got something to do with this. And that photographer has got something to do with you?'

'Yeah! So much for your pure sport, eh, Ken? Drug-taking, police raids . . . it's got the lot!'

'Drug-taking?' Had Ken heard him right?

'The old geezer . . . Coke fiend, isn't he? I clocked him at it yesterday – so I had to call the law, didn't I?'

'That's not cocaine, it's snuff!'

'So?' Steve was unabashed. Ken grabbed the front of his shirt and cocked his fist at him. 'This game's even got mindless violence!' Steve laughed.

'That old geezer's my father!'

'Is he? That's even better – my editor's going to love this . . . ''Shame of Poet Laureate's Family''! See Ken – all's fair in war and journalism. You rubbish my darts, I'll do the same to your bowls!'

'So this is your idea of a sports page is it, Stevens? Set up a picture to tell a story – even if it's not true?'

'Yeah, well – it makes the world go round, Ken. 'Course you wouldn't know about that, 'cos you're a dinosaur, aren't you? Still trapped in the days of Roy of the Rovers! But me, I live the real life . . . and all the Roys I know are having it off with the other Rovers wives . . . and snorting coke and knocking back the booze, and doing back-handed deals with their agents! That's my World of Sport, Ken.'

Ken let go of him in pity. 'You poor sod . . . '

'That's right, Ken – sneer! But you know the best thing? It's What The People Want to Read!'

'Well if they read anything about this I'll break you into a thousand pieces and sue every one individually. Now if I were you I'd get lost before I have you arrested, for wasting police time.'

Arthur was furious. He'd been disqualified for disrupting the tournament. And then, to cap it all, one of the policemen, far from explaining everything to the judges, turned to Ken and produced a tabloid from his tunic. 'You are the Poet Laureate of Sport . . . '

Ken wandered into the bedroom to find the curtains closed. He glanced at the bed. Charlie and Mary lay fast asleep, their clothes scattered on the floor around the bed. On the table at the head of the bed was an empty litre bottle of cider. Ken took in the scene silently then quietly closed the door behind him.

Arthur was just off to pack. Ken apologized to him for having ruined the holiday, and his apology was sincere.

'It's not your fault,' his father told him. 'It's the daft bloody world you move in, isn't it. You had a smashing wife and you lost her, but you still get on so well . . . *I* don't understand why you can't be together. What with police on bowling greens . . . your face plastered all over lamp-posts . . . dogs called Russell – I'll be glad when I'm back home!'

'You know, Dad, there's only one thing that keeps me on the rails and you gave it to me.'

'What's that?'

'The love of sport. And the instinct for how it should be played.' They smiled at each other.

Alison was looking for Charlie. Had Ken seen him?

'Er, yes – I suppose you ought to know, really. I just found him chasing butterflies upstairs, with Mary.'

Alison thought for a moment, then the truth dawned on her. She looked horrified. 'Oh God – he's going into pubs, he's swearing, now he's sleeping with girls – what's happening to him, Ken?'

'He's growing up, Alison.'

'Well, I hope he knows about precautions.'

'I think so. I once spent an afternoon with him on Windsor knots and contraceptives. Provided he doesn't get the techniques confused, there should be no problems. Oh, by the way.' He kissed her on the cheek. 'Congratulations.'

When he got back to Fleet Street Ken sorted out Reg's problems with Bryan as well. Several beers had made a few people sing and they kept coming out with the same tune: 'Reg Prosser's had your daughter away'. Bryan was advancing on Reg when Ken intercepted him.

'Have you ever been Crown Green Bowling? You see, Flat Bowling is played in straight lines but Crown Green is full of ups and downs and twists and turns . . . Well, I've been coming to The Inkwell for over a year, Bryan, and I've seen Ruby handling drunks, fights, floods, the occasional fire – the Crown Green side of life. Do you honestly think she can't handle herself? While you've been in prison, Ruby's become an adult. Isn't it about time you treated her like one?' Ken was taller than Bryan as well.

Ken and Reg had a second editorial meeting in the sunshine outside Dr Johnson's House. Reg was complimentary about Ken's handling of Bryan. 'Well done, Ken – you carved him up better than any QC ever did.'

'Well at least your death sentence was commuted.'

'Yeah, to life with Ruby – all I've got to do now is break it to the wife. Still, that's my problem, Ken . . . '

'That's very understanding of you, Reg.'

'Now I reckon you deserve a holiday.'

'Anywhere but the seaside, Reg.'

'Well, how about France? The Tour de? Stay over there as long as you like . . . '

'No thanks, Reg – the archery in Ealing is about as lively as I want to get right now.'

'Really? Fair enough. You know, the other day Frank

had this really stupid idea about dressing people up as
Francis Drake.'

'To brighten up my bowls piece?' Ken knew Frank.

'Yeah, I shot him down in flames, of course. Robin
Hood, though, now *there* was an interesting man – gave to
the poor, you know. You got any of those tenners left,
Ken?'

POWER GAMES

The Summer Season had come round again and Ken, Russell and Steve were at Henley Regatta covering the rowing. Whereas most people only go to Henley for a good day out, Ken and Russell were genuinely interested, particularly in a young hopeful called Geoff Butcher who looked as if he was set for the 1988 Olympics.

They watched from among the colourfully-dressed spectators as Geoff Butcher, equally colourfully-dressed in a distinctive headband and matching sweatbands, won the race and gave his characteristic punch to the air as he did so. Not that Russell approved of Geoff's behaviour. Rowing was an old-established gentleman's sport – not the sort of occasion to go round in your own sportswear and show off when you won. This was Henley, not Hampden Park.

'I see,' argued Ken. 'It's all right to *swill* punch, but not to throw one in the exultation of victory.'

'As for all that stuff he was wearing – I do dislike sportsmen drawing attention to themselves with gimcrack accessories.' Ken took a long look at Russell's striped blazer and boater.

'Yes, I can see how a man of your sartorial restraint might be offended by that – you old fart, Russell. It's about time rowing got a bit of personality back into it . . . do you remember the Thames Tradesmen crews in the seventies?'

'Oh, yes – those long-haired louts . . . '

'They kept winning though, didn't they? And every time some toffee-nosed opponent shouted "Get your hair cut", they just shouted "Get fast!" That's the spirit, and I reckon Geoff Butcher's got it too.'

'I see – another rough diamond for you to get off on.'

'Even if he did go to Cambridge. Anyway, why not if he's good?'

'Yes . . . and he knows it. Come on, Ken – I thought you were in the same boat as me, defending the amateur ideal against the rising tide of commercialism, which rowing, by its very nature, is more equipped to ride than most sports.'

'There you are then – if I write a feature about him, it's hardly likely to have the crocodiles slithering off the river-bank in anticipation, is it?'

It looked as if Ken had been speaking too soon when he talked of crocodiles. Coming towards them was Steve Stevens, properly dressed for once in blazer and tie. They still hadn't let him into the Stewards' Enclosure, apparently, though. Even when he'd told them he was a mate of Stewart's. Russell didn't bother to enlighten him that he needed a special Stewards' Ticket. They'd obviously spotted Steve as a South-of-the-river lad. Anyway, you could see all the action from where Ken, Russell and Steve were standing, on the other side of the river from the Stewards' Enclosure itself. But, as Steve pointed out, the real action wasn't in the water at all; it was in that Stewards' Enclosure – birds, booze and bad behaviour.

Russell turned to Ken. 'One of the things I like most about the English summer, Ken, is the way sport manages to remain the preserve of the leisured classes – Royal Ascot, Centre Court at Wimbledon, Henley . . . if you don't know the right people, you ain't gonna get in, baby!'

'The right people being ticket-touts in the Personal columns of *The Times*. You can go anywhere you want if you've got the money – top prices for top people. Well, not always top – I dare say there's the odd bent car-dealer over there among all the Bentley owners.'

Steve was encouraged. Perhaps there was a story for him after all among all this. The problem was, how was he going to get across the river to where all the corruption was? It wasn't even as if he could swim.

Ken gave Russell a lift back to Wandsworth and picked up Charlie at the same time. Charlie was coming to stay with him for five days, but from the amount of luggage he was bringing, it looked more like fifty. He dived back into the house to pick up the home computer Russell had given him. Ken was annoyed to hear about this. Apparently Russell had bought it as a premature 'congratulations' present for Charlie's O Level Results. The results weren't out yet, but how could a son of Ken's, at Russell's old school fail to do well? As Ken got into the car and shut the door in a huff, Russell explained to Charlie that he wasn't meaning to squeeze Ken out. For his part, Charlie didn't mind who pampered him so long as somebody did.

'I always thought it was the woman who brought the dowry,' complained Ken.

'What does that mean?'

'I'll give you a print-out later.'

Reg was just off to The Inkwell when Frank came into his office carrying a grey vellum envelope tied with a red ribbon. It was for him. He wondered if somebody thought it was Valentine's Day. It couldn't be his divorce papers seeing as how he'd only left his wife that very afternoon. And it didn't look like a writ. Reg looked at the words 'Prosser. Personal', took a deep breath and opened it.

'Hello – it's from the proprietor.'

'So it's a death warrant,' moaned Frank. 'What's it to be? Firing squad or guillotine?'

It was in fact a personal invitation to breakfast the next day at the Savoy, with Mr Savva himself. Of course, he only ate at the Savoy because he thought it sounded like his name, Frank remarked.

'What of it?' Reg reprimanded his Deputy. 'All millionaires are eccentric . . . and you haven't even got money as an excuse.'

Frank was stung by this. 'So what does a Press Baron want with you? In the words of Brian London – you're just a prawn in this game.'

Apparently the proprietor valued Reg's expertise. In the meantime Reg was to come up with 'five original and visually stimulating sports . . . ' The limousine was to pick Reg up at six the next morning, by which time Mr Savva himself would have put in three hours' work, as well as giving the paper a good going over. Still, as the Sports

Pages would have a cracking piece by Ken on rowing and Mr Savva had made all his money in ships they didn't have anything to worry about on that score.

A harassed-looking Ruby appeared at the door of the office.

'Oh aye, kipping down here tonight are you?' Frank grinned. 'My desk out there's quite comfortable.'

'Go to The Inkwell, eh, Frank,' Reg told him.

'Your command is my wish.'

Once they were alone Reg gave Ruby a big kiss. Things had gone quite well when Reg had broken the news that afternoon to Mrs Prosser about Ruby and he. Instead of hacking Reg to death she'd taken it like a trouper. Her only comment had been: 'How can you leave when you were never here in the first place.'

But it wasn't that that Ruby had come to see him about. 'There's these associates of Dad's just come in . . . and they want to go to the Nat West Final at – where is it? Dukes?'

'Lords. I wouldn't have thought any friends of your father's would have been interested in cricket.'

'These geezers aren't. But they are quite partial to banks. So they're after an executive box for the match.'

'I bet they are – Lords'll be swarming with bank managers, all getting boozed and indiscreet . . . Oh well, I suppose it makes a change from plotting the fall of the Government behind the pavilion.'

'They're serious, Reg. They reckon Dad owes 'em a few favours. He must have known they were coming, 'cos he did a runner to Spain this morning . . .'

'But not before telling 'em his daughter was going out with a sports editor? Thanks, Bryan!'

Reg agreed to help out and gave Ruby another big kiss. How'd she like to spend the night at the Savoy? In an executive box.

'Can we have breakfast in bed?'

'Sure – as long as you don't mind a Greek tycoon being in there with us.'

* * *

Ken was woken that night by a strange sound coming from his sitting room. He emerged from the bedroom, blinking in the eerie glow of the only light in the room, which was coming from the TV screen. Charlie, pyjamaed, was sitting operating a joystick on the console of his computer, which had been plugged into the TV.

The couch which was acting as his bed was deserted – its covers thrown back. Engrossed, Charlie hadn't even noticed his father come in.

'That doesn't sound like the Open University, Charlie,' Ken shouted above the blips and crunches coming from Charlie's video game.

'Gawd, you gave me a fright!'

'What about the one you gave me? I haven't woken up to colour like that since George Best's coming-out party. What is it?'

'Sir Gawain and the Green Slime. See, Dad – there's these creatures come out of the swamp . . . and Sir Gawain has to rip their heads off before they attack the castle . . .'

'I thought these things were supposed to improve your mind.'

'It is doing – Sir Gawain's an A Level set book.'

'Without the green slime, I hope. Well, if Russell thought this was educational, I'd hate to see the toys he buys you. Good night.'

Charlie turned off the game, turned on an anglepoise lamp that had been placed by his sofa and looked at his father.

'You're just jealous, aren't you?'

'Jealous, me?'

'You've no need to be – Russell says you'll still be my real Dad.'

'That's very gracious of him. I'm sorry, Charlie – the old man feels a bit threatened, that's all. When Russell and your mother got together – and I got over the shock – I was secretly pleased that a lot of responsibility would be lifted off my shoulders . . . and plonked onto his. But now that it's about to happen, I realize that I don't want to give up responsibility for you.'

Charlie was touched. 'Ah, thanks Dad . . .'

'Especially now you're discovering . . . well, the finer things in life.'

'You mean like drink?'

'Drink . . . sex . . . '

'When?'

'Oh, when I walked into our room in Margate and found you asleep in bed with young Mary.'

'Oh, then . . . I thought you were going to say at Angela Bosworth's birthday party last year.'

Ken thought he'd better get back to bed before Charlie enlightened him any further. 'What's that set book called?'

'*Sir Gawain and the Green Knight.* Get it?'

Alison and Russell were in bed composing their wedding list, Russell in his half-moons, sucking a pen and writing on a foolscap pad, Alison leafing through a household goods catalogue for inspiration, a notepad by her side on the duvet. The trouble was, they'd got everything they needed already.

'There must be something,' Russell looked peeved. 'Didn't Ken take a few household items when he shipped out?'

'Yes – Wisden Almanacks and Rothmans Football Year-books.'

'No, there's no point in putting them down – I'll bring all the ones I want . . . '

'Oh good, that's a weight off my mind.'

Oblivious to Alison's sarcasm, Russell mused about how wartime Wisdens were very very rare and would make a nice present. 'Add them to the list would you?'

'Wis-dens – any particular colour?'

By now Russell *had* noticed, and was hurt. 'Making fun of this won't get us very far, Alison – when you have a wedding, you have a wedding-list. My friends are expecting it. Especially as it's *my* first time . . . '

The way things were going, it looked as if Alison would have to do what Ken and she did – have separate wedding lists – Alison's consisting of sheets, pillowcases and napkin

172

rings and Ken's of malt whisky, and Beatles LPs, (pre-*Sergeant Pepper*.)

Of course, they had yet to fix the day. Alison assumed Saturdays were out unless they could find a match with a morning kick-off or there was a team Alison didn't mind seeing in the afternoon. There was, though, Russell pointed out always the two weeks he was taking at the end of August.

Alison gave Russell a smackeroo of a kiss at this, crushing the heroic couplets he'd written about the regatta. Once a year, as a party piece, Russell wrote his column in verse.

'I'm surprised the official "Poet Laureate of Sport" doesn't feel got at,' laughed Alison.

'Ah yes – talking of Ken – I thought it might be a nice gesture if we invited him to be Best Man . . . don't you?'

Alison stopped laughing.

Ken had arranged to have lunch with Geoff Butcher the following Monday in a wine bar off Fleet Street. Geoff arrived wearing the same headband and wristbands and expensive-looking pastel-coloured leisure-wear. He'd been doing a photo-session for *Vogue* – he modelled his own clothes. The 'Geoff Butcher Look'. Ken offered him a glass of Chablis, but Geoff refused. He didn't drink. Or take drugs of any sort. Ken ordered a bottle of Perrier.

'Sorry, but that's all some journalists want to know about.'

'I know – I've met him. But I'm only interested in what you do *on* the water . . . though I'm glad to hear what you don't do off it. Do you mind if I switch on the tape-recorder?'

'Go ahead.'

The waitress arrived with the menus but Geoff ordered an avocado salad without more than glancing at what there was on offer. Ken had the same.

'Please don't skimp for my sake,' he told Geoff.

'No, that's all I want.'

'They'll be querying my expenses for this meal – it's too cheap.'

'Well, I was going to pay for it anyway.'

'No, hang on, I invited you . . .'

'Yes, but I probably earn more than you, Ken – besides, no one queries *my* expenses. I'm a one-man company. GB Sportswear.'

'I get it – wear the flag.'

'Right – it's early days yet, but it should really take off if I do the business in the '88 Olympics. My earning power now's nothing compared to what it's going to be when I crack a world audience.'

Ken was taken aback at his use of the word 'audience' and picked him up on it.

'Why? I may be an amateur sportsman, but I regard myself as a professional entertainer. You're not one of those old women who thinks I shouldn't make any money out of rowing, are you Ken?'

'No, not at all – how can I? I earn *my* living from people like you . . .'

'Right, and you're exploiting your own talent. Okay, so I'm locked into a low-profile sport, but that doesn't mean I can't be a high-profile person. A rower may move backwards, but he knows where he's going . . . do you mind?'

'No, no, of course not – if you can combine success with, well, for want of a better word, dignity . . .'

Geoff was getting more and more defensive and took this the wrong way. 'Look Ken, if a by-product of my being super-fit is having an ace body, why shouldn't I model clothes? This stuff isn't rubbish you know.' He took Ken's hand and made him feel the material.

Ken laughed. 'Geoff, I wasn't having a go! Look, I'll rewind the tape . . . then we can talk about sport . . .'

Reg had a good working breakfast with Mr Savva – if you like moussaka that is. When he got back to the office Frank was getting edgy. He'd begun to think Reg must have got the sack, or even that Frank himself might have to vacate the premises. But no, Mr Savva had been very cordial about the Sports Pages and had engaged Reg in 'Meaningful Discussions'. It seemed that Mr Savva had decided that the printed word was dying but that there was a place for people such as his Sports Editor and Deputy Sports Editor in the sunrise media world of tomorrow, provided they could come up with the right ideas. Hence the five new sports. The conditions were, they had to look good on television, and they couldn't have been done before. That ruled out dwarf-hurling – the Aussies had beaten them to it.

Frank was racking his brains and wondering why *he* had to be doing this, when Ken came in and Reg delegated another job. Ken was just dropping off his Geoff Butcher interview for one of Reg's dolly secretaries to transcribe before going on to join Charlie at the Earls Court Computer Exhibition. Earls Court, thought Reg – Perfect! Ken could stop off on his way and have tea with another up and coming sportsperson. Or rather sports*woman*. A bit of a dolly herself, by all accounts and really looking forward to meeting the Poet Laureate of Sport. Ken had been looking dubious, but at this he agreed.

'I don't suppose another hour would be enough for brain damage to have set in on Charlie.'

'Gotcha! Brilliant, Reg!'

'The simple art of delegating, Frank!' Reg beamed.

Ken's sudden doubts about this venture were confirmed when he found himself on the exotic roof gardens above Kensington High Street where he was to rendezvous with the mystery sportswoman. A flamingo strutted past him. He took in the scene of several fashionable people sitting on wrought iron chairs taking tea and wondered which of them was expecting him.

'Yoo Hoo!' He looked round to see an attractive mediterranean-looking young woman waving at him. She was suntanned, dressed all in white and wore a large, floppy sunhat.

'Miss Simons?'

'It's Mrs, but call me Deborah . . . and I'll call you Ken. Now what would you like to ask me, Ken?'

'Well, sports journalists have a reputation for asking

obvious questions, so how about "What am I doing here, Deborah?"'

'I don't understand – didn't Mr Prosser tell you?'

'Only that you were a sportswoman who'd make an interesting feature.'

'That's absolutely right, darling – that's all there is to it! Now what would you like to ask me, Ken?'

Dutifully, Ken put his tape recorder on. This was ridiculous. 'Well, Deborah . . . what sort of sports do you do?'

'Oh heaps – I ride, I swim, I play tennis and I ski.'

'Who for exactly?'

'Sorry?'

'Who do you represent?'

'Myself of course! I've got several Pony Club medals for my riding, but I still like skiing best . . . ' Ken pulled at an earlobe thoughtfully, then turned off the tape. 'What's the matter – was I going too fast?'

'No, no – you were fine – it's just that, well, if you don't actually play for a country, or a country, or even a club – it's a bit difficult to find a peg to hang the article on . . . '

Deborah looked at him. 'Do you mean an angle?' she asked professionally.

'Yes, very good, that's right.'

'Well, what else can I tell you – I'm twenty one, I was born Deborah Savva, my father owns a lot of ships . . . and your paper, of course . . . '

Ken turned the tape back on quickly. Now that was an angle.

Reg and Frank were in The Inkwell, trying to come up with ideas for the 'Savva Games' when Ken caught up with them. Frank had hit upon blowing up hot-water bottles until they burst.

'That's a circus trick, not a sport,' objected Reg. 'Besides, people can get hurt like that! I heard a story where a hot-water bottle backfired and it was the bloke that burst.'

'But that's the beauty of it, Reg! Every sport must have its element of danger – the possibility of something going wrong. People pay a lot of money to see things like that.'

'Not if it's on a video meant for family audiences, Frank. These games have got to appeal to a complete cross-section of society – every Tom, Dick and Aristotle.'

Frank looked gloomily at his notes. There had to be something with Shetland ponies.

Ken had brought Charlie with him, partly as moral support, and partly as he was supposed to be looking after him that afternoon and had already left him too long at the Earls Court Computer Exhibition. Charlie had never been to The Inkwell before and was very impressed. It was just like Dungeons and Dragons, he said.

'Yes . . . let's see if we can find Sir Frank and the Black Knight, after we've got you across the drawbridge.'

When Ken introduced his son to Ruby at the bar Ruby took an immediate shine to him. While Frank immediately nicknamed Charlie, The Young Pretender. Not that Reg admitted to feeling threatened. He just got up very quickly from where he'd been talking to Frank and went over to Ken and Charlie – after all, he needed to know how Ken's interview had gone.

'Charlie,' Ken said to his son. 'Go and sit with that gentleman with the wild eyes, while Reg and I have a little row . . . pow-wow.'

'That boy looks under age to me, Ruby,' said Reg. '*And* he shouldn't be drinking.' Ruby gave him a pout and disappeared round the other side of the bar.

'Reg, why didn't you tell me that I was taking tea with the proprietor's daughter?'

The answer was simple. 'Because I knew you wouldn't have gone.'

'And you'd have been right. I now have two interviews on this tape . . . on one side a young sportsman who talks about wealth, and on the other a wealthy young woman talking about sports. Guess which one's worth printing on the sports page, Reg?'

'Sounds like they complement each other very nicely . . . anyway we'll be running both of 'em. Especially the last one.'

'Look Reg, I'm not naïve – I realize Mr Savva has the power to run a national newspaper as a family album. I don't mind his wife's beauty hints turning up on the Woman's Page – ''The Face That Launched a Hundred Oil-Tankers'' – but why the hell should his daughter be foisted on us?'

'Because she's about to take part in a major new sporting event.'

'What might that be? The Sloane Square Dressage Tournament?'

'No, a modern pentathlon. Well, a modern version, anyway. We still haven't quite got the format of these games nailed down yet . . . '

'Well don't come looking to me for help, Reg, because you won't get any.'

'All right, all right – just write the piece about the girl, and we'll leave it at that.'

'I'm sorry, Reg – I don't think I can do that either.'

'Fine! Here I am, about to start a new life with Ruby, kids to support in the not-too-distant . . . and when I look for loyalty from my chief sportswriter, who I plucked from obscurity on a Sunday subs desk, he stabs me in the back! His principles matter more to him than my career! Fine.'

'Well speaking as an ex-sub, Reg – there were six factual errors in what you just said.'

'But I was right about the main point, Ken – if you don't do that interview for me, I'm out on my ear. Bye-bye Inkwell. Bye-bye Fr . . . '

'That's enough emotional blackmail. Under protest, I'll write you a Deborah Simons profile.' Reg beamed. 'But I'll do it my way and write it exactly how I want . . . so that if anyone's head goes on the block it'll be mine.'

With that Ken went over to collect Charlie who'd been giving Frank some suggestions for novel sports, based on his knowledge of Computer Games. Not that his father was to know that Charlie had been helping out, Charlie warned Frank. He was in a funny mood.

'Dad's the word.'

Ken gave Frank a curt nod and dragged Charlie off home to where his typewriter, Excalibur, awaited.

* * *

Ken played back his tape recording of Deborah's interview in the flat. 'Gstaad's my absolute favourite, of course,' oozed Deborah. 'Ooh, look! There he is again . . . I love flamingos, don't you, Ken?'

Ken set to work typing furiously: 'She broke off telling me about her experiences on Europe's most demanding nursery slope – financially demanding that is – to ask whether I liked flamingos. Fried or grilled, I was tempted to ask, but thought better of it, suspecting that Mrs Simons wouldn't have come across either term in her spoon-fed life . . . '

Charlie had been reading over his father's shoulder. 'Looks like someone's getting the boot put in on them.'

'No, I'm far too gentlemanly for that – the iron foot in the velvet slipper, maybe.'

'It's good stuff anyway. But won't you get into trouble slagging off the boss's daughter.'

'This is mild compared to what I'd like to write. The trick is to let them condemn themselves out of their own mouth.'

Charlie couldn't help noticing and pointing out the difference between the way Ken worked and chatted to Charlie at the same time and the way Russell behaved whenever he was 'composing'. Everything had to stop when Russell was writing. He said he wanted to hear himself think.

'No, he just wants everyone else to hear him think.'

'He even switches the fridge off to stop it humming! What are we doing about food tonight?'

They decided to go out for a Chinese from Queensway, preferably sweet-and-sour flamingo, once Ken had finished. He then got back to work, switching on the tape: 'Now where were we, darling? Oh yes, Gstaad,' Deborah gushed at them.

Of course, Reg couldn't run Ken's article as it was. The proprietor would close the whole paper down, let alone the Sports Department. The only thing that was feasible was a re-write. Not that Ken would ever agree to it. It was then that Reg asked Frank if he'd ever seen a film called *Becket*.

'There's this king, see, who wants to get rid of this priest, but obviously he can't do it himself, right? So he thinks about it aloud, in front of a couple of his loyal henchmen . . . and they go off and do the dirty deed for him. But like I said, it was only historical . . . '

Reg closed his eyes for a long moment. When he opened them again Frank and the piece had both gone.

'Long live the King.' Reg murmured to himself respectfully.

Russell was getting tired of having all his possessions in one place and living in another. He was just off to cover some cricket and he couldn't find the appropriate Wisdens. Alison rather mistimed breaking the news to him that a date had been fixed for him to endow her with all his worldly goods. Thursday, August 29th, at 11.15.

'11.15? That means we'll have to provide a lunch . . . and a long one too. The boys will be expecting a major piss-up.'

'How sweet of you to think of others, rather than ourselves at a time like this.' Alison was resigned to sorting everything out, ordering the invitations, checking out a few places for the do. Russell did offer to hire a marquee from Trent Bridge. But it wasn't even as if he could help over asking Ken to be Best Man now. According to Ken's column, which had appeared through the letterbox that morning, he wasn't going to be at the cricket. He'd be covering the 'Savva Games' instead.

'That doesn't sound like Ken's cup of tea,' said Alison. She hadn't been married to him for eighteen years for nothing.

'No . . . the piece doesn't sound like him either: All about the proprietor's daughter: "The sizzling dusky bombshell sat sipping iced champagne . . . " If my future wife weren't present, I'd call it an exercise in bum-kissing. Still, needs must, I suppose. I'll leave you to contact him then, shall I?'

When Ken caught up with Reg in The Inkwell that morning, Reg blamed the re-write on Gremlins.

'Not Gremlins, Reg,' Ken was firm. 'Gremlins are mischievous little creatures. Whoever did this is a calculating, cowardly, evil-minded bastard . . . ' He stared at Frank pointedly.

'I only wish I'd been there, Ken,' Frank shrugged. 'I wouldn't have let it happen. But I was at the pictures last night . . . a film called *Becket*.'

Anyway, as Reg put it, there was no harm done. They'd even had a call from Mr Savva himself saying how much he'd enjoyed the piece.

'I'm sure he'll be just as pleased when I write about these 'Savva Games' which, according to what I didn't write this morning, are to be my next assignment.'

'Well, in that case we'd better tell you what they are! Reg was shameless.

'They're an exciting new development in the sports-and-media arena,' added Frank.

'Word perfect Frank,' Ken congratulated him. 'I'm flattered you pay so much attention to my column . . . ' Frank looked away.

'Look, Ken – Mr Savva thinks that it's not enough for us just to report sport – we've got to go out there and make it happen ourselves. And with the help of television, that's what we plan to do.'

'Don't spoil it for me Reg – let me guess who's going to be taking part. As well as dusky Deborah, there'll be a few forgotten pop stars, a couple of over-the-hill footballers, a sprinkling of redundant newsreaders, and a disc-jockey on the make! In short, the sort of people who'd stand on their head in a bucket of shit if the money was right.'

'He's been looking at your short-list, Reg.'

'Not closely enough, Frank. You left out your flavour-of-the-month athlete – Geoff Butcher! He was very happy to sign up for a day of tip-top entertainment.'

'That's only because you've found his Achilles heel – publicity. He's not to know what a fool he's going to look. Sorry Reg, wild Shetland ponies wouldn't drag me there. When sport and showbiz get into bed together, their illegitimate baby's called Junk.'

Then Ruby appeared looking worried. The heavy geezers

had been on the phone to her again. Now they wanted Reg to fix them up with anything else they could lay their hands on: boxing at Ally Pally, snooker at Wembley, Springsteen at Wembley, World Cup in Mexico . . . ' Ken said they could have his ticket to the 'Savva Games'.

'Bloody Hell, who do they think I am?' complained Reg. Frank smiled to himself. 'Reg Prosser, Ticket Tout.'

At least Ken could unwind a little over a lunch with Alison at one of their favourite haunts.

'If it wasn't for the wine, I'd be crying,' he laughed when he'd finished telling her the Deborah Simon story. 'And of course the company's a big help . . . ' He smiled sadly at her.

'Now come on love – don't start getting maudlin again. You're right to dig your heels in, because it sounds like a load of rubbish.'

'That won't stop the paper promoting it as a load of fun.'

'But if you've made your feelings clear and you're not having to write about it, why worry?'

'I'm afraid that it might be the thin end of the wedge, Alison – and sitting over there is the fat end . . . ' Ken pointed across the room to a table where, sitting alone, drinking a bottle of wine, was Steve Stevens. 'Remember the kidnap attempt at Charlie's sports day? And the drugs raid on Dad at the bowls? Well that's the man behind them. He may look harmless enough, but you don't know what they've done to his brain, Alison . . . and what they might do to mine. If I'm honest, he haunts me. And now they're starting to re-write my column . . . Today the readers have been told "Ken Wordsworth is ill" . . . what's to stop them announcing "Ken Wordsworth is dead" and appointing a new Poet Laureate?'

'So what if they do? You can always walk away – in a month or so you won't have Charlie and me to pay for, so you can work where you're happiest.'

Ken looked at her affectionately. It was good to be having lunch together. 'Look, love – I've already told Charlie this, but it goes for you too – I hope there'll still be a place for me in your new life . . . '

Alison took his hand. 'Of course there will, Ken . . . you're very important to me.'

Ken gazed at her. 'I know I'm a bit pissed . . . but do you fancy an afternoon in bed, Alison?'

She smiled. 'Thanks for the offer, but I've got to go to Rymans to get some wedding invitations.' Her hand stayed in his. 'A wedding at which Russell and I would like you to be best man.'

'Let me think about it . . . over another bottle . . . '

When Alison had gone, Steve came over. 'That bird was a bit special, Ken.'

'Yes, she was.'

'Are you, er, in there?'

'No . . . Russell de Vries has beaten me to it.'

'Cor, you posh writers can't half pull! And what about the piece the other day?'

'I didn't write that.'

'Not the piece – the piece! The boss's daughter. She must have been another notch on your typewriter. I mean, you did go a bit overboard . . . '

'Steve, that wasn't my work! It just had my name on it.'

'I thought you looked as if you'd seen a ghost-writer. Don't worry, Ken – it happens all the time! I'm lucky if fifty per cent of what I write goes in the paper.'

'You're under pressure as well, are you?'

'It's your fault, Ken – if you weren't so shit-hot I wouldn't have to fight so dirty. I spend half my time trying to knock down what you build up. And it's even tougher this time of year for us real journalists – the silly season. Where's the real rancid meat I can get my teeth into, Ken?'

Ken suddenly began to get interested. Perhaps there was a way the article he wanted to write on the 'Savva Games' could still get published – if not by his own newspaper. 'Have you had lunch yet, Steve . . . ?'

Reg's office was being redecorated and refurnished, new

push-button phones installed and new, matching desk-tops put up, when Reg got a phone call from Deborah Simons. She'd liked Ken's article on her so much, she wanted him to cover her successes in the Games, personally. Reg tried to tell her he was ill but her only response had been: 'Make him better.' Reg moaned to Frank. If only Frank hadn't done such a good job on the re-write.

'Leave it to me, Reg – I'll come up with something.' Frank stopped midway through the door. 'The Boy Wordsworth!'

'Yes, that's who I want to be there. Now take off the earmuffs Frank and put your thinking cap on.'

'No, no – not the Boy Wordsworth – the *Boy* Boy Wordsworth! That's how we get to Ken . . . '

Which is why Ken arrived back at his flat to find Charlie and Deborah Simons there, playing *Trivial Pursuits*. Charlie moved Deborah's counter round for her. 'Art and literature . . . or sport?'

'Ooh, sport please.' They were both so engrossed in the game, neither of them had noticed Ken.

'Aw, it's a doddle, this – "Which Austrian won the Men's Downhill at the 1976 Winter Olympics?" '

'Niki Lauda,' Deborah announced with great confidence. 'Do I get a wedge for that?'

'No – he's a motor-racing driver!' laughed Charlie.

'Wasn't it Franz Klammer, Charlie,' Ken interrupted. 'I thought you might have known that, Deborah – I read in the paper that you were a great ski-ing buff. Still, it's only a game.'

'And I read in the paper that you were ill,' returned Deborah.

'So I've brought you some really nice fruit. And my personal physician's standing by, to make sure you're fit for tomorrow. Now, don't be a spoilsport . . . '

'That's a bit of an inappropriate word, in the circumstances.'

'Why, if you're stopping Charlie from seeing his super ideas brought to life . . . '

'What do you mean?'

'Mr Prosser told me that Charlie was a great help in conceiving some of the Games . . . but don't worry, I'm not telling Daddy.'

Ken glared at Charlie. So much for not telling Daddy.

'Aw, come on,' Charlie said. 'All I did was talk to that mad bloke about computer games . . . can we go?'

'Simons Sez, remember,' Deborah said pointedly. Ken looked at the two different smiles beaming at him.

'I suppose one sort of Trivial Pursuit is much like another. And there is a certain morbid fascination in seeing what happens when Tron meets McNab.' Ken had given in again.

The Savva Games were just as Ken had imagined they would be – and worse. There was a Sinclair C5 Sprint and a Dry Ski Slope Jamboree and an imcomprehensible game with a trampoline and water-polo nets. The contestants were a grim assortment of Beauty Queens and faded popstars and Geoff Butcher, punching the air in his sweatband, and Shetland ponies . . . and ticket touts.

Ken's one consolation was that he could point Steve in the direction of all this nonsense. Steve was already on the job, though.

'See those four suits up there?' Steve pointed at Reg and Ruby's 'friends', 'You've heard of *Police Five* – well, there's four of 'em.'

'Perfect . . . Sport, showbiz and now crime . . . It's all yours, Steve – write it from the heart, for me.'

Ken was sitting in front of an empty sheet of paper in his typewriter when Charlie got back to the flat, munching a bag of savouries.

'What happened to you? You missed a lift home, in Deborah's limo – it's got a telly in the back!'

'Saves having to talk to her, I suppose . . . '

'I might be seeing her later – there's a post-Games party at the Hippodrome . . . I thought you wouldn't mind, 'cos you've got to write . . . '

As if Ken needed reminding.

'How's it going?' There was no answer. 'Good laugh this afternoon, wasn't it?'

'Yes. In the same way that drawing a moustache on the Mona Lisa would get a laugh.'

Charlie pulled a face, knelt down in front of the television, inserted a new computer game cassette and switched it on. The room was immediately filled with blips and crunches.

'Do we need that?'

'Getting like Russell, now. You'd enjoy this, Dad – "Brian Jacks' Superstar Challenge" – it's got a whole lot of sports – canoeing, swimming, cycling. Here, have a Scampi Hoop.' Ken took the packet, looked inside, then began reading the back.

'God Almighty. "Ingredients – wheat flour, vegetable oil, including hydrogenated vegetable oil, with antioxidants E310, E321, maize seasonings, flavourings, flavour enhancers, monosodium glutamate, acidity regulator E262, acid E330, soya protein, potato starch, emulsifier E412 . . . "'

'I've got some Prawn Cocktail ones if you don't like them . . .'

'Bloody hell, Charlie – look at you! Surrounded by crap! It's a summer's evening – why can't you go outside in the park and play with a ball – and eat an apple!'

'What're you taking it out on me for? 'Cos you're stuck?'

'Yes.' Ken sat down and looked at the piece of paper in front of him for a long, sad moment. 'Sorry, Charlie – I shouldn't be attacking you when it's the Green Slime I'm really trying to kill off.'

'I thought they let you write what you liked.'

'It's what *they* like now . . . '

'When's your deadline?'

'Half seven.'

'Well you've got to write *something*.'

'Yes.'

Ken sat down and started typing while Charlie turned off the computer, threw away his Scampi Hoops packet and went off for a walk in the park.

* * *

Reg was reading Steve's Savva Games article aloud to Ruby in The Inkwell. ' "Why are these four gentlemen covering their faces, you may ask. Are they shy because of their reputation in London's underworld. Or can't they bear to look – and who can blame them – at the farcical goings-on masquerading as sport, organized by a certain national newspaper yesterday afternoon?" The proprietor's going to be seriously underwhelmed by this, Ruby.'

It wasn't even as if Reg could go round buying up all the copies. He'd probably be out on the streets selling 'em very soon. And where was Ken? He'd already missed the first edition. But then a grim-faced Ken came down the stairs, carrying an envelope.

'Where's my bloody piece, Ken?'

'I haven't written it – I'm resigning.'

'What?'

'I've tried to explain in the letter . . . of course it may need subbing. 'Bye Ruby . . . ' And that was that.

When Ken took Charlie back home, Charlie presented him with a present to thank him for having him to stay. It was a copy of *Sir Gawain and the Green Knight.* In Middle English. Charlie hadn't been able to get a translation. Ken was touched. 'Never mind. It's the "thughte" that counts.'

Alison wondered if he'd decided whether or not he'd be her best man yet.

'Yes – I'd love to.'

'Ah, great. Are you going to be there?' Charlie grinned. 'Smashing.'

'It's on the 29th of August, are you sure you'll be free?'

Ken smiled a long, sad smile. 'Oh, yes – I think I can manage a day off work . . . '

OUR MAN ON-THE-SPOT

Dear Reg,

I think the time may have come for me to take a change of direction. It seems I can't write what I want, and as I'm unable to write what *you* want, there doesn't appear to be much future for me on the paper. Therefore I am giving you one month's notice of my leaving, and taking one month's leave, which I think will be best in the circumstances. Besides, you owe it to me. Tell Frank he can have my mug.

I hope by the end of the month to have found a job in sports journalism where the status I have earned is more appreciated.

Yours

Ken Wordsworth

This was Ken's letter of resignation. As for a job where the status he had earned would be more appreciated, it looked as if LBC might offer him just that. He was to have an interview with Val Barnett, the Head of Programmes there, the following Wednesday.

Ken sauntered past the commissionaire at the LBC/Independent News Offices with a smile – but was hauled back and made to sign the Visitors' Book like everybody else. Val Barnett was in her office, waiting for him. She was a well-dressed, professional woman in her early forties, who, when the secretary had closed the door behind Ken, came across to him and gave him a less-than-chaste kiss. They were old friends. When Ken had escaped he looked around the room at the walls lined with bookshelves and the dexion racks of programme tapes in boxes. A stereo system with speakers at either end of the window-sill behind Val's desk was broadcasting the station's output.

'You old sod,' Val stood back to look at him. 'How do you manage to stay so slim?'

'And how'd you manage to stay so horny?' They laughed together and Val turned off the stereo. 'Don't do that on my account,' said Ken.

But Val was glad to have an excuse to turn it off. 'To my mind, birching is the only answer to people who put their rubbish in other peoples' skips,' she mimicked. 'Still, it's an easy way of filling the airwaves – they even pay for their own calls.' She poured them both large whiskies.

'We all do it, Val – twice a week we pad out our sports pages with angry letters from the readers, deliberately provoked by ourselves. "We Say – England Manager Must go" – they say he must stay, the next week we want him to stay, they say he must go. It doesn't matter which, as long as the letters keep coming, because it's free copy! At least when I wrote to the "Hotspur" as a kid I got a ten-bob postal order and a biro! Well, I've had my fill. I say "Ken Wordsworth Must Go!"'

Ken couldn't believe the relief it was to talk to someone like this. All that bitterness had been building up inside him for too long.

Val looked suspicious. 'And that's why you're prepared to take a dive into radio?'

'No, no – I took the dive eighteen months ago when I joined the paper. This is my attempt to get up off the canvas. You see, Val, what I've always tried to do as a writer is report what I see, and what it's like for the competitors involved. But it looks as if that isn't enough anymore. Now it's all about what I see in it for the company, and "competitors" means the rival rags. You were smart; you got out of papers ten years ago. Tell me it isn't like that on radio.' The last was a cry from the heart. Ken wanted a job.

And Val was prepared to try him out for one. After all, he had a lovely voice. What their Sports Editor would probably do would be to assign him to cover some major event in the next few weeks, London-orientated of course. And then, if the try-out was satisfactory, he could proceed to a regular freelance contract.

'Er, the London-orientated bit?'

'What about it?'

'Well, that implies that you've got a sports editor like mine – travel narrows his mind, or at least the prospect of paying for it does.'

'On the contrary, we encourage our correspondents to go abroad. Just as long as there's some local interest for our listeners.'

'So if some teenager from Tower Hamlets forces his way into the World Marbles Championships in Hawaii, I'd be in with a shout, would I?'

'Absolutely! We've come a long way since we used to send people out to the nearest phone-box with a Reuters wire report, and get them to pretend they were actually on the spot.'

Ken smiled at Val. He wondered if she knew that he and Alison had split up. Although of course she was married now, doubtless with two . . . well, two lovers probably. And had she heard about Alison and Russell? Russell had been an old flame of hers, too, hadn't he? Well, perhaps not so much a flame – more a pilot light.

Reg sat in his office gazing longingly at the 'Ken Wordsworth – Poet Laureate of Sport' logo. After a few pensive seconds he checked that no-one was around, picked up the telephone and started dialling a number. Frank wandered in and Reg slammed the receiver down.

'You were phoning Wordsworth again.'

'No I wasn't.'

'Yes, you were. I can read it on your face – that grovelling look.'

'If you must know, Frank, I was calling my beloved – about the plans for our love-nest in the Barbican.'

'So it's true about you and . . . Kenny,' said Frank, looking at the logo.

'Ruby, Frank – I was calling Ruby. Now have you checked all the letters we've had about him?'

Frank put a sheaf of handwritten letters on Reg's desk before him. 'Aye, they're all genuine, all in different handwriting from different addresses. He's been very clever.'

'So that's thirty-seven letters now, Frank – all of them worried about what's happened to the Poet Laureate of Sport. The last time we called for the sacking of the England manager there were only half a dozen. And – I've heard a strong rumour that Ken's in the running for the Sports-writer of the Year Award.'

'Ha! Well if he is, it's only thanks to my headlines – if it wasn't for the icing, nobody'd notice the cake.'

'Nevertheless – if he does win it, and all we've got in the shop window is a plateful of crumbs, how are we going to look?'

Frank gave it some thought. 'Stupid?'

'That's the first bright thing you've said since you came in here. Which means we've got to get Ken back. Convince him he belongs with us. Reassure him that his stuff won't be tampered with from now on. Guarantee that there'll always be a place for his ideals in our pages.'

'Okay, you do that and I'll chip in by giving him his mug back.'

'One other thing you can do, Frank – just in case my words fall on deaf ears, give Steve Stevens a bell and see how little we can get him for. After all, if we can't hang on to the Poet Laureate we may just have to settle for rhyming slang . . . '

Ken broke the news of his resignation to Alison, Russell and Charlie over dinner in Wandsworth. Charlie looked disappointed.

'Does that mean you're going to have to get a proper job, Dad?'

'Yes, I start work as an estate agent on Monday. Of course not – who'd have me? I'm unemployable as anything other than a journalist – or a barman, perhaps. That's why I'm going freelance.'

Alison smiled at him. She'd seen this coming. When they'd had lunch together, he was obviously, well, in the mood for a new challenge. In other words, depressed.

Russell got down to the nuts and bolts of the situaggers.

'Where are you going to work, old son? I don't mean to be offensive, but after eighteen months of that place you are rather like an ex-con coming out of gaol, and having to readjust to society.'

'In that case,' said Alison, giving him one of her looks. 'Ken's got a good chance of writing for those trendy periodicals you keep trying to get into!'

'Sorry?'

'Well, they prefer someone with a criminal record, don't they?'

'I thought you weren't supposed to start arguing till *after* you got married.' Charlie could see the potential for a windup. Ken frowned at him.

'Stop it, Charlie. Anyway, my rehabilitation may have started already – I've been told I have the perfect voice for local radio.'

'Oh yes,' Russell guffawed. 'Reading the dog results?'

'I'd have liked to – but actually I've been asked to cover a European title fight in Zagreb next week.'

Russell, Charlie and Alison all looked anxious.

'Don't forget my Stag Night on Tuesday.'

'Or my O-level results on Wednesday.'

'Or my wedding on Thursday . . . ' Alison looked crossly at the other two.

'Don't panic – when did I ever let work interfere with having a good time? Let's see . . . the fight's on Wednesday evening, but they're three hours ahead in Zagreb, so I should be back in time to celebrate with my son that night, and commiserate with my ex-wife the following morning!'

'We'll see who's doing the commiserating after the stag night,' beamed Russell. 'I'm planning an epic piss-up that'll make Sodom and Gomorrah look like Bournemouth and Boscombe!'

'Oh, jolly D . . . ' Alison cleared the plates noisily.

'Where are we booked into?' asked Ken. 'The Reform Club?'

'God no – it's got to be somewhere the mayhem won't be noticed! Fortunately I remembered the perfect place, Ken – and I know you'll feel at home there . . . '

Frank ordered a bottle of ink to be put on ice at The Inkwell. He was having a business lunch. Ruby hardly recognized him in his best suit and tie, smoking a cigar. A safari suit – Frank was going head-hunting. When Steve Stevens arrived, Ruby insisted Frank sign him in, much to Frank's annoyance. Discretion was of the essence. He'd just have to write illegibly.

'I don't want this to be one of your long lunches,' Ruby warned him. 'There's a Stag Night in here next Tuesday . . .'

'Hello, Ruby,' grinned Steve. 'Very cosy,' he said, taking in the corner where Frank had reserved a table. 'This where you and Reg did your courting is it?'

Ruby decided not to answer that in case she ended up on Steve's front page.

'Champagne, eh . . . nothing but the best for you lot.' Steve was impressed.

'Aye,' agreed Frank. Until now, that is, he thought. He looked at Steve sternly. 'Now officially this meeting is not taking place at all. I am not out to lunch . . .'

'That's not what most people think.'

'But you see . . . a friend of mine may be about to lose a friend of his . . . though he's no friend of mine! . . . and so he's asked me – this friend – to have a friendly chat with you . . . to see if you might be interested in becoming his *new* friend. What do you say, pal?'

'Well it depends how serious a friendship he wants, doesn't it?' Steve took out a pound coin and started playing with it. 'I mean these little dubreys are my only friends in life . . . and I'm a bit lonely right now. So if your friend wants me to be his, he's going to have to think about finding some more friends for me . . . about thirty thousand of 'em to be precise. How would your friend feel about that?'

Frank winced. 'Say we agreed to these, er, friendly terms . . . how soon could we expect the pleasure of your company?'

'Oh, I make friends very quickly.'

'Within twenty-four hours if it came to it?'

'No problem. Right! Now that's over with, I'm ready for

a bite of grub.' He reached for the champagne bottle. Frank quickly withdrew it.

'Don't be silly – I told you before, this lunch isn't taking place.'

Ken was just practising talking into a tape recorder when his entryphone buzzer went. It was Reg. Again.

'And the answer's still no.'

'Come on, Ken – give us five minutes, eh? Just for a chat . . .'

Ken gave it a moment's thought. '*Three* minutes – this is a professional fight.'

While Reg was coming up the stairs, Ken played back a bit more of his tape: 'Welcome to Zagreb, where the whole of Yugoslavia holds its breath as it waits to see if Ken Wordsworth, the former Serbo-Croat Laureate of Sport, can overcome all the odds and regain his crown . . .' One bad joke and three cliches – he was getting the hang of it already.

'Are you alright, Ken?' asked Reg. 'I thought I heard you talking to yourself. Must be the strain. This month's holiday'll do you good. You'll be fit as a fiddle when you come back.'

'I'm not coming back.'

Reg completely ignored this and looked round the flat approvingly. 'Nice little place, Ken. You obviously landed on your feet when you were chucked out of your marriage. Hope I'm as lucky with my pied-a-terre. Suppose that's where it comes from, "pied-a-terre" – landing on your feet! Mind you, these second homes – real drain on the old pocket aren't they? A man'd need the guarantee of regular full-time employment to manage both successfully . . . don't you think?'

'I'm still not coming back, Reg.' How many times did he have to tell him? 'For one thing, Alison, my ex-wife's getting married again next week, so she's no longer a burden to me. And as I won't have to pay the Ali-money, I can afford to be choosy about the work I do! Which I couldn't when I signed up with you.'

'That's what I'm going to miss most, Ken – the razor-sharp speed of your mind! You can pluck words out of the air like . . . well, I dunno – that's your job . . . '

'Well if you're that much of a fan, Reg, you can hear me plucking them out of the air next week, when I do a report on the Stubbs/Avramovic fight in Zagreb.'

'You're working for TV? In Poland?'

'Radio in Yugoslavia, actually – the TV comes later, I expect.'

'But Ken, you're a writer,' fumed Reg. 'Radio and TV are sworn enemies of the written word! We in Fleet Street are the protectors of it!'

'Unless you happen to disagree with what's written – in which case words are smothered in the still of the night by Frank and his dark cohorts on the subs desk.' Ken looked bitter. 'Sorry, but if it means what I say comes out the way *I* want it, that's the price I'm prepared to pay.' He glanced at his wristwatch. 'Three minutes.'

'Okay Ken, let's talk prices.' Reg looked fevered. 'How about a five grand rise and a company car?'

'Good afternoon, Reg.'

'And a word processor . . . '

'OUT!'

As Steve told Reg at his interview in Reg's office later that day, whereas some sportswriters (mentioning no names) just report what they see, the way Steve looked at it, it's what you *don't* see that makes the better story. Anyone looking into Reg's office would have thought they were just having a friendly chat, but the Steve Stevenses of this world would have got round the other side of the window and been able to read Ken Wordsworth's resignation letter in Reg's In-tray! The thing was, Reg explained to Steve, he wasn't really looking for a cat-burglar. Steve said he was a cat who could change his spots – specially for thirty thousand little brass ones. So Reg decided to give him a one-day trial with a money-back guarantee. Was Steve free to go to Zagreb the next day?

'Zagreb,' Steve thought. ' ''Today we were privileged to

witness the fiercest fight Zagreb has seen since the peasant partisans swept down from the mountains to attack their Gestapo invaders . . . '' *That* Zagreb?'

Reg looked non-committal. 'That'll do for now . . . ' he said and showed Steve out.

Tuesday was Russell's Stag Night in The Inkwell. Ruby was suffering at the hands of the posh geezers' Wandering Hand Trouble. Russell was by far the worst. You could tell he was the one getting married. Ken was there as well. Frank couldn't believe Wordsworth's nerve showing his face in The Inkwell and then not inviting Frank to join in. Reg, on the other hand, seemed remarkably unperturbed by all the commotion. Ruby gave him a huge kiss as she passed by on her way to get more drinks.

'That made the sun come out . . . '

'Sorry, I can't stop, Reg – I'm rushed off my feet.'

'Don't worry – it won't be long before we have a lot of time to ourselves. I saw the estate agent this afternoon and signed the papers for the flat . . . '

'Ooh, can we stay there tonight?'

'No – it, er, needs a few days to get things straight, then I'll carry you over the threshold.'

Frank was looking morose. Ruby gave him a squeeze. 'Even you'll find somebody one day, Frank.' Frank seemed unconvinced. At that moment a brassy looking airhostess came down the steps into the haze, dressed in full uniform. 'This might be her now. Go on, seize your chance . . . '

Frank came over all shy. 'Can I help you, pet?'

'Is this The Inkwell?' asked the airhostess.

'Aye – have a bevvy!'

'No thanks – I'm looking for Mr Russell de Vries.' Frank turned back to the bar sourly. Trust his luck.

Ruby explained that Russell was over in the corner, but that it was his Stag Night and he'd have all the girl's clothes off if she wasn't careful. But the girl seemed unconcerned.

'I'm part of the entertainment – an Airhostessogram. I give the sort of in-flight service that men only dream about . . . just a giggle, really.'

Reg eagerly escorted her over while Ruby scowled at the two of them. Frank leaned across the bar and looked seductively into Ruby's eyes.

'Hello – I'm Frank . . . fly me . . . '

The Airhostessogram went through an entire routine, removing her tunic, jacket, skirt, shirt, scarf and flight-bag and then, in her bra, panties, suspenders and hat, spoon-fed a willing Russell an airline meal from a plastic tray, sitting on his knee. Russell was by now also wearing a fully-inflated orange airline lifejacket round his neck. He'd never known airline food could taste so good.

'Have a nice day, Mr de Vries,' said the airhostess, giving him a big sloppy kiss and getting up off his lap. As the cronies applauded, the girl started putting her uniform back on, which had been neatly folded and put on an empty seat next to Ken.

'Do you want a sweet to suck, Russell, to make your ears pop?' Ken joked.

'I'll tell you what – everything else has nearly popped! Good Lord! Did you have anything to do with this, Wordsworth?'

'No – I was as surprised as you were – it was probably Alison's idea.'

'Yes, I always suspected her feminism was just a posture – no doubt wanted to give the old man a decent send-off before she shackled him down till the end of his natural! My word, though – what a fantasy!' While Russell was fantasizing, Ken offered the girl another glass of champagne before she went off to attend to another passenger.

The incident had set Russell thinking. 'That's the trouble with life today, Ken,' he told his ex-husband-in-law-to-be, 'not enough fantasy, too much bloody reality . . . '

The Airhostesssogram overheard this. 'Ken!' she exclaimed. 'That's who you are . . . Ken Wordsworth! I thought I recognized the name. The Poet Laureate of Sport? Have you retired? I really miss your column. What's happened?'

Ken looked at her. Here was someone who had some grasp of what he was going through. 'Journalists are like airline pilots really,' he explained. 'They have to keep switching routes to avoid boredom setting in. But I'm hoping to go into radio, so you'll be able to get me in the kitchen, the bathroom and the bedroom.'

'Three times a week?' The girl took Ken's arm seductively.

'Maybe more.'

Russell looked at all this and wondered what he was doing marooned in a lifejacket. His sex-life was starting to pass in front of him. He began to see all the opportunities he'd missed out on in the past . . . Celia Davenport at Oxford . . . she had looked lovely that morning after the May Ball . . . hair in ringlets, cascading onto her shoulders . . . how come he'd never got his hands on her? He realized he would have to face it. He would never fly again.

The air hostess's flat didn't have a very lived-in feel, Ken couldn't help noticing.

'No, well, I'm not here very often. Only when I'm in town – I really *am* an air hostess, you see. I don't get many nights off and so when I do, it seems a pity to waste the uniform.'

Ken approved of the mixing of high-life and low-life. Very enterprising.

'Would you like a drink?' She looked round the room, but couldn't see any. 'Oh – I seem to be out . . .'

There was an awkward pause. Ken didn't quite know how to break this to her. He had to catch the 10 a.m. flight to Zagreb the next day, and what had earlier seemed like a good idea didn't seem quite so good any more.

The girl was adamant. 'We can share a taxi to Heathrow. 9.30 to Tel Aviv, me. And I'll set the alarm . . . ' She took off her airline hat.

'Oh, well – just this once. Do *I* get a lifejacket as well?'

The next morning Charlie got his O Level results. He was sitting looking unhappily at them when Russell wandered in gingerly, wearing his dressing gown. He looked, and was, wrecked. Vaguely acknowledging Charlie, he made his way through to the kitchen and mixed himself an Alka Seltzer.

'Remind me to tell that bloody postman to stop whistling in future.'

'He can't help it,' replied Charlie. 'He obviously enjoys delivering bad news.'

'Anything in the post for me?'

'No, nothing for me either.'

'Then what's that?'

'My O Level results. Five score draws . . . three home defeats.'

'Is that good?' Russell was in no state for brainteasers.

'No – I failed Maths, Physics and Chemistry.'

'Well, that's no loss – I never got maths and physics and look at me.' Charlie did so, unimpressed. 'And as for chemistry . . . Alka Seltzer's all you need to know about that . . .'

Apparently Charlie's school didn't look at it in quite that way. He needed six passes to stay on for A Levels. 'So what do you think I should do, Russell?'

Russell looked harassed. 'Oh, I dunno, ask your mother.'

'I did – she said ask you.'

'Did she? Why?' Charlie looked hurt, so Russell thought he'd better explain. 'Oh, I'm sorry, Charlie – I'm not in mint condition at the moment.'

'Can I talk to you later then?'

'Yes, all right – oh no, hang on – I'm going to an hotel for the night.'

'Why?'

'It's bad form to sleep with the bride on the eve of the wedding. Look, why don't you give Ken a ring.'

Charlie got up. 'Because he's gone to Yugo-bleeding-slavia!' he moaned and stormed out.

Russell looked mournfully at his Alka-Seltzer. It had gone flat. Lucky-bleeding-Ken.

But Ken hadn't gone to Yugo-bleeding-slavia. He emerged groggily from the bedroom of the flat. The alarm clock had stopped and he couldn't find his watch. The air hostess appeared to have gone. He poked his head into the kitchen but she wasn't there either. He went across to the stereo, turned on the radio and twiddled the dial.

'And finally, for motorists heading to Heathrow on the M4 – the AA warns of serious delays following an accident on the Westbound carriageway near the Heston service area. So if you've a plane to catch, please allow an extra half-hour to make sure you're on time . . . ' announced a voice. But what *was* the time? 'You're listening to LBC, where it's just coming up to six minutes past ten . . . '

Ken hit the roof. Ten?! He looked desperately round the room, spotted a telephone, rushed into the bedroom, emerged with his jacket, socks and shoes, reached into his jacket and produced a passport with an airline ticket inside it, ran across to the telephone, clasping the ticket, and started dialling a number he'd found on the back. The radio meanwhile droned on.

'Sport now, and apart from yet another call for the England manager's head, the main news today concerns the chances of the young South Londoner Lloyd Stubbs when he takes on the reigning European Light-Heavyweight champion Bogdan Avramovic . . . we'll be having regular reports on the fight, live from Zagreb throughout the afternoon – so don't miss that!'

Ken was trying not to. Holding the telephone to his ear, he reached for the radio and turned it off. The telephone was answered.

'Yes, hello – look, I was booked on the ten o'clock plane to Zagreb . . . yes, I'm aware of that! So can you tell me when the next flight is? Thank you very much . . . is that six o'clock our time, or their time? No, thank you – that's absolutely useless.'

He slammed the telephone down, put on his socks and shoes, then his jacket. Fed up, he made for the front door.

It wouldn't open. The silly cow had left the Chubb on. He crossed the room to the window and pulled back the curtain. Perhaps he could climb out. But he was on the twentieth floor of a high-rise block. Terrific.

* * *

'Yes, it *is* the last round, but you don't understand! There are lots of Yugoslavians on their feet in front of me, it's absolute bedlam here . . . What do you mean "go"?! . . . And, er, if you've just come in . . . The big news is that Lloyd Stubbs, the twenty year old from Lewisham is only a few seconds away from becoming the new Light-Heavyweight Champion of Europe . . . And he knows it!' Ken took a deep breath. 'And suddenly Avramovic has got nowhere to run! It's all over bar the shouting! In they go, left, right, those twenty year old fists, and the champion's reeling now! But he's as brave as they come, this lanky father-of-two, and he's still absorbing the punishment as he hangs on the ropes directly above my head!' Ken reached across to an anglepoise lamp and pinged the shade several times with his pen. 'That's it! It's all over! And Stubbs' arms go up in triumph, no need for the judge's decision, he must have won a clear points victory . . . they'll be lighting bonfires in the streets of Lewisham tonight . . . ' He stopped as he realized he was off air. 'Hello . . . was that all right? . . . Oh – thank you very much, I look forward to the next one . . . I'll give you a round-up before I leave for the airport . . . bye.'

Ken hung up and dialled another number. 'Lanky father-of-two' indeed. He sighed. 'Hello. Extension 516 again please . . . Hello, Terry . . . no that's all right I don't need it now – I just had to wing a live commentary on the last round. What happened?'

Ken didn't enjoy his meeting with Val Barnett. As he himself admitted, he deserved to be on those proverbial bonfires in Lewisham. Val didn't take it as seriously as Ken had done. In her eyes he'd shown he was a professional by ringing a story through, even if it was false, rather than getting a caretaker to let him out immediately he found he was locked in. After all, he'd only actually been caught out because Lloyd Stubbs had been knocked out. And thanks to events that afternoon Ken had joined the living legends of Fleet Street – like the Vietnam war correspondent who was found filing front-line copy from a Paris bar. And he'd given LBC a new expression. Anyone not where they should be would, from now on, be deemed to be 'in Zagreb'. Not that any of that got him the job.

'I only hope she was worth it . . . ' Val shook her head ruefully.

'Do you know – I can't remember. Frightening isn't it – another half-minute and I'd have fooled everybody.'

'Not quite everybody – among our phone-in callers this afternoon, there were two guys who were absolutely convinced that you weren't actually there . . . ' Ken looked at her suspiciously.

Reg wasn't very happy with Steve's piece, even *after* Frank had beefed it up. He was the 'Young Face of Sport' alright – a six year old could have written what Steve had culled for them. As for Frank's headline, what was 'Goodnight Zagreb' supposed to mean?

'Well, it's near Vienna isn't it?'

'Zagreb happens to be in Yugoslavia, Frank . . . Vienna's . . . ' Reg thought for a moment. ' . . . Nowhere near it.'

'What's the matter with you, gaffer? This is supposed to be the start of a new era.'

'I dunno, Frank . . . there's just something missing . . . magic.'

He couldn't ring Ken *again*. Perhaps he'd wait till Ken had got the forget-me-nots he'd sent up.

Steve sauntered in carrying a duty-free bag. 'Hello lads!'

'Hello, Face.'

'How are you, gaffer?'

'Disappointed about the Stubbs fight . . . ' Reg replied meaningfully.

'Yeah, bit of a choker wasn't it – still, he'd have lost anyway.'

'What?'

'Well I happen to know that when he got cut in the seventh, his corner used an illegal cement on it . . . The Slavs clocked it and were going to protest – so even if he'd won, he'd have been stripped of the title next week . . . '

Reg looked at Steve and then at the back page and then

back at Steve. 'I don't see any mention of this in the story.'

'Come off it, Reg – you told me you wanted Shakespeare, not shit!'

'Yeah well – I've handed up with neither haven't I?'

Thursday dawned. The day of Alison's wedding. She went to the hairdressers, then back home to put on her wedding dress, and then to the Registry Office, accompanied by Ken and Charlie. There were a handful of well-dressed friends ready to meet them, and they chattered happily to Alison. A telephone rang in an adjoining room. A woman appeared.

'Is there a Mr Wordsworth here?'

'It'll be for me . . . ' joked Charlie. 'They've done a recount on my maths, physics and chemistry.'

Ken followed the woman down the corridor.

It was Russell. He was in Zagreb. Ken thought he was winding him up at first. But he really was in Zagreb. He couldn't go through with the wedding. Over the last days he'd been doing a lot of thinking, he said, and he'd decided marriage just wasn't for him. He'd make a rotten husband anyway. It was just that he still felt one of the lads really. That's why he'd decided to head for Zagreb – a sort of homing instinct to be with them all. Only they weren't there. As Russell's dinars ran out he made a quick plea for Ken to say sorry to Alison for him.

Ken walked slowly back up the corridor, through the milling guests. He looked sadly at Alison, taking her by the hand. She stood up, sensing what had happened from his expression, and started to cry. Ken put his arms round her and Charlie looked as if he wanted to hit someone.

For a change it was Alison who suggested they watch television when a silence fell as Ken, Charlie and she were having a cup of tea.

'Where was he anyway?' asked Charlie.

'Yugoslavia,' said Ken.

'It's quite flattering that he should go so far!' Alison laughed.

Charlie for one hoped he'd stay there. He could change his name to Russel Dubrovnik.

Ken had some whisky in his tea. 'I suppose Russell was pissed?' asked Alison.

'Funnily enough, I don't think he was.'

'Really? It takes a special kind of man who can fly two thousand miles and make a phone-call like that without a drink . . . '

Charlie went off to take his suit back to the hire shop leaving Ken and Alison alone.

'Charlie's had a rough couple of days,' Ken observed.

'He'll be all right – I spoke to the school this morning. They'll take him in the sixth form because he got good grades in everything else. I wasn't going to tell him till after the wedding? I think he'll be doing English, Economics and History. Creative writing, handling money and thinking about the past – I'll have another Poet Laureate of Sport on my hands! On second thoughts he'd better leave school now. I've had my fill of journalists for the time being – I might take up with a fairground attendant – you know, somebody more reliable.'

'You don't have to put on a brave face for me, love.'

Alison smiled bitterly. 'It isn't brave, Ken – just realistic. What do you expect? "He was the only man for me"? "He's broken my heart"? Well he wasn't and he hasn't, so don't put me on the spot, because all I'll come up with is clichés I don't feel like saying.'

'Yes, you're right . . . sorry. That's the reason why me being on the radio didn't work . . . well, one of the reasons – I talked rubbish and hated myself afterwards.'

'So what are you going to do?'

'Well, Reg still wants me back, so it'd be a pity to disappoint him. Besides, I've got a family to support again . . . Don't worry, though. This time I'm not doing it because I have to, because I want to . . . '

Ken and Alison looked at each other. If ever there was a moment for an affectionate hug, this was it. But something stopped them.

Charlie came back in and looked rather disappointed. 'Oh great – I leave you two alone for a minute and you *still* can't get back together . . . '

So that is how Ken came to be shaking hands with Reg on Friday morning. Reg was made to swear on one of the Wisdens. Foreign travel, expanded budget, no editorial or sub-editorial interference, a £5000 pound rise and a company car. And the word processor. Reg also handed him a letter. It was an invitation to the Sports Journalist of the Year Dinner – and they'd reserved a place for him on the top table.

'That means you've won it.'

'Don't be stupid.'

'Well, a lot of other people value your contribution to journalism – it's not just me, Ken . . . '

'Do you think so, Reg?' Ken felt quite chuffed.

'Sure. And you'd have been wasted on radio . . . and d'you know why? Because the pen is mightier than the word.'

Ken won it, too. He had to go up and collect it and make a quick witty speech and be applauded by Reg and Frank and Steve and all the big nobs in sports journalism. He'd felt like crying. Then, after the dinner, Ruby suggested they go back to Reg's and her new flat in the Barbican, and have a celebration knees-up-cum-flatwarming. She couldn't understand why Reg was so reluctant . . . but Ken did when they arrived there, and Reg unlocked the flat door and switched on the light. The place looked very familiar. Frank and Steve made a beeline for the drinks on the sideboard – nice to see that some had been got in since Ken was last here, he thought.

'What do you think, Ken?' Ruby asked nervously. 'Do you like it?'

'Yes . . . I feel very much at home here,' said Ken slowly, as he spotted something else on the sideboard. 'In fact – that's my watch . . . '

'It can't be. The caretaker found that down our toilet last week – it can't be Ken's can it, Reg?' But Reg had already gone out the door.

Ken hared out of the flat. Reg was at the lift, desperately pressing the button.

'Prosser!'

'I only did it 'cos I cared, Ken . . . '

Ken thundered towards him, brandishing his Sports-journalist of the Year trophy.

'Open wide, Reg . . . ' He grabbed him, raising the trophy above his head.

'Come on, Ken . . . be a sport, eh?'